Brinks in Time:
The Legend of Valendri's Relic

TOM ROGAL

ACKNOWLEDGMENTS

This being the first of an epic tale, I made sure to have good people looking over my shoulder ensuring I stayed on track. I couldn't have done it without the support and encouragement of my family and friends. I had spent many years writing, revising, and re-revising, then adding. They helped me along the way. Special thanks to Jayme Zobel for making me look good in my author photo. Also thanks to Michele Blackstone for copy editing my work. A special thanks to Indie Designz for making a beautiful book cover. Enjoy the story!

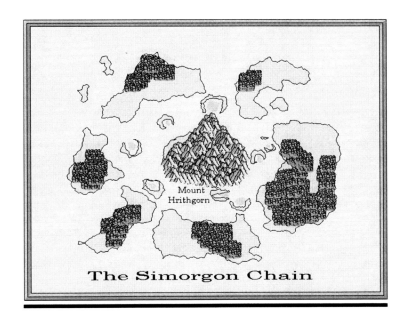

The Simorgon Chain

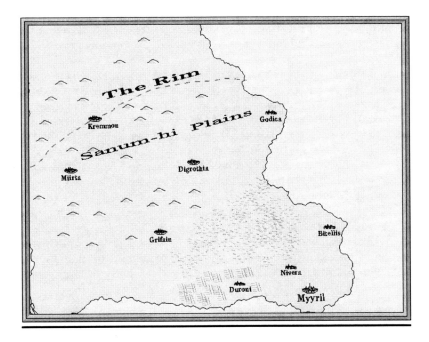

<u>Prologue</u>

Dark skies in strange seas were never a good omen.

That was the first thing Captain Aaron Civise had learned from the previous captain of *The Forthcoming Sun*. He inherited the prized vessel when his captain received The Kraken's Vice, a sea sickness that was slow and painful always resulting in death. It happened to crew that remained on the sea for too long without the proper provisions. They were currently on the thirtieth day on sea, a week overdue.

Taking the northern route was a slower trip. If they had taken the Southern Route like everyone suggested, they would have been home already. The former captain explained he had nearly died there months before, refusing to listen to reason. Death still found him despite going the complete opposite way.

His first mate, known as Horim, asked, "Is that it?"

Civise replied, "I'm not sure. Doesn't look like it. From what our Elf Eye has said, it's much smaller. Bring him to me."

Horim didn't delay as he looked for the elf. He was a lifetime first mate, knowing the seas quite well. He just never developed the skills one needed to captain a ship. He was a short and stout man, slow to act generally because of his physical limitations. Under pressure, there was no one else he would rather have at his side. There was never a captain who ever regretted having him aboard. Aaron was the same way.

Aaron grasped the wheel trying to steady her from the rough currents. He was a strong man, tall and fair . . . or so the ladies usually said. By now, like the rest of the men onboard, he was scruffy and probably smelled worse than a dead carcass after having not showered in weeks. It was hard to see all the water surrounding them yet none to wash themselves with. They needed to save the water they had on deck for drinking. Aaron scratched his beard as he got the ship straight.

Their destination was the elf stronghold of Hiierland, but they should have known this trip was doomed when their mast broke hours after leaving port. They had returned to repair it, but much good that did. It broke again during the latest violent storms they ran into. With another of their sails damaged as well, Aaron was running dangerously close to losing his crew. They had to be close . . . just had to be. Life would have been much easier if the elves had kept all their island fortresses up. At least they could have stopped on the way. Now, Hiierland and Fort Za, much further south, were all that remained of the once greatly touted Western Island Wall.

The Great Western Ocean was a dangerous place, located in between the mainland and the continent that was being called Dragonia by the elves. Sandwiched somewhere in between them was their target . . . along with thousands of miles of ocean. It was such a small blip on a map that it made finding it that much harder. Normally elves were only allowed to make deliveries there, but as they were still trying to recover from the Ettui Island Wars it left them contracting many human vessels as well. This alone made it essential to have a competent Elf Eye aboard.

Horim finally returned with Higalmos. Like every elf, he was taller than anyone else on the ship, though by far not the tallest he had ever seen. This was only his second trip on the water, so he spent most of his time below deck. It was just Aaron's luck that they were given a greenhorn Elf Eye to lead them. He was certain that he knew the way, but every time he pointed them in a direction they ran into a storm that turned them around.

Aaron said, "Good of you to come. We seem to have run into some land up ahead. Please tell us that it's Hiierland."

Higalmos looked in the direction the captain pointed as he joined him. He could tell him right away that was not their destination. It was much too large. Plus, Hiierland didn't have a mountain. This one seemed to have the largest he had ever seen. It could only be one place . . . a place they would much want to avoid.

Higalmos answered, "I'm sorry to disappoint, but that is not it. We should go. We will not find any good on that island chain."

The elf and Horim began walking away, but not Aaron. He kept staring at the mountain. He couldn't take his eyes off it. He heard what Higalmos had said, but how did he know?

Juulomasula.

That's right. They needed food . . . and water . . . and there was something there that he wanted. What was it?

Aaron said, "We are stopping at the islands."

Both stopped as they stared at him. They were nearly halfway across the ship, but his order was loud and clear. Was he being serious? Landing on those islands was the worst idea in the history of bad ideas.

Higalmos pleaded, "Captain, I highly recommend that we not head . . ."

"We are going toward that island. It has everything that we need. If you'll not listen to me then go back below deck."

Horim wanted to stop him. Every sense that he had in his body screamed for him to do something. Yet, for some reason, he had the strange desire to go there as well. What harm could it do? Just to set on real land would be a relief and a blessing.

Higalmos looked on worried. He didn't like this. He knew where they were and he knew what was on that island chain. It was not a good idea at all to go there. He was going to have to put a stop to this.

As he walked toward the captain, three of the ship hands walked in front of him, not saying a word.

Higalmos commanded, "Let me pass. I must speak to the captain."

The largest hand, a tall burly man, responded, "The captain is busy. Can't you see he is steering us? He has no time for your useless words."

The elf was taken aback. What was going on? Why were these lowly ship hands trying to block him? Next to the captain and his first mate, he was the third most powerful person on this boat.

Higalmos yelled more forcefully, "Let me pass. Now!"

It was then that he felt it: A strong magical presence. He looked to the south, the direction where it was coming from . . . right at the islands they had found. He had to get them out of here.

"Captain, you must turn around now!"

The hand said, "Men, secure the elf."

They tried to grab him, but he was much too fast. Everyone on board had turned against him. *The Forthcoming Sun* was not an overly large vessel, but it was full to capacity, which made moving around difficult. That was Higalmos' problem now.

Most were trying to catch him with their hands, but others were using boards and nets to apprehend him. The island was getting closer, as were the dark clouds. He would rather be stuck in another storm than on that island chain.

As he ran in between two boxes, two of the crew tried to pincer him. When he got close to the one in front, he leapt over him, causing the two to collide. Captain Civise was now in view. He saw a strange hunger in his eyes as they narrowed toward the islands. This whole time he had tried to contact the nearest elf he could. They were probably about two hundred miles away from Hiierland, so well within the range of his Elf Speak. Yet, as they got closer to the island, he couldn't seem to reach out to anyone. He could feel the power strongly now as well. He could hear it calling to them. Was it blocking his abilities to contact another elf as well?

He began to run for the captain when a rope suddenly lifted, tripping him hard to the deck. Even before he was able to know what was going on, three nets were on top of him and held by eight crew members. Higalmos struggled, but it was no use. Elves had many advantages over humans, but strength was not one of them. Especially when they were so many days out to sea and no elf food in sight.

Higalmos pleaded again, "Captain Civise! Please turn back! There is nothing on this island!"

Aaron replied, "It is here somewhere. I can feel it. It wants us to find it. Why else would it have guided us here? It is ours."

They were within three miles of the island and coming in fast . . . too fast. Everyone could hear the sounds underneath the ship. Higalmos gave one last attempt to escape. There was still time, but it would have to be now. He used what little he had left, but they countered by throwing more men on the net. There would to be no stopping it now.

Even with the sounds of water entering the ship from below and the men screaming, the ones on the deck and the captain made no attempts to slow down. They showed no remorse . . . only an unheralded desire.

It happened about a mile off shore of the northern island of the Simorgan chain. A large impact rocked the *Sun* as it caused everyone to fall. *Damn, now it was too late.* Higalmos knew from the shock that the bulbous bow was destroyed. If they had stayed the course, then they might have landed on the coral, keeping her at least afloat to some extent. That didn't happen. Captain Civise wanted the ship on the coast. He had to get it to land whatever the cost.

Aaron ordered, "Full speed ahead! Keep going! We must get it! It wants us to get it! Come on, you sea dogs!"

Higalmos now looked terrified. When he meant landing, he meant on the rocks. At their speed, the ship was going to be unrepairable and lost. Anything but that! Not on this place!

There was nothing he could do. The crew seemed just as hungry for it as their captain. They didn't even know what they wanted, but whatever it was called to them to locate it. As the ship crashed into the rocks, everyone on deck was thrown into the water.

Higalmos struggled as he was still tangled in the nets, which was keeping him submerged in the water. Even though he could last longer than a human underwater, he could still drown. That was never a good way to die. After doing everything he could, he was finally able to free himself and get topside.

The scene was bleak. Crew members who did drown floated face down in the water. Some fell on the rocks, dying instantly or barely moving. There was about fifteen of the eighty crew member still floating, including their captain. They had no choice; they had to turn south and he would need to find a way to reach his brethren from on land.

As he turned to swim south, he could see clearly the mountain that they saw in the distance before. It was a sight he had hoped to never see with his own eyes. He was born just after the Island Wars, so he only heard of this place in stories from his parents. They were now in the shadow of Mount Hrithgorn, and a storm was coming. And for them, the survivors of *The Forthcoming Sun*, he knew their nightmare had only just begun.

1

On a hot, late summer day, the last place Neeza wanted to be was sitting in his council chair. It was elevated slightly above the rest, making it just that much hotter than the rest. He wiped his brow. It was situations like this he wished mages wore something else besides robes. Nearly all the persons on the council were aged men and women too, so they all were going through the same. *This meeting would be over soon*, he reminded himself. They had already been there for a few hours. Just needed to last a little longer.

Neeza was not a young man by any stretch. He was 816 years old, his name day only a few months away. His face and skin had been wrinkling more and more each year. His white beard was almost iconic now, having been the longest reigning leader of the magic using Mage people for over half a millennium. It was a burden he was happy to be lifting, but that still didn't end his troubles.

"Honorable Neeza. Are you ready to move onto the next subject of discussion?"

He had lost his train of thought again. It was a reoccurring theme with him over the last few years. Thank the gods that his retirement was only a couple months away. Five hundred years as Myyril's leader had certainly taken its toll on him. It would to anybody. After he officially called it quits, a steward would take the helm as leader of Myyril and the mage race. That was until his daughter would claim it, but he knew Divi was far from being able to do that.

"I am sorry," apologized Neeza. "Yes, we can continue."

"Are you certain? You seem unfocused today. We can always go on tomorrow if you are unwell."

"No, I am fine. Let's move on."

Bezini, the councilman representing the School of Divination, nodded. The council was made up of fifteen members. Seven represented each school of magic that Myyrilian mages could learn. The other seven were won during an open election every ten years. Sydis didn't lead any of the magic divisions, but he was the second most influential person on the council because he was just that much more powerful than the rest. All except for himself, that is.

Darcoul headed the School of Black Magic and was in a position that usually required an aggressive man. He was at the height of his abilities and an even more hardened man than most. His face was chiseled, easily seen through his trimmed beard. He was tenacious as a teacher, many saying he was worse out in the field. He was not one to mess with. Neeza and Sydis were probably the only two that would be able to defeat him cleanly in a battle.

Dinermar, a man of Neeza's age as they were in many of the same classes when they went to school, lead the School of Illusions. He had been a trusted friend of his throughout his career. Dinermar was going to retire the same time Neeza did, but that didn't stop him from taking on one last student before then. He couldn't remember her name, but she came from a reputable family.

Colletti, the youngest councilperson as her blond hair was not white yet, lead the School of Restoration and White Magic. It was one of the few school positions that were given to a woman because Myyrilian females usually made the best doctors. Neeza's late wife was a great example. The only mark against her was that she let her emotions get the best of her at times. It didn't affect her doing her job, but those moments were interesting times to deal with.

Herodit was representing the School of Telekinesis, the only school he'd been able to get his daughter to attend because it was the only school his wife encouraged her to attend. He was the only head that didn't have a personal student, but that was because he held other tasks outside of teaching that needed to be performed. His beard was growing quite long now having the position for a couple hundred years. Ghorris, the headmaster of the School of Geomancy and Surnius, headmaster to the School of General Knowledge were absent.

Sydis continued, "Very well then. The next object in our agenda is what to do about that rebel mage group, Ferigor's Hand. They have been terrorizing some of the small settlements for years, as we all know. Thanks to the Kittara, we've been able to keep these attacks silent, but they have been growing more daring as of late. They attacked Grifain, which is only fifty miles from the capital here. We won't be able to keep it a secret for long."

This rebel group had been a pain in Neeza's side for nearly a hundred years. They wouldn't attack non-mage convoys as they didn't want any other nation getting involved; especially the humans, who the mages held a very brittle truce with. They were looking to end the current form of government, replacing it with an entirely elected one instead of appointed or handed down by birth. Although the group was small, they had been growing bolder in their targets.

Milfury, one of the elected officials, answered, "We must remain diligent and keep trying to stop these attacks before they happen. If we send our military mages after them it would be viewed poorly by the general populace. We have been promoting the safe environment for years in the capital, but outside our walls the living can be harsh."

Sydis replied, "Indeed they are. Whether it was wise to hide these attacks is not the discussion here. We must seek some solution."

There he was, at it again. He always would second guess him, usually disguising it cleverly through the rhetoric. Sydis was never shy about letting others know he was eyeing the position of High Mage. *Everyone* knew this. How frustrating it must have been for him when nearly 100 years ago his wife gave birth to Divi, thus ending any hope for him to assume the throne after Neeza stepped down. He was worried early on that he might try having her killed, but he hadn't tried anything and at least now Divi was at an age where she could defend herself, even if she did refuse to learn magic.

Neeza answered, "We did so because they started out as simple thieves. This resorting to violence is a recent development, which leads me to believe they have new leadership. One that isn't afraid to take a life for their cause."

Colletti asked, "What are we to do then?"

Neeza hated to have to make the decision he made, but this would give them the appearance of a larger military as well as giving the students a great opportunity for experience. Plus, the council would never agree to send any of Myyril's available 7,000 combat mages to the outlying villages. Those kept the capital safe from the poorer communities and discouraged any notion of a revolt.

"I want you to send newer recruits that have just entered their military training to meet in key cities and villages around the capital. We will tell them that this is an experimental training exercise and they will be stationed there a few months. If successful, we can keep some there as outposts to avert attacks."

Just by the faces they made, he was right about their reaction. It was the right call for this situation sadly. Even Sydis didn't object, which he was famous for doing. Yes, he was sending in greenhorns, but if the increased numbers would prevent even a single attack, then it would have done its job.

Neeza continued, "Very well. Inform their Kittara mentors of the plan. It should be in effect immediately."

The other mages nodded in agreement. At least that went by fast. Normally, any discussion involving the Ferigor's Hand lasted hours. They must have sensed his desire to not stay much longer, too.

Neeza did have one thing he wanted to follow up on, so he asked next, "Has anyone heard from our Paladin candidate? I believe her name is Amber."

Herodit answered, "I last heard she stopped at Fort Za for food and supplies. That was a little over two years ago. I do feel her life force though, so she still is alive. Given her quest, that alone is an accomplishment."

That was good. Neeza actually liked her. She brought a fire the day he initiated her Paladin quest. Normally appointed during a large celebration, Amber requested to have it small because she only wanted the celebration if she returned. None of the others cared too much to discuss the half-mages. They couldn't be avoided forever, he knew. He always wanted to form some type of alliance with them (they did have mage blood in them after all). But the council would never have the ears for it as they considered them abominations not even worthy of living. Paladin trials were their way of dealing with the supposed half-mage 'problem'.

Sydis continued, "I'm glad you brought up the half-mages, Honorable Neeza. This issue has been brought to us by the head of the Kittara. Apparently, the half-mage population has been steadily on the rise. More and more mage women are giving birth to half-bloods. The Kittara are running thin, and are requesting immediate approval from the council to strengthen their numbers. I think this would be wise. We are pushing more and more on them that if they are to keep up with their duties we must increase their size."

Another increase . . . he had already increased it by 500 people in the last year. He understood why Sydis would approve such a measure. Many of his students he taught decided to stay with the Kittara after their military service. Many more probably would too if Neeza didn't put a cap on their numbers. But, since the Kittara was not an official branch of the military, his influence on their decisions was small. They had certainly overgrown their original function, and that worried him greatly.

The council, however, seemed to agree with the idea. Before he retired, he needed to make it a priority to find some reform to take away some of the Kittara's powers. It wouldn't be today, unfortunately.

Before Neeza was able to answer, Haldirin, his personal messenger and confidant, opened the council chamber doors. It took everyone by surprise, wondering what on Gyyerlith he was doing there. Neeza was very curious too. He had told him to only interrupt the council meeting if something of dire importance arose. He even seemed out of breath, despite being young enough that he hadn't even grown a full beard yet.

Neeza stood up and asked, "Haldirin, you have news for me?"

After he finally caught his breath, he replied, "Yes, Honorable Neeza. I was told to retrieve you as quickly as possible. It involves that private project of yours. I was informed it was most urgent."

Haldirin's words sank in the mage leader's throat. By the gods, did she finally have another lead for him? She must have. She wouldn't have sent for him if she didn't. Neeza looked over at the rest of the council trying to mask his excitement.

"I apologize. I must see what Haldirin has for me. Continue your discussions and leave a parchment in my quarters. I will look them over tonight."

The others stood up as Neeza stepped down to leave the council room. Sydis watched with great curiosity. He had heard about this 'special project' that Neeza was conducting. He had been trying for years to find out its nature, but the only person he knew associated with it was Haldirin, and he wouldn't talk. If he could only find out whom he was talking to. With the telepathic block on the council room during meetings, he couldn't even get his student, Cyprinus, to keep an eye on him. Oh well, there would be other times.

Sydis continued, "So, as before, the subject about the half-mages."

In the hallway outside the council chambers, there were a few people walking around, mainly the couriers. It wasn't uncommon for the council men to send messages right after each meeting, normally to inform parties they were representing of the good or bad news. None were in as much haste as Neeza and Haldirin. They had to be careful when they talked about the more specific natures of Neeza's project. He realized it may be a selfish quest, one could even say it was an obsession of his, but one that he felt he needed to finish for his soul to die in peace.

When he felt they were safely out of earshot of anyone, Neeza asked, "Did she tell you anything? Anything at all?"

"I'm sorry, sir. She told me only to get you and bring you to the meeting place. As I said, it seemed very urgent."

And when she said something was urgent, she usually meant it. She was not one to call false claims on something. The only way they were going to find out more about it was to see her.

"So, what is it that you have found for me, Inno? It has been years since you've contacted me about my project."

Inno was still dressed in her alchemical aprons when Neeza entered Mierena's old shop, the former business of his late wife. Haldirin waited outside in a plain robe to ensure no one would surprise them and to be sure no one could identify him. Inno's involvement in this project was one of the closest guarded secrets Neeza had.

Inno was Mierena's assistant for years and rarely talked. Because of her adventurous nature, his wife would always send her to get supplies and ingredients. As he later found out after her passing, she also had more secretive tasks assigned to her as well.

Mierena's death was hard on all, but the two people in this room were a few affected the most. They worked tirelessly behind the scenes trying to find a way to save her from her Gerrun disease infliction since Mierena was willing to help others before saving herself. Unfortunately, there was not enough time. Gerrun's disease was tough to cure because there didn't seem to be a way to reverse the decay physically and mentally. He was certain she would have been touched by what he was doing, but the rest of the mages wouldn't. He used many funds to form expeditions or missions blanketed as training exercises, almost all coming up empty. He couldn't even tell Divi what he was doing. If she unintentionally said something to the wrong people, it would have dire consequences for him and possibly his family. That is why it never went past Inno and Haldirin. They were trustworthy, and more importantly, extremely loyal to him.

"I'm sorry, but the nature of our project is such I have to be discreet while *not* being discreet."

There was little doubt as to Inno's complicated task. She had to gather data mostly outside of the mage territories. So she was frequent in the human port cities, under guise that she is looking for ingredients. He was just happy no one had wooed her on her numerous trips. She was quite an attractive mage that would have made any younger mage quite pleased . . . or human for that matter, though she wouldn't do that. She may like being silent, but she understood the consequences of such an action.

"You are right. So tell me."

Inno finally said as she continued to work around the shop, "I was just over in South Cordca. A very strange rumor has been going around. There is a series of islands surrounding a mountain in the western seas that any sailor who floats near them is driven mad. Many even crashing their ships into the stones saying they had to find it."

Neeza had learned to take any seafarer's tales with a grain of salt as normally there were many embellishments, leading to nothing but a wild garlon chase. He had never seen Inno this excited while telling one, however. Did she find proof that these tales were not fiction?

"Did they name the island chain?"

Inno nodded and replied, "The Simorgon Islands."

The Simorgan Chain! But she couldn't possibly mean the same he was thinking about. Those islands he heard were not very inhabitable and that they should be avoided at all costs. It had to do with something about the land being quite dangerous now.

Neeza confirmed, "You mean the same chain that houses Mount Hrithgorn?"

Inno nodded. This didn't make sense, he thought getting ready to dismiss the tale. Mount Hrithgron had a short, albeit interesting, history. The stories told long ago, spoke of it as an elf stronghold. Lost after their victory against the Ettui, he was led to believe it was deserted. But if sailors that are once sane all of a sudden grow mad, perhaps there is some black magic afoot there. The distance eliminated the idea that he was embarking on a solo mission.

"Are there any elvish tales that might explain this?"

Inno answered, "Just one. The Legend of Valendri's Relic."

He in truth couldn't recall it. Then again, there were many elvish legends out there, so it was entirely possible he had simply forgotten it. He would have to do his research tonight.

Neeza asked, "Were you able to confirm about this Relic? I mean, many elf tales like our own usually concern of lost artifacts that can never be found. I just don't want to commit a trip if there's nothing for us to find."

"I knew you would say that, so I talked with my Elf Eye friend. He told me he has seen the shipwrecks first hand. When I mentioned the Relic, he grew silent and would speak nothing more other than he felt a dark presence about that place."

That is an odd reaction indeed coming from an elf. Elves usually loved when someone asked about their legends and their tales. For one to not want to speak about them with the recent goings on was strange. That dark presence also worried him too. What could possibly be there that was driving these captains to the brink of madness? However, to Neeza, all this information was unimportant. There was still one important question that needed to be answered.

"So, what does this Relic do?"

Inno thought he would never ask. "It has the power to return the dead to the living. And not like the way a necromancer would, where an empty shell of the person's former self would return to life. We're talking living, breathing just like death never happened."

Now *that* had Neeza's attention. He had very few regrets in his time as the leader of Myyril. One of those was that he was unable to save his wife. Mierena gave him everything, and he couldn't help her the one time she needed it. That was the nature of his special project. Nearly 300 years ago, he failed a mission to acquire a long, lost Myyrilian object that could have saved her, thwarted by the Cordcan forces before he could finish the ritual. She died 290 years later, but the sickness had won in his eyes after that day. He would not get another chance in his lifetime to perform the ritual. Inno's lack of new informatiom since then had him lose further hope. If what she said was true, then there was still a chance, even if slight, to bring Mierena back. This truly was exciting news!

"What does one need to make it happen?"

Inno explained. "A personal effect of the person and then to complete the necessary procedures and rituals. This shop is littered with her personal belongings, and I'm sure we can figure out what is needed to be done with the ritual."

Neeza asked, "Will she still have Gerrun's disease? I don't want this to bring her back only to have her inflicted again with it."

Inno responded, "If we can bring her back to life, she would have already died from the disease, meaning it would become dormant in her, creating antibodies. With those, our half-elf friends might be able to finally create a cure for Gerrun's disease! Mierena had always said she would be the key to eradicating it. And as fate would have it, she might have been telling the truth."

The news kept getting better and better. Thank the gods the half-elves had discovered the existence of antibodies. It was a relatively new discovery, but it had helped them discover cures and preventative measures to many diseases that had high mortality rates. He hardly saw a reason why this wouldn't be a good idea to at least try.

Neeza, to comfort his own decision, asked, "You are certain of all of this?"

Inno gave him a disbelieving look, almost afraid she was going to give him the silent treatment. It would have truly been a shame to never hear Inno's beautiful voice again.

"Who was it that told you about the Sealed Cave on Dyyros? Me! If I wasn't sure, I wouldn't have told you."

That answer would have to do. He didn't want to anger her, even though they were all-for-one in this project. Oh, he was so happy the only thing he could think to do was go to Inno and hug her! It was not common for mages to engage in physical contact unless married, but given the circumstances of the news, he felt it was appropriate. As he let go, he had a large smile on his face.

"My, we have much work to do. We have to get a boat, I have to select a team, oh my, this is exciting! But I am curious of one thing. Why didn't you just wait to tell me this? I mean, I am thrilled you didn't, but why pull me out of the council meeting?"

Inno suddenly went mute, looking down toward the ground. That wasn't good. He was hoping her excitement of the relic was all the urgency that she had, but apparently there was more.

Neeza asked again, "Inno?"

Inno finally looked up with a worried expression. "The sailors also told me that I have not been the only one to ask about the relic. You might not be the only person after it.

2

Neeza was nearly to the dock. When Inno told him there may be others going after this relic, he knew he had to act fast. He was not going to allow another chance to bring his beloved back go by the wayside. He failed her once, once too many. Never again.

The dock was relatively small as Myyril never really did much sea travel. For whatever the reason, mages were not good swimmers. Even for the rare ones who could, they struggled. Neeza at a younger age could swim decently, but that was before he grew his beard. Still, there were a handful of mages that called themselves seasoned veterans of the seas. Most of them were viewed as crazy, but that was exactly what he needed at the moment.

Myyril was like any major city of the times, with slight differences of course. It had a grand epicenter where the palace and Mage Schools were located, surrounded by the much poorer families. Located on the Gunjumi Peninsula, it was the furthest city in the south on the east coast of the mainland. They enjoyed everything south of the Sea of the Unifier and up to the outpost of Barnat . . . where the elves' territory started. Everything north of that belonged to the humans minus the Great Northern Desert. Especially with the Human territories, it was land being wasted as far as the mages were concerned. The mage lands were grassy, serene, and beautiful . . . well, grassy at least west of the Rim. To call everything west of the Rim serene was a stretch even he couldn't hide behind. At least they weren't destroying their forests to make way for industry and other selfish means like the humans were.

Humans and Mages had not gotten along since the Great War seven hundred years ago. It was sad that nothing changed in all those years. He had tried to resolve this gap with the humans many, many years ago. They didn't look much different. After the Dyyros 'invasion' as they called it, any efforts he made to form a treaty with them died with his wife. They were one of the reasons he couldn't complete the ceremony, thus they were one of the parties he blamed for being unable to save her. He wasn't going to forgive them for that. *Enough of dwelling on the past for the moment.* He had to focus on the here and now.

Despite his far distance away from the dock, he could see a line of people standing next to a medium-sized boat. He hoped Haldirin did well in his recruiting efforts. He had notified the heads of the various Schools of Magic that he was going on a mission, and if they wanted to volunteer anyone, Haldirin would be by to collect them, and any supplies needed. He also sent private messages to the mage seafarers to see if any would sign up. This was risky, because he had to tell them at least where they were going. If one didn't, a captain would most likely turn you away.

The real risk of course was that they, or someone who overheard them, could tell Sydis. It was imperative that they leave before he found out. He knew he would not only try to stop them, but also try and use the mission against him saying he was reckless to chase after shadows. With the Kittara on his side, there was a great possibilty he could overthrow Neeza. If he could bring the relic back, however, Sydis would lose all arguments. So, he was quite eager to see the team assembled for this journey.

Haldirin made sure he met his ruler before they reached the lineup. He felt bad for his messenger as he doubt he got much sleep last night. He knew he barely got any himself, but he began to wonder if his assistant had gotten any at all.

"Good morn, Honorable Neeza!"

"Good morn to you as well. I see you were successful in recruiting a team and captain. Great work!"

Haldirin replied, "Thank you, but I can't take credit for the captain. He was the only one that said yes. The others told me to go jump in a lake, to put it nicely. They said Mount Hrithgorn is cursed, and we are fools to be going on such an errand. The rest all were assigned by their headmasters or volunteered."

Neeza replied, "Well, let's get acquainted. I am eager to see what was given to us so generously."

Haldirin seemed hesitant, but finally chased after Neeza. When they were finally in the eyesight of his companions, he stopped. Nearly every person was around his daughter's age, if not younger. Was this seriously what they were going to be giving him for this important mission? Kids?

"I see you got your first glimpse at who will be accompanying us."

"They're so young. I was hoping they would send us some seasoned mages. We don't know what we are going to face out there."

Haldirin explained, "I know, but being as I couldn't tell much about why and where we were going, they took it literally as a training mission. They sent out apprentices and early students. I know they are young, but I think we have a fine, ambitious group of people. Meet them, and you may change your mind."

This was not a very good start. He had hoped the urgency of his letter at such a late hour would convince them to send a wiser group. Instead, he had to babysit for a bunch of younglings, most likely just starting their advanced training. In terms of mage training, advanced was one of the lowest levels of development just past basic. He certainly prayed they would mature on this trip, otherwise he would possibly be returning with a lighter boat.

As Neeza arrived, the people stopped their chatter and looked forward. He began to pace in front of them, analyzing them. Only two of the men were old enough to have grown their beards, and for one that was being generous.

The first man he stopped in front of was the most serious one of them all, so he assumed he was from the School of Black Magic. He had short brown hair with a red jewel in his staff. He also wore a maroon robe. Although a mage's robes usually hid the physique of the wearer, he could tell the boy was quite fit.

Neeza asked, "What is your name, my young friend?"

"My name is Lindaris, top pupil of the School of Black Magic, Honorable Neeza. You will not regret having me on this mission."

"Funny, I thought Callianus was the top pupil? Darcoul spoke highest of him."

Lindaris responded, unflinching, "Top pupil of the novice class. I was held back for what they called erratic behavior. They were all lairs, though! I will prove it to you."

Neeza would have sighed, but it would have been a waste to do so now. He was expecting more candidates like him as he got further down the line.

He only replied, "Welcome aboard, Lindaris. I am expecting you to remain true to your word in this mission."

Lindaris didn't react as Neeza continued to the next person in line.

"And you are?"

"I am . . . I am . . ."

The young mage shook with nerves. Neeza feared he would faint at any moment. His hair was short with an orange jewel in his staff. He wore dark blue robes that seemed a little too long for him.

Haldirin introduced, "This is Vindar. He is the newest student of Zarca in the School of Divination. He can be a shy one, but also a large fan of yours."

Vindar finally breathed heavily and said, "It is such an honor to meet you finally! Your actions in the Nesseis dispute were masterful! I will do what I can to help with this mission we are on."

Neeza only replied, "The honor is all mine. Welcome aboard."

Vindar gave a large sigh of relief as if he just relieved a heavy load off his chest. Well, if anything, at least he would be loyal. He walked up to the next person in line, almost not realizing it was a woman because of the way she had her hair.

"Yours, sweet lady?"

"My name is Dyenarus, top pupil of the School of Illusions. I volunteered because I was told your missions bring out the best in whomever you bring. I will do whatever is asked, Honorable Neeza."

At last, someone of repute. He should have known by her infamous silver hair. Her staff had a purple jewel in it and she wore a partial robe that went down to her thighs. The coloring of her milky skin brought out her exquisite hair. He had heard many great things about Dyenarus from Dinermar, who took her in as his last student. She was top of the class and a very accomplished mage, from his understanding. If there was any school he would have wanted the most veteran mage to come from, it would have been from the Illusions school. And he had one of their best.

He was very proficient at the rest of the magical abilities, his family being one of the few who could. It was one of the perks to having the rare pureblood-type known as sacred-blood. Thought to be ancestors of the Myyrilian gods, these mages could master all schools of magic. He wouldn't even know he had that much power had the last leader not told him his origins. He often wondered how powerful Divi could become, but until he got the idea out of her head to not learn magic, he would never know.

Neeza smiled, "It is great to have you on board."

As he walked to the next person, he met the first member that was beyond being an apprentice. He recognized him only from afar. He had much darker skin than the rest, a trait found normally on the mages from the far west near the elf territories. A dark blue jewel was in his staff, his robes a light brown.

"My name is Gerran. I am an esteemed mapmaker and navigator. I am formally of the School of Telekinesis. Also known for my photogenic memory. It is my great pleasure to be here."

Haldirin explained, "We needed to find someone independently as the captain didn't have his own. I was told by many in the inn that he is one of the best. He promised his fee would be very reasonable as he just wants money for his family. Times are hard out west."

Neeza felt a little pity for the man. What parent would name their child so closely to the disease that killed his wife and many other mages? He began to wonder if his profession was by choice, or if he had no other options. His name would have been ridiculed in school. He'd seen it before, even participating in the razing once. It was not one of his proudest moments.

He moved next to the first man to have grown his beard. He hoped they were finally giving him a mage with experience, but judging by his clothing, it would be nothing of the sort. His clothes were shabby, and his staff had a strangely forged light blue jewel. His skin was quite tanned, meaning he must have worked outside most of the day.

Neeza nodded and asked, "And who is this?"

"My name is Biverin, local farmer from the neighboring village of Duroni."

He looked at Haldirin, who looked at the ground. This one must not have been intentional.

Haldirin finally explained, "He overheard my conversation with Gerran. Since he knew everything, I couldn't turn him down."

"And what do you do well, Biverin?" asked Neeza.

"I am a master mage of water spells and can grow anything on any ground, no matter how bad of shape it looks. Looking to do my part!"

Neeza smiled and turned without saying a word. What a collection so far. Not the one he had in mind when he was looking to establish this team. He finally stepped to the next member, another woman. She had brown hair and wore an off white robe. Her staff jewel was even white. Everything about her appearance screamed a healer mage.

"All right! Who's next?"

"My name is Condarin. I am a budding apprentice in the School of White Magic. I am very eager to come with and learn as much as I can."

This one was going to be in for a surprise. Their mission was going to be anything but a simple training session. She would gain plenty of experience, though. He had a feeling she would be healing many people on the expedition.

Before reaching the end of the lineup, he noticed Condarin and Vindar smile at each other. Neeza faced Haldirin, who seemed to know what was happening.

"Those two are dating. When Condarin was selected by the Honorable Colletti, Vindar forced Zarca's hand. Those two are inseparable from what they say. At least they will watch over each other for this trip."

Neeza would have to keep an eye on them as the journey progressed. Love could make one do strange things. He knew first hand what one would do for love when he met his wife. Back then it had almost cost him his life.

He reached the final person in the lineup. He was very short, but definitely was not a boy. He didn't have a beard, but had lots of facial hair. Neeza was curious what this one would contribute to their ruffian group. His staff jewel was green as was his robe.

"My name is Joakon. I'm an apprentice in alchemy. My teacher saw that I was much better using my magic toward potions and tinctures, so I started that. He volunteered me hoping this mission would help with my indecisiveness."

"How long have you been doing alchemy?" asked Haldirin.

Joakon answered, "Five months."

Neeza smile and nodded. He just didn't know what to say. Although he had nothing against alchemy (it was his wife's profession after all), he saw little use for one in this journey. They weren't going to have the tools for him to do his craft where they were going.

He finally reached the last man, who stood separate from the group. He was obviously their captain, and Neeza recognized him instantly. His name was Mimerck, considered the strangest of all the captains. He tended to take many risks that scared any mage that had ever traveled with him. Then again, to take all these risks and to be around to tell about them meant he had great sailing skills. The one thing about risks, however, is that eventually luck would run out. Perhaps he would be more careful knowing the mage ruler was on board. He had a long beard and wore an old, worn hat.

"Hello, Your Honorable! Captain Mimerck at your service! I have the best vessel in the mage territories. *The Sea Dragon* has never let me down! And since your coin cleared, you will get to Mount . . ."

Neeza quickly shushed him, "Not yet. Not until we are on our way."

Mimerck shrugged, "Not my place to question. If we are nearly ready, I say let's get a move on. The quicker we finish, the quicker I can spend my fee. All aboard!"

Haldirin stayed with Neeza as he watched every recruit grab their belongings and climb aboard *The Sea Dragon*. It was not like he had to, but he could feel what Neeza was thinking.

"We are in trouble, aren't we?"

Neeza smiled slyly. "I hope I'm wrong, but yes. Yes we are. Still, we must work with what was given to us. These men and women have come because they feel they can be greater than what they are. If that desire remains strong throughout this journey, then maybe . . ."

The last of the companions were boarding. He started to move when a voice from behind stopped him. To Neeza's joy, it wasn't Sydis'.

"Honorable Neeza, you summoned me?"

"Ah, Tasi, my boy! How are you?"

He was actually glad to see the young mage. He had told him to meet at the docks, knowing Tasi tended to come early. He was Divi's best friend . . . well, only friend really. He was fifty years older than her, barely having even stubble as a beard. At first he saw his age as a problem. However, the boy was nice to her, and because of his daughter's trust in him, Neeza named Tasi her official teacher. It was a role all parties were reluctant to take. Even the council was hesitant to approve the measure from one so young and no teaching experience. Yet, as her father, he was willing to do whatever it took to make sure Divi learned magic. She had to. None of the other teachers appealed to her and if anyone could convince her, perhaps a friend could. So, in the meanwhile, that task was in Tasi's trusting hands. In his opinion, the boy had the hardest part of this mission, and he wasn't even going to be leaving the mainland.

Tasi replied, "Doing well, but I am quite curious as to why you called me to meet you here."

"Understood, but time left me with little choice. I need you to do a favor for me. These other students and I will be going away for a couple weeks. I wouldn't go if it wasn't of great importance. I need you to watch over Divi for me. If you can convince her to train in that time, you would have my eternal gratitude."

Tasi laughed and said, "I can do the first part, but I hope you won't be disappointed if you come back and all she can use is her telekinesis."

He wouldn't be, of course. It was a dream that he wanted to see come true in his lifetime. He still had a good 50-100 years left, but as he learned, years can go with the blink of an eye if you chose to let it. Unfortunately, it seemed he let the last 500 years of his life go like the turning of a page.

Neeza replied, "Many thanks, Tasi."

He was about to turn to step onto the boat when Tasi suddenly said, "She's not going to be very happy about you leaving again so suddenly. You do know this, right?"

Neeza held his head low and closed his eyes. Of course he knew. It pained him every time he had to do it. He wanted to be with her, but because of all the time he missed with her growing up, he really didn't know how to anymore. She had to realize that what he was doing today was for both their benefits. If this mission was a success, they could be one happy family again and he could erase the 'tough love' he put Divi through, the true reason why she was mad at him.

Neeza just replied, "I know, but I must do this."

Tasi, persistent as ever, asked, "Why do you continue to do it then? Go to her and tell her yourself. I know she would appreciate it, and it might start the healing."

Again, he wished he could. He wished he could just cast a cure spell and all the damage would go away. It wasn't that simple, he had to realize. Tasi had been trying for years to correct his situation, but how could he possibly know what to do? He was on the verge of working this out the way he saw best. He loved his daughter more than anything in the world. And once this mission was a success, the true healing could finally begin.

Neeza answered, "Please, Tasi. Just do as I say."

Tasi bowed and said, "Of course. Just be sure you come back. I always fear the conversation I will need to have with her should you not return from these trips of yours."

He turned around and began heading toward the capital. He certainly hoped so, too. The other expeditions he led were nothing compared to where they were going this time. Mount Hrithgorn held more dangers than just the mountain. He had researched all the poems and tales on the scrolls they had in their library last night. The mountain was going to be the least of their worries if what they spoke of was true.

Haldirin asked, "Neeza, are you okay?"

Collecting his thoughts, he replied, "Yes, my apologies. Let's go."

Haldirin allowed him to go first. For once, he agreed with Tasi. He wished Neeza would just try and resolve the problems with his only daughter. He knew he cared about her, but he never showed it. Maybe he just didn't know how. Mierena had always been the one to take care of their daughter, despite her deteriorating state. Which is why the loss was equally hard for both Divi and Neeza. They were both reliant on her to take care of Divi. When Neeza was forced to be a single parent, the only thing he saw important was legacy and tried to raise her the way a teacher would. He just couldn't comprehend how a father would act, but he would never listen to reason. This is why he remained mum.

As Neeza and Haldirin stepped on the ship, the ramp was instantly taken away telepathically by Mimerck, under Neeza's orders. He didn't want anyone getting cold feet at the last minute. With the ramp gone, there was no way off until their destination. Thankfully, none of the recruits paid much attention to its leave.

Mimerck reported, "The winds seem kind and the sea calm. Conditions are perfect to set sail. Honorable Neeza, when you are ready."

Neeza instantly ordered, "Let's go."

Mimerck yelled, "All right everyone! Hold your robes and staves! We are going for a ride!"

He finally raised the anchor. The ship jerked violently as the first large gust of wind hit the sails. Most of the students fell to the deck. Mimerck gave a hearty laugh. Vindar and Biverin joined in on the laughs.

Neeza commented, "And so our journey begins."

Mimerck suddenly asked, "Just so I don't get in trouble later, should we have listened to that mage back on land telling us to stop?"

He was so focused on getting the ship going, he never noticed Sydis standing on the edge of the banks, yelling at the top of his lungs for them to stop. They must have just taken off moments before he arrived.

He turned confidently toward the captain and said, "Not a chance."

Mimerck shrugged his shoulders and responded, "Very well. I heard nothing if you didn't."

Neeza was already beginning to like this man. But then again, he was paying him a lot of Magari to make the trip. He expected nothing more but complete cooperation from their captain.

"How long will it take to complete the trip there?"

Mimerck answered, "Normally a week. But I've made special modifications to this thing."

The captain took his hands off the wheel long enough to show him the hollow center leading to a central pipe. The pipe led down to the water. Quite innovative. It allowed him to use his magic to add some extra power to the boat.

Mimerck continued, "This is a mage powered boat. We'll be there in four days, five if we run into weather, which one always seems to do taking this route."

He held onto the wheel as traces of blue light filled it, the magic spell cast hitting the water propelling them further. Between the wind and Mimerck's invention, it appeared they might make it there in record time. Good. The quicker they got there, the better.

Condarin looked back to also notice Sydis, "Hey look! Master Sydis came to wave us to a good journey!"

Nearly all the recruits went to the back of the ship and began to wave back toward Sydis. He was well known among all the students because he would often drop in during classes. They knew he was much tougher on his personal students, but to them, he was much nicer than their general teachers. Some students even referred to him as Uncle Sydis. Lindaris stopped waving after looking harder at what he was doing.

He commented, "Are you sure? He looks kind of pissed."

As the ship began to go deeper in the distance, Sydis dropped his arms. He was too late. If only he found out where they were going moments sooner, he could have halted this nonsense. Mount Hrithgorn . . . Neeza was losing it. It was suicide to go there. Other forces were in play and now he was getting the mages involved in it. But there was nothing he could do. None of the other captains would dare go near there, and he didn't want to try and sink the ship with his magic. Too many people watching. They would get the wrong idea. All he could do was sit back and wait to see what happened. He hated to think it, but in his heart of hearts, he felt very soon Myyril would be leaderless.

****

They finally were well off from the mainland, taking the infamous Southern Route. Because of the currents and heavy winds, it was always the fastest, most direct way to get from the east side of the mainland to the west. That goes to say it didn't have its risks as well. Some of the strongest storms originate in this path, making life and death all based on the skill of the ship's captain. One could not imagine how many ships were lost in these waters. Neeza prayed to all the Myyrilian gods that they would not suffer the same fate.

The students seemed to be enjoying themselves for the moment. Although the sea was a scary place for a mage, he could understand how journeys like this would be a change of pace to the normal wear and tear of a mage's training schedule. For a few, this might have even been their first time leaving home. Even though he considered himself a professional at it, he still loved seeing the world. But as Haldirin stepped next to him, he knew it was time to get to business.

Neeza yelled, "Mages, gather around!"

All except Lindaris moved toward Neeza. He wanted to reprimand him more forcefully, but decided against it. Black magic students were more rebellious by nature. Darcoul was the same way. As he learned with the head of that school, he would need to win him over if he expected Lindaris' attention. Since he was still very much in earshot, he would just go on. Another thing he had to consider was not making his School department heads look incompetent. According to Haldirin, most thought the mission was just a glorified training mission because of how he worded it. He had to speak carefully . . .

"I wanted to first thank you all for being here. Your participation is appreciated, whether you were chosen or volunteered. However, I think that your teachers and headmasters may have toned down the importance of the mission you have embarked on. They are not to blame for that, it is I. Thus, I saw it right to enlighten you about our destination. Afterwards, I suggest we rest, as we will need to be strong physically and mentally."

They all listened attentively. He thought that was tactfully said. At least it left his teachers and schools out of any immediate criticism. Most of his missions were just that, minor and not requiring much skill.

Dyenarus finally asked, "Where are we going?"

Neeza looked at Haldirin before answering, "We are enroute to Mount Hrithgorn."

Based off their reactions, they almost all heard of this place as well. Most were chattering in disbelief, while some contemplated quietly.

Gerran asked, "You mean *the* Mount Hrithgorn?"

Haldirin added, "I know of no other by that name."

Biverin meanwhile asked, "What's Mount Hrithgorn?"

Condarin asked, "Why would we need to go there? There are tales that the mountain is cursed."

"Curse? What do you mean a . . . curse?" Biverin asked.

There was the reaction Neeza was expecting. Stories of Mount Hrithgorn's fame went long back. He recalled reading them as a child after re-reading them the previous night. Tales of curses and deformed beasts cluttered page after page. But in all these years no one could prove that a curse was ever in place or that anyone was even on the island at all. Now might be different based on recent events . . .

"I would not have risked such a journey if the benefits didn't outweigh the dangers. I will say that it will potentially be very hazardous. No one has supposedly stepped on that chain in 800 years as the elves that occupied the Mount mysteriously disappeared. Anything can happen."

Joakon asked, "So what is there?"

Neeza replied, "There is a relic, one that has most recently been driving human merchant ships and their crew to go mad and crash into the rocks of the island chain. As we've confirmed from surviving Elf Eyes, there is a strong magical presence there. It has always been there they tell us, but has grown stronger the past few weeks. We are going to enter the Mount, find the relic, and bring it back so we can try and examine the source of its magical power."

A few of the candidates were deafly silent. They were scared, and he didn't blame them. Very few mountains on Gyyerlith incited as much fear as Mount Hrithgorn did. Even fewer had the reputation their current target had. With its brief but strange history, it definitely earned it.

Vindar finally spoke, "What worries me is that we'll be entering an elf territory, I assume, without their permission."

Haldirin quickly corrected, "Former elf territory. As far as we're all concerned, it's free land. The elves could have re-settled it, but chose not to."

"You mentioned that this relic has been calling human sailors, leading them to their deaths. We aren't after this to make a weapon against the humans, are we? If we are, then I refuse to partake in this expedition," said Dyenarus.

Mages sure have grown resistant. Gone was the time of students agreeing with their elder unquestioningly. She did have a legit claim this time, however. Many of the mage sponsored campaigns in the past were a guise to secretly get ingredients to make better weapons. Most of the others seemed to share her same sentiment, though not some.

"I can assure you all we are not seeking this relic to use as a weapon. As mages, it is our responsibility to catalog, research, and characterize any new forms of magic that exists in the world. This is a new type of magic, and we must find out what is causing it to be so lethal to some and not to others."

Haldirin added, "Besides, your teachers must have thought highly of you to choose you for such an important mission."

"That is Hurip fodder."

Everyone turned to face Lindaris, who had a scowl on his face. Of all the people, he was the only one who was angry.

Lindaris continued, "We're here because our teachers thought most of us were too much trouble, so they sent us with hopes we'll be fixed when we return. Don't try and make this sound better than this is. I heard the words from Darcoul's own mouth."

He was still sensing uneasiness in them. He had to do something quick or else he risked losing them for this entire journey.

He turned around to see what Mimerck was talking about. A large tidal wave, at least a hundred feet high was coming their way. So that was what a 'blanket' was. There was no time to waste. Neeza rushed toward the bow of the ship. The meat of the wave was more toward port, but there was no way to avoid it. Their only hope was to go through it, with a little magical advantage. As he reached there, he stood in the center. He looked to his left and right, where Lindaris and Dyenarus were in front.

"Hold me down! I need to be as straight as possible!"

Both walked forward and grabbed the mage leader's robe as he tightened the grip of his staff in his right hand at a forty-five degree angle, while holding his left hand out. The turquoise jewel in his staff began to glow lightly. No normal spell was going to get them out of this. He needed to use one of the Eirborenz spells. These were powerful spells that only sacred-bloods like Neeza could perform because they required a lot of energy. These were approved by the gods to be used sparingly. It was only the twelfth time he'd ever had to use them in 500 years. It was much different than the Forbidden spells. Those were spells of the gods that were only to be used once in twelve lifetimes, so never. All the Forbidden spells could destroy cities and end ways of life. No mage in recorded history had ever had to perform one.

The wave continued to get closer. Biverin and the rest began to panic. If that wave hit, there was no way the boat would be able to stay on its course without capsizing. Mimerck was probably the safest person because he could grab onto the wheel as leverage.

"We're going die."

Dyenarus yelled, "Don't lose hope!"

Neeza could hear what was going on, but he couldn't comment. He needed extreme focus to pull this off.

Neeza finally began to chant, "*Guronnon Forintia. Hurip Supura. Ielio Hempanan. Guilliom Veronta!*"

Out of Neeza's palms a mighty energy blast pushed forward, hitting the wave. Lindaris and the others were amazed. The energy of the spell was actually pushing the wave backwards. Eventually, the wave crashed back into the water as they harmlessly moved on.

Lindaris seemed the most impressed by what had occurred, "I so want to learn how to do that."

Dyenarus asked, "Are you okay, Neeza?"

Neeza nodded; he was too tired to speak at the moment. That spell took a little more out of him than he thought. Dyenarus brought him toward their end of the boat making sure he was secured.

Mimerck yelled, "Much obliged, Neeza! Maybe when you retire you'll think of coming with me full time! All right ladies and gents! The worst is behind us now! Five waves more and we'll be through!"

Joakon yelled, "You said that twenty waves ago!"

"Well, bound to be right one of these times!"

Mimerck began his maniacal laugh again as Vindar looked and Condarin again, trying to comfort her, "That guy is crazy!"

3

"Land ahoy!"

All the mages looked toward the starboard side of the ship. There it was, after five days of travel: The Simorgon Island Chain. Although they couldn't see the mountain yet except for its peak, the outlying islands appeared to be tall and rocky. From what Neeza could see, there was not a beach to land their vessel. The islands were just north of the elvish territories on the mainland, so they had to move far enough out past Fort Za to reach their destination.

The students all went to the side of the boat to try and catch their first glimpse of the fabled mountain. To think, they would be the first mages to lay eyes on her in . . . well, ever. None would admit it loudly, but they were glad to be here. It was more exciting than reading scrolls and practicing on dummies all day. Real life experiences were usually the best training. It was their first time off the mainland, so there would be a learning curve, but they had Neeza. Whatever they did wrong, he would correct them. If they were going to be marooned to a foreign shore for an adventure, they were glad it was with him.

Mimerck said, "Looks like we are in the clear as far as the elves are concerned, which is a relief. Would really like to avoid confronting them if all possible."

Joakon asked, "Why would they be mad? I thought they no longer inhabited the islands?"

"You have much to learn about the elves, my boy. Once they own something, they seem to think it's always theirs, whether it's true or not. They still consider Barbata theirs even though the Ettui have controlled it for over a thousand years," explained Mimerck.

Seeing that the student understood his statement, he walked over to Neeza, who was standing next to the stern of the ship.

"Well, Honorable one, here we are. Mount Hrithgorn and all its damned glory. You feel it too, don't you?"

Neeza commented, "Yes, it's a very strong magical energy. None like I have felt in my life."

Mimerck added, "This is your last chance to turn back. We shouldn't be here. Whatever is flowing from that island is dark energy. I don't like it one bit."

Neeza didn't answer, instead he walked toward the rest of the students. He was surprised at Mimerck's change of heart as he was here mainly for gold and that damned glory. Returning without even trying was not an option for him. They got that far. It wouldn't be fair to the students who were starting to gain some confidence, and it wouldn't be fair to Mierena. He was doing this for her. Giving up would be like killing her again.

"Just find an adequate landing spot," advised Neeza halfway to the other side of the boat.

Vindar suddenly asked, "You told us that sailors who have sailed near these islands went mad. Why, it can't be more than ten or so miles away. Why are we okay?"

Neeza was about to answer, but Mimerck did first, "Powerful magic affects the races differently. Those that are weak to sensing magical properties like humans are easily influenced without knowing it. Mages and elves are very sensitive to magical energy, so we can sense and control it better when confronted with it."

"You should be able to feel it," commented Neeza.

Dyenarus was the first to answer, "Yes, and you're right. I know I'm still young, but I've never felt this kind of energy. We may have found a new magical source."

Their ship slowly began to creep toward a break in the outer islands. As they did, they all got their first glimpse of the infamous Mount Hrithgorn. It certainly didn't look special other than its enormous size, but the surrounding islands and atolls made the view unique and beautiful. The sky was cloudy at the moment, giving it the ominous appearance that the stories told about. As they neared the gap, a scraping sound could be heard coming from underneath the ship.

Gerran asked, "What's that noise?"

Mimerck cursed to himself before replying, "The coral reef. The water is too shallow for me to take the boat straight to the mountain, even as small as it is. Unless the other gaps are different, we might have to land on one of the larger islands and walk from there. Can't risk holing the ship up, otherwise we won't make it back to Myyril."

He should have assumed as much. Elf strongholds tended to have very few points of entry. If all the points between the islands were that shallow, no enemy would be able to reach the mountain without earning it.

Neeza ordered, "Dock at the first chance you can. We'll walk toward the mountain if we have to and see if we can find a place for you to bring the ship closer. Students! Get your things from below. As soon as we land, the trek toward Mount Hrithgorn begins."

The students did as told with no questions asked. He could feel their mixed emotions of excitement and fear. The realization that they were advancing on a place of legends began to overcome them. Neeza only stared at Hrithgorn and its ominous peaks. He didn't care how difficult it would be, or what resistance they might meet. He was getting in that mountain, and he was getting that relic. Nothing was going to stop him, not when he was so close.

Neeza whispered, "Hold still, Mierena. I'm going to bring your salvation."

Mimerck heard the whisper, but opted to say nothing. It was clear to him why Neeza was here. He only hoped this wasn't a foolish quest that would cost them their lives.

Mimerck landed on the largest island on the southeast of the Simorgon chain. It was the only one that they could find after an hour of slowly moving around the perimeter. It had an eerily quiet search. It was as though all life had failed to exist. Not even the sound of the insects could be heard.

When the ship docked, the students began to unload onto the short beachhead. Just from there, Neeza could see much uphill walking in their future. Wasn't going to be doing his old knees much good, but then again, neither did that adventure in the storm. When he recovered from the spell, he had felt exhausted and rested the remainder of the day. There was no denying it. He was beginning to feel his age. It only needed to last a few more days. Then he'd be back in Myyril hopefully with the answers to his problem.

"You sure you're going to be okay? You looked pretty bad after we got out of that storm."

He turned to see Mimerck looking at him with a sly smile. "I'll be fine. It's just I haven't had to use one of those spells in a long time. I appreciate your concern."

"Well, I'm just making sure my investment is healthy enough to return home to pay me. You're no good to me dead. That's why I'm going with you."

Neeza refused, "No, we need you on the ship until we can find some way to get you closer. I want the ship as close as we can get it in case we need to get out of here quickly."

"You still don't trust me, do you?"

Neeza responded, "Well, you did admit you were here for the gold."

Mimerck looked hard at Neeza before giving a hearty laugh. He didn't understand what the captain had in mind. He normally didn't take private ships, and this reminded him why. The captains tended to have agendas.

He finally responded, "So I did. You afraid I'll get the gold first and run? What good would it do me? Everyone knows I took you and the students. I'm certain there would be nowhere I could hide. If I was you, I would keep my focus on Mount Hrithgorn. I'm the least of your worries."

Mimerck looked toward the students, most of them already off the boat. Biverin was finishing his one bag, looking out of place as the other students at least had three each. Condarin and Vindar were helping each other with theirs. He could see the budding relationship with those two. Even their schools of magic complimented each other. He never discouraged two mages having feelings for each other during missions. After all, that was how he met Mierena. It was from that first time that had Neeza concerned for these two students. He nearly lost Mierena and himself on their first mission together. What if something happened to one or the other?

Gerran had more map scrolls than anything in his backpack. It reminded him of his younger self a little, exception for the map part. He would spend hours in the library studying tomes and spell histories, trying to learn whatever he could. It was something he had tried teaching his daughter. He knew she went to the library as requested, but that was as far as it usually got.

Dyenarus and Lindaris were probably the most prepared, as they packed their rations and tools in a certain order. She was obviously more polished at this point in her training, but Lindaris had such great potential. He made a good point earlier. Darcoul would often send his 'troubled' students on these missions. These expeditions were the best form of learning to use attack spells. If things went to plan, Neeza would be returning to Darcoul a much improved pupil. Time would tell.

Let's see, that is every . . . wait, where was Joakon? He finally saw him coming down the ramp carrying three large backpacks that made a noise of glass rubbing against each other with every step. The straps were loose and slipping from his shoulders, making it difficult to balance himself along with the other bags he carried. Condarin and Vindar saw his struggles and chuckled.

Neeza commented, "Funny. I don't remember seeing him bring all this on the ship before."

Mimerck cleared his throat and replied, "He was the first one at the docks. He loaded that *before* anyone else got there."

He continued to struggle with his bags full of alchemy potions. Dyenarus shook her head before looking at Lindaris. Oh, how much the Black magic mage would have loved to just watch Joakon try and get it right. This was the closest thing to entertainment they had in a few days. But Dyenarus' nod told him it was probably best to help him. Being the faster of the two, he grabbed the two bags Joakon held in his right, while Dyenarus grabbed the other from his left, patting him on the shoulder. He still looked tired and disoriented, but thankful.

Mimerck gave a heavy sigh and said, "Neeza, I wish you good luck. You're going to need it."

They journeyed throughout the afternoon, mainly under the shade of the tall trees. Neeza was always wondering on the boat trip how this part would turn out. Under normal circumstances, the mage students usually got along without a hitch. They were mainly from the same schools of magic and knew each other quite well. With exception of Condarin and Vindar, it appeared this group barely knew one another, if at all. It would have been better if they had because then the group would have an established unity and chemistry. Then again, this was definitely not one of those normal times.

Neeza had to stop a few times to rest. He wasn't tired because of the distance they walked so much as the travel was uphill. The island didn't seem that high from the boat, yet it seemed like they never went downhill at all. They never realized the perspective of how high they were until they reached an open plains area offering a clear view of Mount Hrithgorn. They would have been about a third of the way up the mountain had they been climbing it.

Neeza stopped to admire the mountain. It was much larger than he had anticipated. One couldn't see the western set of islands barring the northern tip because of its gargantuan size. Gerran saw what he was doing and stopped next to him.

"Looks so close, like you can almost touch it."

Gerran observed, "Sir, the sun is setting. We should find a suitable camp for the night."

Neeza agreed, "Yes, we will travel a little further until we find a good spot to make camp."

Gerran relayed the order to the students who moved ahead. Haldirin, who stood by, looked at Neeza and patted him on the shoulder before moving forward. He was definitely worried about his boss. His spirit was never stronger, but he was slowing down with his age. As he knew from painful experience, it was hard to convince a mage that they were getting too old to do things. Haldirin was certain he would probably be the same way when he got old and grey. One thing was certain: he was going to need to keep a tight watch on his boss' health because Neeza wasn't.

Night hit an hour after they found a suitable place for camp. They chose a clearing near the top of the highest hill, located on the southern part of the island. Dyenarus was worried it would make them easily visible to anyone, but so far, they had not run into anybody. Many were even privately dismissing that there might be any locals living there.

Biverin took care of the fire as well as getting food prepared and distributed. Neeza laughed it off at first, but having Biverin was a blessing. The farmer mage was a great cook, and more beneficial than that, he could spot poisonous plants and berries with just a glance. Without him, they might have either had some very sick mages or some very dead ones. He had just finished concocting a stew with some of the available plants and whatever he brought with. They were not likely to have a finer meal than this while they were here.

Neeza sat near the edge, overlooking Mount Hrithgorn. It was three miles from the island they were on, but because of the atolls, it was going to be an obstacle getting to the elvish base in Hrithgorn, much less getting a ship there. One could see everything from their vantage point on the east side of the mountain. The island chain consisted of six large islands surrounding the infamous Mount. Atolls surrounded the inner circle and because they lacked a small boat, those were going to be their bridge toward their destination. From the look of it, they needed to reach the extreme south of the current island they were on to make it happen. That was the only part where he saw the land close enough for them to use.

His focus once again returned to Hrithgorn. It seemed to growl at him, warning to abandon his quest. He knew he couldn't. He had to see this mission through. *It was going to take more than a parlor trick to scare this mage away.* A quiet obsession was welling inside him as he refused to let the stories of the place deter his desire.

"Are you all right, sir?"

Neeza turned to see Haldirin, sitting next to him, "Yes, just thinking about what to do next."

"Sir, I will just say the words because I am concerned. Not just about this mission, but about you. Since you cast that spell on the boat you've been physically sluggish. Tiring faster than you normally would."

Neeza replied, "I appreciate your concern. The spell took a lot out of me, but what you are seeing is just age. You'll understand when you reach it."

He stood up to walk toward the students, who were now sitting around a decent size campfire. He observed Neeza sit down, still in the distance so as to not intrude on their current conversations. Haldirin didn't like Neeza's avoidance of his question. Of all the people on the mission, he was the one with the most to lose. He had to see that. His moving closer to the kids meant their conversation was over.

At the campfire, the students were laughing as Biverin told a tale about his old teacher's reaction to his deciding to become a farmer. Condarin and Vindar were sitting next to each, while Lindaris and Dyenarus sat on the other side. Gerran sat next to Biverin while Joakon sat opposite of the flame.

Gerran finally said, "Great story! I never thought that about you. But you continue to surprise."

Vindar suddenly said, "Well, as we each come from different schools, I know each of our teachers taught us something unique. Don't be afraid!"

He started with a ricocheting light show. If the fire didn't already draw anyone's attention, that would have. Condarin followed by casting butterflies of light that had a soothing feeling as they passed through everybody. Biverin showed his talents by planting a seed and having it grow nearly instantly. Gerran relied on his telekinetic powers to juggle four big stones, tossing them over the edge so they splashed in the water. Joakon used a couple of his mixtures, one that produced a heavy smoke and the other negated smell for a few moments. Dyenaris showed her skill by sitting up from behind a nearby log, revealing that they had been talking to a copy of her the whole time. Lindaris, however, refused to participate, thinking it a childish game they were playing. He learned Black magic so it would be destructive, not entertaining.

When the laughter settled down after Dyenarus revealed her secret, Biverin finally asked, "I wanted to ask, since it seems everyone else knows more about it than I do. What happened here? In Mount Hrithgorn, I mean. I'm not in the schools anymore, so I'm not sure what the popular stories are. When I went there the tales involved a land of shadows to the east of the human lands."

Those tales were still prominent, but never proven. Quite frankly, it was never even worth exploring, at least in the eyes of the mages. There were no magical powers they could feel, and if they wanted to trade with the elves, their farthest trading partner, it was quicker by land or taking the Southern Route. The ones for Mount Hrithgorn began circulating for quite a few years as well, picking up more steam because of the rumors. As Dyyros didn't do much trading outside Cordca, not even the humans had much desire to see if these tales had any validity to them. The mainland had everything each race needed. Someone would eventually find out, but most likely wouldn't be in their lifetimes.

Dyenarus replied, "Well, I mainly know it as a bard song that I heard as a youngling that I remember. Vindar, you have that flute with you that you were ever so doting about?"

Vindar pulled out the flute from under his robe and replied, "I never leave home without it."

Lindaris commented, "You mean you've had that underneath your robe this whole time? Kind of scared to find out what else might be in there."

The group laughed as Condarin patted him on the shoulder, trying to heal the slight bruise of ego. Dyenarus finally continued.

"Can you play for me 'Shadow over Hrithgorn'?"

Vindar began to play a melodious introduction while the other students waited attentively. Neeza was very curious as well. He had not personally heard the song, but then again it was one bards only told. He was not one to go to taverns and bards were very discouraged from coming to the capital. Nesseis, on the other hand, was frequented by them. Everyone sat quietly as they listened to Dyenarus sing the tale:

In time of fear, an island bore was surreal
Islands of fire, through the sea and mire
Through the brush and the thorn, born Mount Hrithgorn

The elves they did came, seeking more to tame.
Losing their home, with no place they were alone
Finding through these shores, a new place of elvish lores
No more fears or distress, a new impenetrable fortress.

Through the First Golden Age, the enemy came
Bearing teeth and steel, the elves' fate they came to seal.
They fought and they rallied, the fortress did bleed
In the end the foes gone, on the shores of Hrithgorn.

Attack they did more, on the bloody shore.
Four years of tear, no end seemingly near.
From the forsaken halls, to the Gate of Huiilumal,
The Ettui sworn, to take the keep of Hrithgorn.

In the Year of the Beast, when hope seemed its least,
The elves turned the tide, the enemy nowhere to hide.
Smoke and fire filled the land, turning their foes into sand,
Defend itself til it was lorn, fought the Mount of Hrithgorn.

After years of peace, it began to cease.
A plague sent from stone, arose the coffin's drone
And like lights in the sea, the elves disappeared, a mystery.
And now they are all gone, consumed by the Shadow over Hrithgorn.

All the students clapped, whistling their approval. Even Neeza had to applaud. She had a lovely singing voice! It reminded him of Divi's. She was a great singer too, when she felt inspired to do it. Sadly, it had become more and more infrequent.

Biverin continued, "So, basically this used to be an elf stronghold and the people disappeared. Other than that, what's the mystery?"

Vindar interrupted, "Not just any elf stronghold. This used to be *the* elf stronghold. Way before Fort Za ever received the reputation it has now. It was established to keep defense of the Wood Elves' territory. A large battle was fought here by the Ettui, but the elves were victorious. Ironically, that's when things began falling apart."

"What kind of things?"

Joakon explained, "People went missing. Talks of a whispering shadow that would call to them when they slept. It has been said that perhaps this land was once owned by an Eratuu god and the giant battle displeased him, so he cursed the land."

Neeza's ears perked up when he heard about whispering shadows. That definitely fitted with the current situation. However, if that was true, why would it be calling to sailors who just happened to sail by with no intention of landing on her shores? And he didn't believe that an Eratuu god existed.

Biverin continued, "The line that intrigued me was the one about the plague sent from stone, something from the coffin's drone. What does it mean?"

Dyenarus tossed some small wood on the fire as she answered, "That line is the greatest mystery of the song. The plague suggests to what possibly killed the settlers and the defenders of Mount Hrithgorn, but it's all speculation. No one knows what the coffin line means."

"I find it interesting how the song makes no mention of the natives," added Gerran.

"Natives?" asked Biverin.

Dyenarus commented, "Oh, don't fill his head with that rubbish."

Neeza was amazed it took this long for them to even be mentioned. He didn't truly believe they existed based on the legends. But he hasn't always been right about everything. When it came to *them*, he hoped by the gods he was right.

Condarin explained, "They came during the chaos after the Battle of Simorgon. Giants sprouting from the mountain. They were told to be strong, tough, and faceless. Their ruthlessness was legendary. They are supposed to give horror a new name. We call them the Garchai."

Biverin asked, "What does that mean?"

Lindaris finally contributed saying, "It's old Myyrilius. Means 'unholy ones'."

"They're nothing more than legends. There's been no proof that they existed. Even the elves don't recognize them in their versions of the story," added Joakon.

Condarin said, "I've always believed. Elves are tough to take down. What else could have wiped them out so suddenly? Their race is super resilient to diseases, so I find it hard to believe a plague could have made them disappear."

Lindaris began to laugh as the entire group gave an uneasy stare. Neeza saw lots of good qualities in him, but there were also many bad ones . . . ones he would need to grow out of if he wanted to complete his potential. He didn't mind his lone wolf persona. That was a common trait amongst students of the Black Magic School. What he didn't want was for him to put down the group, whether he was better than them or not.

He finally said, "Listen to what you're saying! Legends this and legends that. I'm really hoping the Garchai are real. Pray to the gods, give us some action."

Great. Not only was he cocky, but it seemed like he had something to prove as well. Although that has led people to do many great things, more times than not, it led to the person's destruction. *Time for him to intercede.*

Neeza cautioned, "Never pray to put you or your team in danger. I don't know if the Garchai exist or existed at one time. I do know one thing: We would find ourselves fortunate if we don't run into any resistance until we reach the Relic. I would get some sleep soon. I would like to reach the shores so we can begin finding a better spot for Mimerck to dock."

All the students could feel it. There was something he wasn't telling them. Since they arrived, they could feel a combination of excitement and uneasiness, throwing a major pinch of nervousness in the mix as well. Was there someone else going after the relic that he knew? Would he tell them at all?

Dyenarus stood up and walked to Neeza, who looked over his shoulder to face her. "I know there is another reason you're here. I also know it's most likely none of our business. Just promise me that if there is something that could put our lives in danger, you'll be open with us."

Neeza smiled and said, "Of course."

4

They continued on early, just as Neeza had hoped. The good news was the ground was more level where they were. At least the uphill climbing was over. The only place they had to go was down. The area was full of life and heavily forested for most of the morning journey. As they moved further north, the density of the forest lessened, but the sun was still covered by the shade of the leaves.

As they moved out of the coolness of the thick woods, it became more humid. Which was most unfortunate. If it got much worse, they would need to stop and find a place to cool down. The last thing they needed was to have a bunch of overheating mages. He looked at Haldirin, who was thinking the same.

"Students! Take a seat. We should rest and try to keep cool."

Vindar sighed in relief, "Thank the gods! It is hot out here!"

Lindaris, despite sweating heavily himself, commented, "Don't be a wuss."

"All right, we're all feeling the effects of the heat. Find a shady spot, get something to eat, and relax," reprimanded Haldirin.

Everyone found spots in a relatively shadier area except for Condarin, who brought up the rear. Being the youngest of the group, she probably had never experienced what heat exhaustion was like. At least this was not too bad. In his time, Neeza had felt a lot worse. He nearly had died a few of those times. She would get over it.

Joakon asked, "So how much farther do we have to go? The islands didn't look that big when we were sailing to them."

Gerran replied, "Well, I would say ten miles. The terrain is jagged and we've had to double back a few times, so it has slowed our progress a lot. Plus, this is the largest island in the chain next to Mount Hrithgorn."

Biverin cast a small water spell toward his face, cooling his warm skin instantly. As a farmer, he was probably the best equipped in this situation besides Neeza. The long hours in the sun to do his job probably prepared him the most to the heat. Dyenarus, who saw what he was doing, requested a douse, which he gave unquestioningly. As she wiped the water over her face, she walked over to Neeza, who was discussing their next direction.

"Honorab . . . I'm sorry, Neeza, Haldirin. Can I ask you both something?"

Haldirin replied, "Of course."

Dyenarus continued, "It has to do with the magical usage of mages and how it affects the use of the forbidden Dark Magic. It's my thesis. I was told that you would be the only person who might know much about the subject. My thesis is reliant on it."

Haldirin added, "Odd subject for any one of the Schools."

She agreed, "Indeed. But I found out that Dark Magic originated from a teacher in Illusions, so there must be some kind of connection to our two schools. Granted that doesn't mean I want to learn it, it's just become an interest."

Nor should she *ever* want to learn Dark Magic. It was made forbidden because of the simple reason it was so dangerous. Most mages who learned it never reached their 200th name day. Was it a powerful brand of magic? Oh yes, frighteningly powerful. To have so much power, came with a price. Since they were forced to move to the mainland those thousands of year ago, he had not seen Dark Magic cast. Although, he knew there were tiny cults hiding on Myyrilian lands that still practiced it.

Neeza replied, "I would be more than happy to share with you what I know. I do hope it will be enough for a thesis. There isn't much."

Dyenarus' eyes lit up, and she replied, "Anything would help! Thank you, Neeza! I really . . ."

Her sentence was interrupted by a female scream. As Dyenarus was with them, there was only one person it could be.

Haldirin softly said, "Condarin."

Everyone rushed toward the screaming. Vindar was panicking, calling out her name and telling her he was coming for her. It was coming from behind a thick brush, which Vindar cleared first. He found her on the ground crying profusely. He bent down to comfort her.

"Its okay, Condarin. I'm here for you. What's the matter?"

She didn't speak. She just pointed. As Vindar looked to where she was pointing, he stood and stared with horror, "By the gods!"

The others crashed through the bush to check on her condition. But even their concerns were stymied at the sight in front of them. As Neeza and Haldirin stepped through, what they saw engulfed them with surprise and fear. On yellowish rods that served as spikes, heads were impaled at the tip of them. The one closest was only about five feet tall. The rest were on metal at least twenty feet high, all with a head impaled on them. The spinal cords hung lifelessly from two of the heads. Flies hovered over the decaying flesh.

Biverin said, "Please tell me those heads are fake."

Lindaris added, "Don't bet your life on it. I wish the smell was fake, though."

Haldirin stepped forward and began to examine the shortest impaled head. He had been an assistant to their local medical physician, Frari, for many years, so the sight of such things didn't make him queasy. Still, it was never easy tending to any part of the dead.

"What do you think?" asked Neeza.

Haldirin examined, "Definitely human. Based off the decay, these look to be seven days old. All of them. The cuts were clean, so it took only one shot to do the deed. Those two with their spines attached met a far more painful end."

Damn. Others were coming. The people had arrived there only a couple days before they did. Then again, they could have been survivors from one of the shipwrecks, trying to find salvation on the island.

Gerran suggested, "Perhaps there were two competing parties here for the Relic and this group lost."

Lindaris commented, "Don't be dumb. Another group going after it wouldn't have went through all this trouble. The people that did this live on this island. These are their trophies."

Vindar and Condarin arrived at the same conclusions, and being they were the only two to really believe in the Garchai at last night's campfire, it was doubly horrifying.

Condarin muttered, "Then it's true. They are real. The Garchai. They are real! By the gods, they are real!"

She began to cry again as Vindar returned to trying to comfort her. Haldirin stepped back to get a view of the larger scene.

"I wouldn't jump to conclusions, but I am curious about how they got them this high. The metal stakes are too heavy for normal men to lift, even if you had a hundred of them. Whatever did this is large," stated Haldirin.

Although he agreed with his messenger, he wasn't seeing the big picture of this situation.

Neeza finally clarified, "I don't know if this is the work of the Garchai or not. One thing we know for certain we're not alone on this island."

Travel for most of the afternoon went slowly, more cautiously. The realization that there was something out there, potentially fitting the description of the Garchai, hit the students hard. Up to this point, they had it easy. But with the forest of heads they encountered, they now knew the seriousness of where they were. Condarin and Vindar were the most quiet. Neeza worried about them most because mages, with their personalities, tended to freeze up in the beginning on decisive decisions. One lapse like that could mean none of them would be going home.

It was evident the way everyone was moving that they were tired, but no one wanted to stop. If they did, whoever lived there had extra time to find them. As night fell, there was no fire, no laughing. It made for a tense and uneasy feeling that caused most of them to lay the night awake with fear.

Neeza and Haldirin watched from a short distance. They saw what was happening. Yet, neither knew the best way to handle it. A teacher like Sydis or of that ilk would know. Neeza played the role of teacher a long, long time ago. However, as he was considered too strict, his student was pulled from him. It was the leading factor driving him to his current life in politics when he befriended Myyril's previous leader.

"We are in a real bind here."

Neeza turned to Haldirin. He had lost himself once again dwelling on the past. He needed to maintain focus too. His mind was starting to wander more than he would care to want.

He replied, "Indeed. If the students will not fight, it will make this mission more difficult."

"More difficult? Neeza, it would be impossible! I will help you as much as I can, but you know as well as I, we need them. If they are unwilling to face the situation put before them, we must turn back."

He shook his head and looked at the ground. Things were not looking good, that much was true. The odds were always against them. But unlike everyone else, the options were different for him.

"It seems like an easy decision, doesn't it? Pack our things and leave this place behind. It is an option you all have, but not me. Mount Hrithgorn holds a treasure that I need; one that I am willing to risk my life for. If I must do it alone, then so be it. But I cannot leave. I wouldn't be able to live my last days not knowing what could have been. I'm sorry, Haldirin, but I am staying."

Neeza walked off toward his makeshift bedding as Haldirin looked toward the mountain. As much as he didn't want to go, he was not going to let Neeza go alone. He owed more to the Myyrilian leader than just his life. He was not going to break his oath. He shared Neeza's fate. Giving a heavy sigh, he began to head for his bed. Little did they know, the student closest, Dyenarus, was wide awake, hearing every word they had said.

What a difference a night made. When they awoke, the students were already up and ready to go. They didn't say a word. They didn't flash a defiant or relentless eye. It was almost as if they all accepted they were there. Whatever the reason, he was happy for it. At least he would not be alone in his fight for the Relic.

They made their way more north, thankfully moving downhill with every mile. There they could survey the inside part of the sea surrounding Mount Hrithgorn and relay the info to Mimerck. He wondered what the sea captain was up to. It had to be boring staying on the ship this whole time. Then again, he already had Lindaris complaining how they'd seen no action yet. He could imagine their captain being much worse.

As they reached a clearing, Neeza felt something was odd. A small, yet recognizable magical presence. Still, in that place, he didn't trust anything that wasn't their own.

"Stay close everyone!"

"What is that?" questioned Biverin.

The group looked west toward a shiny object in the distance. Should they have just looked the other way and continued their journey? That would have been the wiser thing to do, but all mages were naturally curious about everything. An unidentifiable shiny object in the distance certainly fell in that category. Neeza knew this, but he was still unable to control the urge to check it out. It might be important, after all.

As they crept closer, all the students could see what looked to be a yellowish shield, and beautifully designed. He knew the designs well.

Neeza analyzed, "It's an elvish shield. That explains the magical presence."

Vindar continued, "Probably left over from the stronghold. But why hang one out here? This is the middle of nowhere!"

Neeza stepped forward. Mainly because of the close relations his daughter had with the elves, he knew most of the clans and their armor craft. He was curious if it belonged to Prince Thamalos and his family, but based off the shield design it did not. He believed it was more Orothai, but he wasn't too sure. As he took one more step closer, a loud, un-natural snapping sound was heard.

"Neeza, look out!"

All he felt was the power of someone tackling him to the ground followed by a loud gong of wood hitting metal. The sound of that collision sent an echo resonating throughout the entire area, causing any wildlife to scatter. As Neeza came more to his senses, he found it was Dyenarus who had taken him down. *My, was she strong!*

"Are you okay?" she asked.

Neeza replied, "Yes, what in the holy heavens was that?"

Haldirin and Joakon examined the large log attached to a rope. Lindaris, while they were looking up, looked down to notice some strange device. Judging by what was above ground, it appeared to go underground much deeper. When he stepped on it, it must have cut a rope that was mainly subterraneous as well. The tree behind them cleverly hid the now taut rope.

Lindaris finally commented, "It was a trap."

Joakon revealed, "And that shield's magic must exemplify the sound of something hitting it, which means . . ."

Haldirin finished his sentence, "They know we are here."

In the close distance a group of loud shrieks were heard. The students were frantically trying to find the source, all of them raising their staffs to prepare for an attack.

Neeza commented, "Level your staves more. Maintain posture!"

Haldirin added, "Sir, is this really the best time to be giving a lesson?"

No, he guessed not. It was a preference of his, that he felt made mage's magic more potent. He was right, though. This was not the time or the place to be playing teacher. Whatever was coming was surrounding them. The shrieks were echoing off the trees and carried by the wind.

Vindar said, "We should run. We stay here we're sitting ducks."

Lindaris added, "Where to? Sounds like we have no place to go!"

Neeza related to the point, but despite the closeness of the sounds, there was nothing coming in any direction on the ground. Unless the creatures were invisible, something that took too much effort from a mage to be worth casting, there was no sign of anyone.

It was then that it hit him. What they were looking for wasn't coming for them on the ground, but above it. A shadow suddenly engulfed them from above. He looked, but couldn't identify what was swooping toward them.

"Get down!"

The students didn't ask any questions as they dropped hard toward the dry ground, barely missing the talons of the large bird-like creature. As it flew up, Neeza got a better look at their adversary. It had to be at least ten feet long with talons sharp enough to cleave a person in half. The strangest thing was its feathers, which reflected the prism as the sunlight hit it. The only bird he knew who did that was known as the Kyroselip, an indigenous bird to the land of the Wood Elves. Yet, why was it here and how did it grow to such a size? They normally only grew as large as a fist.

Biverin yelled, "Incoming!"

This was just great. A flock of seven began to fly toward them. They didn't have much of a choice here. Vindar was right. To stay put was death.

Neeza commanded, "Run!"

The mages began heading north as the birds swooped down. He knew it was going to take a little more than running to discourage these birds, usually tenacious by nature if disturbed. Haldirin seemed to agree.

He turned around and yelled, *"Triolong Firamma!"*

A white fireball split into three ejected from his hand swooping low to the ground before hitting the lead Kyroselip in the belly. It disoriented it enough to cause it to fly toward the air again. One down, but six still to go.

Gerran, as he was running between two logs, telekinetically picked them both up and waited until one of the birds was in position. He tried to smash one between them, but barely missed. *Man, were they fast!* Luckily, the way the logs ricocheted off each other hit two of the trailing birds, taking at least one of them out of commission. Seeing the older members of their band fighting, Vindar and Joakon tried to fire volleys of spells, but none of them hit their marks.

They were going to need to get rid of those birds and fast. The longer they were chased, the easier it would be for whoever was living on the island to find them. They certainly weren't the creatures that placed those heads on that metal.

Neeza turned around, stuck his staff in the ground, quickly chanting, *"Iczera Temmponi!"*

A wall of ice instantly grew in front of him. He grabbed his staff and turned as the Kyroselip crashed into the ice, knocking itself unconscious. The shards of ice blasted forward because of the impact, hitting Neeza and some of the students so hard it caused some of them to stumble. One bird made an attempt to snatch Vindar and Condarin, but a change in elevation was their salvation as they dropped down a small alcove.

Lindaris was sprinting as hard as he could. For all that he learned, casting magic on the run was not something he was particularly good at as his accuracy was way off. If he could get ahead of the group, he could at least get a couple shots off before he had to start running again. When he got enough distance, he chanted a couple times in succession, "*Firammii morza!*"

One of his fireballs hit the Kyroselip head on. It didn't see the spell as it was trying to reach out for Gerran, igniting the bird's normally beautiful feathers and forcing it to crash to the ground. The second one was different, squawking at the others more than actually trying to catch them. That bird had to be the leader. Neeza shot one more fireball that missed before he started running again.

Neeza wasn't sure how much longer they would be able to keep it up. His older legs were tiring fast, and he could sense the panic in the others. If it wasn't for Haldirin supporting him, he may have fallen a while ago on this sprint.

One of the birds closed in on Dyenarus as she began to sprint harder. Despite that, the bird got closer as its jaws surrounded her. When the Kyroselip closed them, it was surprised to see that it had attacked nothing. A few feet to the right, Dyenarus was bringing her hand down as the copy of herself was negated by the bird. She once again ran toward the group.

The Kyroselips began trying different swooping patterns with the remaining birds. They were trying to hit them from the sides and once from up front. The leader continued to fly swiftly, squawking out orders. As Neeza looked back, he noticed a very strange physical disability on the lead bird as well as the others. They had no eyes. Where the eyes should have been was a crusty-looking material covering them. The squawking was beginning to fill the forest around them.

Before Neeza could try and determine what to do next, him and the other students were airborne, albeit for a short while. The grass and the woods blended together, disguising the alcove in front of them. They all rolled down very hard as the world was spinning from their point of view. They could have been easy pickings for the birds, but they did not come. *The alcove must have fooled them, too.* Not enough apparently as he could still hear them overhead.

After what seemed forever, Neeza was the last to stop rolling. His body hadn't ached so much in years. He must have hit a few rocks on the way down as his arm and left thigh hurt a lot. Since everyone was moving, he was thankful that no one broke their necks from the fall or the roll. Many, though, were clearly feeling the effects from it.

Lindaris commented, "Well, that's one way to lose them."

The squawks were getting louder again. Neeza knew they were in no condition to run again at the same pace after the tumble they took. They were going to have to stand their ground and take on the menace. At least, they only had to deal with four to five instead of the original eight.

"Get together! Be ready to unleash the most powerful spells you know!"

From above, the five remaining Kyroselips began to circle around them like buzzards. The lead one landed on a strong branch, supervising the progress of the others. It began shrieking at them, forcing them to cover their ears. The rest of the birds were nearing the ground.

Vindar finally separated from the group, digging his staff into the ground, "Enough of this! *Galiareni Lucenif Hempata!*"

Out of the jewel of his staff a white light hovered thirty feet in the air, where it exploded into a blinding light. Neeza wasn't sure what good that would do since none of the birds had eyes, but then he remembered the spell had a secondary effect. It just might do the trick. He covered his ears as the students followed his lead.

A loud shriek preceded the bright light, even overpowering that of the mutated Kyroselips. The four hovering ones instantly dispersed. The leader tried to intimidate the spell's effect, but even it couldn't withstand the spells potency. The birds flew high in the sky as the spell fizzled out to nothing. Neeza uncovered his ears and stood up to see that they were all alone again.

Vindar gave a celebratory clap of the hands, "Woohoo! Always wanted to try that spell in a real life situation!"

Condarin ran up to him and gave him a half hug, "You did well!"

Neeza commented, "That was a well-thought spell for the situation. Even with the enemy having no eyes, you were still able to scare them off with the sound. Excellent work."

As Neeza went to Biverin, Vindar looked confusedly over to Condarin, "They didn't have eyes?"

Neeza was joined by Joakon as they helped the farmer mage up gingerly. It appeared they didn't all come up from the fall in one piece. A small sharp piece of wood was jutting out of his side. Thankfully it didn't seem to hit any vital organs- he hoped. The way he moved certainly suggested otherwise.

"Are you all right?"

Biverin commented, "Yeah, but I'd feel better if you took this wood out of me. I'd be much obliged."

He waited until he got the okay from Haldirin, who was the closest thing they had to a certified doctor. He gave a nod and Joakon pulled the piece out carefully. He gave a sharp cry of pain as the other students first realized one of their own was hurt.

After the initial pain softened slightly, Biverin eased his breathing and said, "There, much better. Remind me to never to do that again."

He tried to get up, but Neeza stopped him, "Wait. Let me heal your wounds."

Biverin nodded, allowing Neeza to cast his curing magic. The spells would mend the muscles and flesh, but if it pierced any of the vitals, which to a mage were the lungs, liver, heart and brain, it would slowly kill the mage unless it was replaced. Without having a real doctor here, there was no way he could tell if any had been punctured. Even if they could identify, they had no tools to perform the procedure, nor anything to replace it with. Only time would tell.

After the purplish light of the spell finally diminished, with exception of the blood and hole on Biverin's robe, one would have never known that a wound had existed there. He finally stood up with Haldirin and Joakon's assistance. All the students, even Lindaris, showed their concern for Biverin. He found it amazing how moments such as life threatening wounds could bring even people that didn't get along too well together. He knew that Lindaris didn't care for the mage farmer, and likewise for Biverin. But it warmed his heart to see them put their differences aside to work as one. That's what it meant to be a mage.

Neeza finally said, "Okay, everyone. We should get moving again. I'd like to reach the coast before nightfall."

Gerran commented, "Please don't mention fall."

The other students chuckled as they all began to follow Neeza. Lindaris began to move forward, when he noticed Dyenarus had left a backpack. From what he knew about her, she normally didn't forget much of anything. He ran back and picked it up. Perhaps she left it on purpose. He never really thought about going out with her before now, but after seeing how happy Vindar and Condarin seemed to be, maybe she was trying to tell him something. Why wouldn't a beautiful woman like Dyenarus want to go out with a guy like him? He grabbed the bag and quickly ran back to return her possessions with hope of reward at the end.

The group began to walk through a column of trees all planted in a row. These were intentionally grown like this, but why? Condarin, as well as the others, were using their staves to maintain their balance as they were all still a little shaky after the fall. A close eye would be kept on Biverin to be sure no further injury had occurred. Gerran led the way as he had been working hard on figuring out the way to the sea.

Gerran reported as he talked loud, "My, how very interesting! Notice the trees! This must have been some sort of walkway back when this belonged to the elves. This probably led to a town or a fort. And judging by the width of this, they must have been moving large objects. If we follow this, it should lead us to the sea."

Vindar added, "As long as we are as far away from those birds as possible."

"I wouldn't worry about them anymore. They know what we are capable of. Kyroselips are smart creatures. Should be smooth sailing from here," added Gerran.

Lindaris was nearly caught up with the group when it happened. It was almost as if the ground had absorbed them, then lifted them to the treetops. Lindaris was driven back, hitting the old path hard and knocking the wind out of him. Everyone was confused as they swung from the net. Damn it! How could they have grown so complacent to not see this trap? There was great panic from the students as they were trying to figure out what just happened.

Neeza yelled, "Students! Settle down and be calm. Is everyone okay?"

Dyenarus replied, "I'm fine. Vindar?"

Vindar answered, "Within reason. Joakon?"

Joakon said, "Other than not liking heights, I'm good. Gerran?"

Gerran replied, "My pride is hurt by not seeing this, but okay. Condarin?"

Condarin answered, "Other than my only view is someone's butt, okay. Biverin?"

Biverin caught his breathe and answered, "All good. Much better than falling I suppose. Lindaris?"

"Down here!"

As many that could, turned their heads down to see Lindaris still standing on the ground. Neeza breathed a sigh of relief. At least not everyone was captured in his thing. That meant they still had a chance to escape. As fortunes smiled on them, the one that wasn't caught was their Black magic student.

Neeza yelled, "Lindaris! I need you to hit the point of the rope that is holding us up. It might be by the branch of the tree. A couple of fireballs should do it!"

Lindaris looked up trying to find the base. With the traps sprung, there were so many ropes and wires pulled taut. After a while, he finally found it.

"Okay, found it! Gerran, you ready with your telekinetics so you guys don't hit the ground?"

Gerran replied, "Yeah. Just do it!"

Lindaris focused on the base of the net and chanted, "*Firammii morza!*"

The fireball's aim was straight and true. As soon as it hit the rope, the spell deflected off toward the treetops. That was strange. How did that happen? Lindaris brought his hands back. Maybe he needed a little stronger spell.

"*Firammii piranrza!*"

A slightly larger, but hotter fireball went toward the same spot as the first. Just like the previous fire spell, the results were the same. He didn't understand what was happening.

"Lindaris! Is everything okay?" asked Neeza.

"I don't know! My spells are just deflecting off into the sky the moment it hits the rope!"

Joakon asked, "What kind of rope does that?"

Haldirin answered, "A rope with a magical deflection ability. Only one race I know had this: The elves. Which means this is elvish black rope. Good luck trying to cut through it with a normal knife."

Great. Just what they needed. His messenger was quite right. The elves were the only race to ever develop magic-resistant items, and the net was certainly one of them. He thought he felt a magical property when the net went up. But these items were rare even now because the components they required were native to the Barbatan homeland, which now belonged to the Ettui and Eratuu. Plus, if they wanted to cut through any elvish rope, they'd need at least an elvish knife, which they didn't have.

"It's all right. There is always another way. We must think, however. Lindaris, do you see any other way to get us down?"

The young mage searched all around, but he could see nothing that would help them. The ropes were all made of the same material as the net. Casting on the trees wouldn't help either as they were thick and would take hours for him to burn through the sturdy limbs.

Lindaris' concentration was interrupted, though. *What was that noise?* As he looked forward his eyes grew. By the gods! He was getting out of there. He instantly started to run the other way.

Dyenarus was the first to notice his action, "Lindaris! Get back here! Neeza, I think he's deserting us!"

Although he wasn't surprised that it might happen, he was just as equally disappointed. So much potential, so little heart. As Neeza began to think, the students facing the north froze. Joakon began to tap on his shoulder rapidly, but not hard. Now was not the time for random attention. He had to think of something to get them out of the situation.

Neeza reprimanded, "Not now, I'm trying to figure out our options."

Despite his clear answer, Joakon continued to tap him, harder. Now Neeza was getting annoyed. He was usually much slower to anger than that, but they were in some real trouble, and he needed to think. Neeza began shifting around.

"What is so important that you must interrupt me at such an . . ."

He couldn't even get the next word out. Staring at them through what looked like a cracked yellowish helmet was a large bipedal creature. The eyes . . . again there were no eyes. The helmet covered its face completely, only allowing one to see the nose and mouth. Gnarled hair overspread from its head down to its shoulders. It had to be at least thirty feet tall and was very muscular. Across its chest it had cracked armor much like the helmet, but it looked small on it as if it had outgrown the wears. It had a grass skirt covering the upper parts of its legs.

Condarin kept repeating while she cried, "They are real. They are real."

Sadly, it appeared they were. Just when he thought things couldn't get worse, they did. Flesh and blood had replaced the image of the nightmare. They were no longer myth. The Garchai were real.

5

"What are we going to do? Where is he taking us?"

Gerran answered Joakon's questions, "Not to give us a warm welcome, that's all I know. You remember the heads."

It seemed like hours even though it had only been ten minutes since the Garchai detached the net and slung it over its hairy back. Except for its loud breathing, it was relatively quiet while moving for one its size. Even the footprints were soft and barely audible. That almost explained how it was able to sneak up on them . . . almost.

Hanging from the creature's side was a large mace. It had six blades protruding from the center and looked well-made. Something was odd about the whole nature of these things. They weren't normal giants. Neeza had seen giants before way up on a continent to the northwest on one of his secret missions, but their weapons were normally tree trunks whittled down to make it a club. To make these weapons and especially at this size, craftsmanship was a must.

Vindar responded, "I'm sure Neeza has something up his sleeve. Isn't that right? You must have been prepared for something like this."

"If by prepared, you mean I have a plan to escape a magic resistant net against a foe I never thought existed, then . . . no."

He hated to sound so defeated, but there was nothing they could do while entrenched by the net. Not even Dyenarus would be able to use her illusions while they were trapped in there. The only spells that he could think of that wouldn't be blocked were the spells of the gods, but this was hardly a time to use such a spell, if there ever was such a time. Not only was he sure that it would kill him casting it, but he was also pretty certain it would kill the rest of his party along with the Garchai. *The spells of the gods didn't show any favor toward anyone.* His former Myyrilian leader had given him that wisdom the moment he was taught the powerful spells. Another solution would present itself; he was certain . . . and hoped.

A peculiar scent began to fill the air. They all smelled it. It was more pleasant than their captor who stunk of dirt and sweat, but they all began to understand where they were finally being taken.

Vindar commented, "Guys, not to alarm you, but I think we're meant to be the main course."

Biverin, knowing a thing about cooking, added, "Yeah, little too late for that. I could smell the spices a few miles ago. One thing I know about rations, we're a lot for just one. There must be more."

No one had thought about that until then (or at least would admit to it), but he was exactly right as they neared the makeshift camp. Neeza could see at least two more from his vantage point. That was going to complicate any escape plans. Getting away from one was going to be hard enough. Getting away from three . . . that was going to be nigh impossible.

From what he could see, they were much like their captor. Their eyes hidden by their helmet and all the other gruesome features of their skin and armor. The one on the left was missing a pauldron evident by its bare shoulder while the one on the right had much more body hair than the other two. The original Garchai finally dropped them hard to the ground as it neared the edges of the camp, going over to converse with its friends. This might be the chance they were waiting for.

Neeza whispered, "Okay, let's see if we can get out."

The younger mages all went toward the only exit. He started to, but he was distracted when he heard the creatures speak. It was broken and their voices deep, but there was a dialect that he could have sworn he was familiar with. None of it made any sense. Where had he heard it before?

"Neeza!"

He turned to see Dyenarus standing by him, "We can't climb out or get it open. The ends are sticking to each other like paste. Either the magic on this thing is that powerful or they are just that strong."

She seemed to be right on both ends. He could feel a strong magnetism coming from the ends, holding the two together with a force the mages wouldn't be able to break even if they were outside it.

Condarin asked, "This is how it's going to end for us, huh?"

Neeza and the others looked at her, seeing she was losing hope fast. The mage leader walked to her and put his hands on her shoulders. The touch was surprising, causing her to gaze upon his face.

"I promised all of you I would do everything I could to ensure we all went home. That hasn't changed. We will get out of here, or I will die trying. Never lose hope. You have great potential, but you let your fears consume you. Let go of them and you will continue toward being a great mage of White Magic."

Condarin held her tears as she nodded. Not the strong answer he was hoping for, but it would have to do. Their captor began to walk toward them again.

Biverin commented, "You know, if it wasn't us going in the pot, I would say it smells good. Amazing how they seem to know how to cook like a normal person would."

That was one of many things he was finding amazing about them. If they didn't think of something fast, all this new learning would mean nothing. He turned toward Haldirin as the Garchai dragged them closer toward the pot.

"Are you thinking what I'm thinking?"

Haldirin answered, "I think so. The only realistic chance for us to escape is in the pot. The net might be magical, but the pot is not. Risky because we would be cooking alive, but it might be our only window of opportunity."

Neeza agreed. It wasn't the best of plans, but it was all he could figure that might work. It was going to take more luck than anything to get out of here. Luck, unfortunately, hadn't been on their side lately. One of the Garchai finally tugged hard at the net, releasing the opening. Neeza thought about moving, but another of the Garchai moved its head into their view. As he inhaled deeply, he unleashed a heavy breath on the mages. By the gods! The smell was awful!

"By the Holy Staff of Gadic-Va, don't these things believe in hygiene?" commented Vindar.

Somehow, he didn't think the Myyrilian god of water and cleanliness applied to these creatures. The Garchai began sniffing around, chatting with his other two companions. He felt some confusion between them. Almost like they didn't know what they captured. He couldn't understand why. Mages looked similar to humans, but were much different as anyone with a sense at detecting magic could attest. Then again, the eyes of these creatures were covered, so that wouldn't have mattered. They must track off of smell.

After the Garchai were finished arguing, all three looked down, their noses busy at work. If only he could get a fireball off, he might be able to knock off all three at the same time. But as long as he was in the net, that was wishful thinking. Finally, one of them reached down toward them. Haldirin was doing his best to be the one they grabbed first to protect the children as well as his boss, but Neeza at the last second pushed him out of the way.

"Neeza!"

The Garchai picked him up by his robes, lifting him with two fingers. He was tempted to start casting his strongest spells and pray that it would kill them, but instinct took over. He remained still as the Garchai brought him toward where his eyes would be. He had a stare down with the creature's helmet for what seemed like forever. It once again lifted its mouth up and breathed on Neeza, sniffing the air right after. *Hold true, Neeza, my boy*, he told himself. It was almost time to act, but not yet.

The Garchai growled and spoke in its undetermined language, frustrated. On various sides of the camp, three explosions occurred. The Garchai holding Neeza dropped him, and he hit the ground hard. The way he landed, though, from the dark he could see fireballs coming all toward the camp. The three Garchai were confused and alarmed. After the third volley, which nearly landed by their feet, they began to scatter into the forest.

As the figure stepped into the light, a smile grew on his face.

"We are glad to see you!"

Lindaris hurried and helped Neeza up, "Same here. We must make haste. They don't seem like the type that stays scared for too long."

He was right. They had to get out of there and make for the coast in a hurry. There was no telling how many more they would return with when they did. Neeza found a thick trunk and telekinetically put it into the net. He held on to a piece that was just above the magic-resistance's range. The students grabbed on as he brought them up. They instantly walked up to him, relieved and overjoyed.

Gerran said, "Great work! Where did you go?"

Lindaris explained, "I saw that one coming toward you guys. I knew I couldn't get you out while you were in the net, so I followed you here and waited at least until one of you were out."

"I guess I was wrong about you deserting us. I'm sorry. Is that my bag?"

Ah, the person he wanted to see. He proudly brought Dyenarus' bag in front of him and handed it to her genuflecting slightly.

"Of course, my lady. I saw you left it and retrieved it just because it was yours."

She grabbed it and again thanked him before turning around and joining the rest. Not how he envisioned it at all. He was hoping at least for a kiss or a heart-felt appreciation. He didn't even get that definitive look that women tended to do when they were interested. All he got was a simple thank you. Maybe she was just playing hard to get or she didn't want to put her emotions out there in public. He would ask her later.

Once everyone was safely out of the net, Neeza turned to the group, "Okay, we should get away from here and head over to a secure place, make camp for the night. We will have watches throughout the night to be sure that they don't sneak up on us again. Tomorrow we will head west and make for the coast."

The students didn't ask any questions, just followed Gerran west. He had hoped that going north would lead them to the easier shores, but the further north they went, the more trouble they ran into. He prayed the coast would be better luck for them. They had to hurry too. If they didn't contact Mimerck soon, he might think them lost and leave them there. Especially with the Garchai, he didn't want to risk communicating so far inland because he wasn't sure what else they were capable of. They would reach the coast within a day, then it would be time to start finding a route going toward the reason they were here: Mount Hrithgorn.

The height of nightfall came an hour after they made camp. They ate dry rations as Neeza didn't want a fire going. Their enemy was robbed of sight, but their sense of smell seemed to be what they relied on for tracking. The smoke of a flame would make them that much easier to detect. Thankfully it was a warm night, so there were no complaints. Neeza and Haldirin had the first shift, which was nearing its end. Dyenarus and Lindaris had the second shift. Vindar and Condarin would have the final shift before they would continue moving.

Neeza gave a yawn as he was glad his turn was ending. The first few hours were very stressful, strange noises being heard from the Kyroselips and what sounded like wolves. He really didn't want to find out what the wolves could do. He had enough of the wildlife and locals on this trip.

Dyenarus finally stepped up, giving a strong yawn herself, "Time for you two to get some shut eye. Lindaris and I have got this."

Neeza nodded while Haldirin responded, "Thank you. Most of the activity sounds like its coming from the east, so I would keep your attention to the other directions. Neeza and I concluded the creatures here are smarter than they should be."

She nodded as she replaced Neeza, who went to lie down next to Biverin. He decided to stay by him to make sure he was okay. The farmer mage had been shivering all night despite the warmth. He began to suspect that his lung might have been punctured, even if just slightly. It only gave him more inspiration to finish this quest with more haste than ever. As he lay down, it was obvious he wasn't the only one still up not on watch.

"Getting your break in, sir?" Biverin asked.

Neeza replied, "Yes. Much needed. You need some rest as well."

Biverin laughed and said, "This is the most alive I've felt in years. Sleep can wait. Will do enough of it when I am rotting in the ground."

Neeza wasn't sure how to respond to that last statement. Did he perhaps feel the injury he suffered was worse? In this place, he was the only gauge they had if there was a problem.

Biverin continued, "In case I never get the chance again, I wanted to thank you for letting me come with you. I know I wasn't meant to hear the conversation about this journey, so you didn't have to let me go. I've always been known as being weak and unconfident. I know who I am, Honorable Neeza. I know what people think about me."

"You have any children?"

Biverin answered, "A beautiful young girl named Hirora. She's sixty-five, so still a child. She enters the Telekinetics School in a couple years. Another one on the way too. I'm doing this for them. It's tough going when the parents are known as they are even to the younglings. Once the other students find out that Hirora's father dropped from school and a coward, her life will be made miserable. I don't want her to share the same fate as me. She is a bright girl for her age. I had to do something brave. This is my chance."

Neeza wished everything he said was a lie. Myyril schools were a very difficult spot for a youngling. There were lots of bullying and name calling, mixed with selfish tricks and blatant use of skills against weaker mages. He knew this all went on. He began to think about his own daughter, Divi. Mother passed away while she was young and at her advanced age, still didn't know magic; Prime material for bullying to be done if there ever was. It normally wouldn't because she was the daughter of the leader and was the heir to the throne.

That is where he began to feel terrible. The kids in school only did it to her because he encouraged it. He didn't want to, but he was running out of ideas. She had to learn magic. Not even having her friend be her teacher was enough. Peer pressure was a powerful tool and one he hoped would get her to crumble faster in her decision to not learn magic. Yet, it made her stronger. Definitely was one of the biggest backfires he ever had.

Neeza finally said, "I know for a fact you are making them very proud. When we come back with the Relic, you'll be able to parade through the streets and show all those doubters. Someone told me before we left that those who have gone to Mount Hrithgorn rarely come out the same person. You will be changed for the better."

Biverin asked, "Can you guarantee we'll be returning home?"

Neeza figured he would level with Biverin. He was more mature than the others and would understand more.

"No. This has been much harder than I anticipated. But those who do, will have a great story to tell."

He could tell Biverin appreciated the honesty. He wanted to be able to promise them safe returns, but with the Garchai involved he wasn't so sure he could guarantee them anything anymore. They were living in a fairy tale, only a demented horrible one with real-life consequences. Normally in stories and fairy tales, the brightly colored birds aren't trying to eat you. Happy endings in this place, he was coming to realize, was something he couldn't promise.

Biverin just said, "Sleep well, Honorable Neeza."

Both men fell asleep shortly after. As they did, Lindaris finally joined Dyenarus on watch. She was annoyed by his lack of timeliness and urgency. Having two pairs of eyes was better than one, especially on that night.

"I almost thought you fell back asleep."

Lindaris replied, "I find your lack of faith in me troubling. I may be rough around the edges, but I'm not here to intentionally harm anyone. I know the talk around this little group of ours; that I don't care about anything *or* anyone. It's tough being labeled."

Dyenarus added, "Well, based off your past, it seems justified."

She was going to be a tough cookie to crack. Maybe she wasn't playing hard to get either. Well, he liked a challenge.

Lindaris continued, "You know, we never settled on my reward for squiring your important bag back into your trusting arms."

"Reward? What are you babbling about? I said thank you . . . eventually."

She just wasn't getting it. Maybe she was just naïve. He inched closer to her. She was obviously getting uncomfortable with his actions.

"I think it deserves a little more than a thank you. You know, I could have left it or just left the group, taking it with me. But, I stayed just so you can have it back. A heroic deed should never go unrewarded."

Dyenarus finally got where he was getting at the moment she saw him moving in for a kiss. She placed her hand in front of his face as he kissed her palm. She stood up with a mix of anger and disbelief. Heroic? He considered that heroic! She was appreciative he brought it to her, but she believed he was thinking a little too hard on this matter.

"We have killer birds and natives who would love to see our heads on sticks after us and could come at any moment, and you're trying to ask me to make out with you?"

Lindaris thought about it for a moment and replied, "I said a kiss, after that we could see where it went."

"You're unbelievable! Look, I'm just going to set this straight for you. I appreciate you bringing my bag, I really do. But I'm not . . . romantically interested in you. I just forgot the silly thing! Trust me. I'm not your type."

"And what is my type?"

Dyenarus answered, "How about Guillia? Us girls talk, you know."

Oh dear. Guillia. She was in the Black Magic School with him, only a couple years older. Her eyes were as green as a jade and had beautiful red hair, a trait in a Black magic female that some teachers took as a sign she might be something special. She was very competitive and in order to impress her, he found himself always in duels with other higher ranked Black magic students. He lost every time, of course. He always did love her, but she was almost unattainable in his eyes.

"Guillia . . . just isn't interested. She thinks she's too good. It's okay, one day she'll see how much she would have been better off with me."

Dyenarus asked, "And you think parading me around her would make things any better? She doesn't think she is better than you, but between us, at this point she is more skilled. She doesn't seem interested in you because she doesn't respect you. All you have ever shown her is that you're this tough guy picking fights for the sake of getting in a fight. Whatever your intentions are, good as they may be, she is reading them the wrong way."

Lindaris asked sarcastically, "So what do I do, since you're the *expert* on female behavior and psyche?"

Dyenarus sat down. He really didn't have a clue. He was convinced that woman liked the tough, macho stuff. She had a lot of work to go on this one, but maybe, just maybe, she could get him hooked up with Guillia by the end of it all.

"Did you try flowers?"

Lindaris sat puzzled as he looked across toward Dyenarus, "That actually works?"

Dyenarus wiped her brow. Yep, this was going to be a long night. Thank goodness their shift was only three hours.

On a tree nearby, a smaller Kyroselip listened intently on a tree limb. One thing the elves had never told anyone about these magnificent creatures was they could listen to any conversations and repeat them perfectly to the one it called *miseri,* or owner. It was one way the Wood Elves kept in communication without making it obvious. Seeing how it was not going to get any more information tonight, it flew off silently over the tree tops and toward the depths of Mount Hrithgorn where its master awaited.

The next morning they moved early, trying to keep a jump on their enemies. Neeza was relieved the night went without incident. He was worried that the three Garchai would come back and try to sneak up on them while they slept. Gratefully, that hadn't been the case. Dyenarus and Lindarus reported nothing out of the ordinary and Vindar and Condarin said they heard the birds in the distance, but nothing more. Perhaps the worst was behind them.

The farther west they moved, the thicker the forest became. Good. That way they would be able to hear the Garchai better. The only problem was that they were heading back uphill, which meant that to reach the coast would require them to climb down. Then again, that was better than having to elude the natives.

Neeza stopped and listened to the surroundings. Despite the progress, something didn't feel right. Haldirin walked next to him and began to look around as well.

"What do you sense?"

Neeza said, "I don't know. This place is streaming with magical energy. Give everyone a few minutes to rest. I will scout ahead."

Haldirin moved to the students to relay the order as Neeza moved forward slowly and cautiously. They needed to get off the island. They were spending too much time there. At the rate they were going, someone might beat them to Mount Hrithgorn and the real treasure. He bent down to make his leap off a small alcove easier to avoid injury. As far as he could see, there was nothing wrong, just lots of foliage. His attention was turned around when the sound of birds was heard, but he could see nothing.

He froze, though, when he heard the familiar sound of breathing. To Neeza's right, a Garchai soldier was searching for them. Every few seconds he would breathe out, followed by the customary sniffing. It's amazing how quietly they moved and how quickly. Maybe the magical presence hid them from view as well. The Garchai began to move away.

"Neeza! You ready to go?" yelled Lindaris

The Garchai turned around violently. Neeza had to quiet him otherwise they would be found. He could see him moving toward the alcove.

Telepathically, Neeza said, "Stop moving, Lindaris. No matter what happens. Don't move!"

He was confused at first, until he looked to his right and saw the Garchai running toward him. Instinct told him to run like hell. Maybe the others might hear the monster coming and help him. But that wasn't happening. He could barely hear the footsteps despite it running at full speed. It was nearly on top of him. He tried to keep his body from shaking, but he had never been so afraid in his life.

Without warning, the Garchai stopped a few feet in front of Lindaris. Releasing a hard breath, it began sniffing. It was the first time Lindaris got a view of their razor teeth. If he didn't have an iron constitution like he had, he would have given himself away.

Neeza watched with amazement. He couldn't find them! If they didn't move, they were invisible. He still was trying to figure out exactly why they constantly used breathing and sniffing when it seemed to not help them. The Garchai tried it again; frustrated that it couldn't find the source of the noise. After a few moments, it finally gave up and began heading back north. Lindaris gave a sigh of relief, releasing all the air he was holding.

"There you are! We were worried something had happened!" yelled Condarin.

Both Neeza and Lindaris tried to quiet her, but it was too late. The Garchai heard her. Condarin gave a scream and began to yell while the others followed suit.

Neeza yelled, "Nobody move!"

The Garchai began to head their way. Lindaris tapped Neeza's shoulder. It was too late to cover it now. It knew they were there. Least he could do was try and slow it down.

Neeza chanted, "*Herimon Firamma!*"

A larger fireball headed toward its target. Neeza wasn't even going to wait to see if it connected, and he didn't need to. The creature leapt over it and landed softly to one knee, removing its club off its belt simultaneously. Pressing something on the base of his weapon brought out the six blades at the top, making his club a deadly mace. Haldirin made sure he stuck around to cover his boss. No matter how fast they could run, it was gaining on them fast. Other than a slight vibration, the footsteps were silent. Haldirin looked back. By the gods, it was right behind them and had its mace aimed and ready.

"Duck!"

Haldirin forced Neeza down and to the right. The mace connected with the ground, kicking mud and grass everywhere. The two mages stood up and rushed forward again, but didn't get very far before it swung its mace at them, this time over the top. The earth shook violently from the impacts.

Dyenarus stopped and saw what was going on. Neeza and Haldirin were in trouble. They were doing admirably, but eventually that large mace would find its target.

"We have to do something! They won't last much longer!"

To their surprise, Biverin stepped up, already chanting something softly. The last mace attack caused both Neeza and Haldirin to fall in the freshly uncovered mud. It raised its mace for the final blow.

Suddenly, a large vine appeared from nowhere, wrapping around the Garchai's arm. More and more began to engulf key points of the creature as it was doing its best to figure out what was happening. Within seconds the entire monster was nearly blanketed by some kind of plant life, not allowing it to move. As Neeza looked behind him, he saw Biverin finishing his spell.

The other students were impressed as Neeza and Haldirin joined them, "Excellent work. I am much obliged for the save. What did you do?"

Biverin laughed and said, "Weeds."

Joakon asked, "Those are weeds?"

"They are the strongest, most durable plant on almost any world with life. And grow almost anywhere with little sustenance. This should hold him for a while, but it won't hold him forever, so we should get moving."

Of all the things he thought would never factor in his survival, it would have been weeds. He had scoffed at having Biverin along at the beginning, but he had been a key member of their party since they landed. Plus, he was a pretty good guy. He didn't pay much attention to the farming community back home; something that would change when he got back.

The mages began to run farther west away, from the trapped Garchai. Seeing it wouldn't free itself soon despite its awesome strength, he raised his head and gave a loud scream. It echoed throughout the immediate area. There was a silence that followed, but it didn't last long. A loud howling filled the wind, causing the group to stop temporarily.

Condarin asked, "Now what?"

Neeza had heard that sound before. The previous night. They were far away at that time, their howls only as loud as a distant insect chirp. Now, they sounded much closer. Too close for his comfort.

"Wolves. Keep running. Gerran, how close are we to the coast?"

"Should only be couple miles away. You can begin to smell the salts from the sea from where we are now."

Neeza ordered, "Everyone run into the water as deep as you can. If you can reach one of the atolls, do so. Go! Now!"

They all started running as they could hear the cracking of branches and crumbling of leaves. Neeza could sense three, but there were undoubtedly more. It was tough, even with his sharp perception at detecting magic, to feel anything clearly. Did the elves cast a rune on his place before they had disappeared?

The wolves finally made their grand appearance as they went through a clearing. Unlike the other creatures on the island, these actually had eyes . . . three of them. They also had two heads and two rows of razor sharp teeth for each. The fur was knotted in many places, some having spots of open skin that looked diseased. They were also much larger than a normal wolf, probably slightly larger than a man. Upon seeing their prey in the distance, they began to pursue.

Much to Neeza's disappointment, these creatures were fast, too. *Wasn't anything slow here?* He needed to do something to impede their progress. Earth spells wouldn't work too well because they worked best when the caster was stationary. The same went with Wind spells. If they were at the coast, the Water spells would be more effective, but the wolves would reach them well before that. It appeared to him that ice magic was the best option again on this new menace.

Neeza started to run sideways as he chanted, "*Iczera Borruanmun Aquanta!*"

A spray of ice emitted from his hand, creating a sheet of ice below the foliage. Perfect! They were less likely to see it with all the cover. As the wolves hit the patch, they slipped and rolled hard on the ground. The ones behind them crashed into the ones in front. There was one that wasn't fooled. He must have been the Alpha, as he seemed larger than the rest. It stared at Neeza with its three eyes, angry at what he did to the rest of his pack. It lifted its head and gave a deep howl.

Haldirin grabbed Neeza's arm and yelled, "Come on!"

His legs just refused to move. The howl was hypnotic. Even Haldirin's words were becoming distant. All he could think about was the sound. The Alpha finally stopped its howls. *No, keep howling,* Neeza wanted to say, but he couldn't open his mouth. His legs were trying to move closer to the creature.

"*Firammii morza!*"

The three fireballs connected, hitting the Alpha and breaking Neeza from his trance. All of the students attacked the wolves, pelting them with the basic fireball, but it was effective.

Lindaris stepped to the side and chanted, "*Firammii Tidolva!*"

A wave of flames rushed toward the clan, cindering everything it touched. The pack rushed away the moment they saw it. The Alpha waited, though. They could see it through the flames, staring at them. It growled once more as the Flame Wave spell ended just in front of it.

"Damn it! I could have sworn I was close enough to reach it!"

The Alpha jumped into and through the flames, igniting some of its fur coat. It began moving slowly toward them, getting into position to pounce the first chance it got. Digging its nails into the ground, it leapt toward the mages. Neeza pushed Haldirin and Gerran off him and quickly began enchanting a spell.

"*Iczera Voulfan!*"

The ice spell connected with the Alpha, freezing it quickly until it became engulfed by ice. It dropped five feet in front of Neeza; so close that the icy mist of the creature's breath could be felt. That was too close.

Joakon celebrated, "Well played, Neeza!"

"What happened? You seemed hypnotized for a few moments," asked Haldirin.

Honestly, that was exactly what had happened. How a wolf was able to do that was beyond him. The capabilities of the animals on this island terrified Neeza. It's no wonder everyone, including the elves, would stay away. There was no use explaining something he didn't understand quite yet.

"I need to think on it. We must hurry and get off this island before they come back."

Dyenarus replied, "Too late. I can feel them getting closer. And they are not going to be happy when they see what we did to their leader."

Neeza ordered, "Run and don't stop. Go!"

The mages began to sprint as hard as they could west. Even with the wolf pack still far away, they were getting closer with every moment. Despite telling himself constantly not to, he kept looking back expecting the wolves to be on their tail. They weren't that close, but he could see their ghostly eyes shimmer through the trees . . . and they sounded angry. They pushed harder through the brush after seeing what happened to their Alpha. Their howls were ones thirsting for revenge, not control.

The students turned around briefly as they too heard the pack. They were getting closer to them. There was no way they would be able to outrun them for much longer. *Come on*, Gerran said in his mind, *where is the damn coast?*

His feet gave out under him and he began sliding. The other students were taken by surprise as well because they were right behind him and couldn't stop in time.

Neeza was the last to descend down the slope. He suddenly noticed a growl from behind them as a couple of the wolves crashed through some thick bushes and pursued down the slope. Where did they come from? Gerran's scream brought everyone's attention forward.

"Cliff!"

Not good. He had a feeling they would still be too high to actually reach the coast. Neeza braced for another long drop. The distance between the foliage ending and the cliff edge starting was so miniscule there was no chance to stop at the full speed they were going. The other students had already gone over, followed by Haldirin and finally Neeza. As he looked down, he was relieved to see water down below. At least they wouldn't be hitting the solid ground. It would still sting from their height, but it wouldn't be fatal. What would be is if they didn't make it to the shore in time *after* the landing. Mages were not known for there swimming capabilities. Some were going to be weak after hitting the water. Time was still going to be ever important.

The howl from above broke his concentration. One of the wolves had fallen off with them and because of the way it was positioned, it was falling faster. It readied its jaws for an attack. Even in certain death the beast was still trying to kill them. Neeza tried to get his staff, but the fall had disconnected it from his back. It would hit the ground moments after they reached it.

A fireball suddenly hit the wolf. Haldirin's spell had enough power to it to drive the falling wolf closer to the rocks. It was not going to have as soft a landing as they were. Soon all the mages hit the water while the wolf hit the rocks, killing it instantly.

Neeza struggled to get back from under the water. He was seeing many of the other students laboring as well. Dyenarus and Lindaris were the only ones not needing assistance. The water was only fifty feet deep, but smaller depths had drowned many a mage. Neeza grabbed Vindar, who was nearest to him and helped him toward the shallows. Haldirin was able to retrieve Joakon, but had to work much harder trying to take him and the bag of alchemical mixes. Dyenarus had retrieved Gerran and Lindaris was bringing in Biverin. But there was someone missing.

"Help!"

Condarin, seventy feet from their positions, was struggling to stay afloat. Vindar only needed to hear her voice to realize that she wasn't on the shore.

"Condarin! Let me go! I need to help her!"

Lindaris and Haldirin held him back because he was still disoriented from the fall. Neeza had to do something. He closed his eyes. He hated to have to have to use another Eirborenz spell because he was going to feel it even worse than the last time on the boat. At least there he hadn't used much magic during the day. Between the Garchai and the wolves, he casted more than he was used to.

Neeza said, "Someone be ready to get her. I don't know how long I'll be able to hold the spell once I do it."

Vindar wanted to, but Lindaris stepped in front of him. He was the fastest of the students and the best option.

Neeza began to chant, "*Calliyorn Vinscini. Watriiara Dullontra. Hirimar Freeyama. Aquaton Sintopla!*"

The waters in front of them began to split a path directly toward Condarin. The others were amazed at the spell. Lindaris was too, but didn't have the luxury of just watching. The moment the water cleared, he began sprinting. Condarin was finally exposed, landing softly on the now open floor. Lindaris made it to her quickly, swooping her up in a quick motion. As he turned back to run, he could see Neeza struggling to hold the spell. Running back was harder because of the added weight, but also because he was slipping in the mud from the uphill incline.

Neeza couldn't hold it any longer and released the spell. Lindaris was halfway through when the waters behind him began to fall. The students were yelling for him to hurry. *Easy for them to say*, he told himself. Condarin wasn't heavy, but she was an extra burden he wasn't used to running with. He didn't need them telling him he had little precious time. He could hear it behind him. He wasn't going to make it!

Dyenarus found some soft soil to implant her staff, holding it and extending her hand. As the waters covered Lindaris there were a brief few seconds of silence. Discouragement began to settle in. Suddenly, Lindaris emerged with Condarin, under his arm. He was trying to swim, but the current was getting too much.

Dyenarus yelled, "Grab my hand!"

He was trying! *Give me a break*, he thought. He was so close, but he was tiring as well. He may have been the best swimmer here of the mages, but like any mage, if he didn't have enough energy to get to shore, he'd most likely drown. He gave a one final push. Dyenarus was able to barely grab his hand, but her grip was slipping quickly.

"Help me!"

The other mages quickly came to her aid as they pulled Lindaris and Condarin onto the shore. While Dyenarus and Lindaris sat near the water exhausted, the others pulled Condarin up to the dryer area and laid her out. Vindar began checking her vitals.

Vindar panicked, "I can still feel her life force, but it is weak. And she isn't breathing. Come on, Condarin! It's me, Vindar! Don't leave me!"

Neeza was exhausted, but he could see his work wasn't done. What Vindar was doing wasn't helping. She was alive, but wouldn't be for long if he didn't act fast. Neeza pushed Haldirin to the side as he made his way toward Condarin. The other students cleared a path seeing his approach. He nearly collapsed alongside her, but found the strength to kneel.

Without looking, he raised his hands over her face and chanted, "*Aqualorn Abzerba.*"

A red light began to emit toward her mouth. It was a potentially dangerous spell, but it was one of the few ways known to him to save a person from drowning. It absorbed the water inside a person, essentially dehydrating them. If held too long, it could kill them because every person needed fluids in their body to live.

After a few seconds, Condarin coughed up a bunch of water, which dried up quickly because of the spell. He could hear the students crying tears of joy and happiness. He must have saved her. Good. That was the last thing he remembered before collapsing.

6

Neeza woke up later that night, still tired, but awake enough to eat. Haldirin explained that after Condarin recovered, they carried him into a small cave along the coast. It was not easily seen and small enough that the Garchai couldn't reach them. They set a fire, mainly for cooking, but also to dry out a bit. From what Neeza could tell, everyone else seemed okay. That was good. More importantly, they had reached the coast. Now it was time to find a better place to land the boat and it was onto Mount Hrithgorn.

As she finished the last of the soup that Biverin prepared, Condarin silently walked up to Neeza and Haldirin, bowing her head.

"May I request a sit down, Neeza?"

Neeza replied, "Of course. I told you for the rest of this trip you don't need to include any of the formalities. Just sit."

Condarin raised her head, smiled, and sat in front of them. At first she said nothing. He could feel she was a little nervous. He guessed that no matter how much he was tried to be one of the crew, he was always going to be seen in their eyes as the Honorable Neeza, leader of the mage people.

She finally said, "I just wanted to come here and thank you for saving my life. They told me how you nearly spent yours trying to get me from the water. You've saved my life twice already, and I don't know how I can repay you. I'm not a great mage like Dyenarus is, but I always repay my debts. I just wanted to let you know that if there is any way I can make it up to you, let me know."

Neeza replied, "You may not be a great mage yet, but you are still young, and I can guarantee you, once we are done with this adventure, you'll be more advanced than your classmates. And don't worry about repaying a debt. How can friends be in debt?"

Condarin smiled, nodded, and went back to Vindar. Neeza watched as the students began to joke around again. They finally understood. They were at last accepting they had a job to do and until that was done, they would just have to deal with the hardships. Condarin was one of the last to realize this, but he thought now the circle was complete. They were no longer students in his eyes. They graduated into something more, but they were still not done.

Haldirin asked, "What are you thinking?"

Neeza responded, "Just thinking . . . and realizing the validity that anyone who comes here rarely comes back the same."

"Indeed, but we still aren't out of the woods yet. We still have yet to enter the mountain. I'm sure more dangers exist there."

"Let us hope then that we can find the Relic quickly," added Neeza.

Gerran suddenly came over with Neeza's staff. He was testing it to see if it was damaged during any of the earlier events. He was convinced he lost it for good during the fall, but Gerran was able to telepathically retrieve the staves the students may have dropped during the plunge. One of Joakon's bags was lost for good, though.

He said, "Well, it looks to be in good shape. No physical damages and Vindar tested the crystal for leakage, but found none."

Good. He was definitely glad to have a member of the Divination School with him on the expedition. One of their specialties was being able to detect less visible damage to a mage's staff, which was their life blood. Without their staff, their spell power decreased and most gradually would lose touch with their magical abilities. One might as well just call them human at that point. Neeza could technically do it too, but in his weak state it wouldn't have been accurate and the earlier the detection, the better.

Neeza answered, "Thank you, Gerran."

He nodded and returned to the other students.

"So, are you finally going to tell me what you felt back there with the wolves?"

Neeza looked at Haldirin, trying to find the words to say, "It was . . . strange. It was as if that howling was calling to me. I could hear your voice, but all I cared about was that howl. You could feel none of it?"

Haldirin shook his head. That was interesting that the creatures could target a single person. And why it targeted him instead of Haldirin was beyond him as well. Was it possible it they could sense he was the strongest, so they tried to take control of him?

"No. Other than its accursed howling, I heard or felt nothing strange."

He needed to ponder on the strange phenomenom more carefully. If anything, it proved to him the faster they went for the Relic, the better.

Neeza finally said, "There is a danger here. A real danger. There is an awesome magic happening here. One that I can't even comprehend. Tomorrow, we contact Mimerck, and by nightfall, I want to be at the base of Mount Hrithgorn. I want to be out of here the next night."

Haldirin couldn't have agreed more. He could see, that for the first time this trip, the weight of the mission was beginning to be felt by their leader. He was not one that liked surprises, especially ones he couldn't explain. Every hour on these islands seemed to bring a new surprise their way and it had Neeza, if Haldirin dared to say . . . afraid.

Finally overtaken by exhaustion, Neeza lied down and closed his eyes. *Good, he needed his rest*, thought Haldirin. Again, he was lucky to be alive after casting another Eirborenz spell. For a younger mage, those set of spells weren't an issue. Unlike a normal spell, the Eirborenz required more concentration and borrowed a person's internal life particles to make them more powerful. Only a few select mage families could even perform them. Neeza's sacred-blood line was one of them. Divi, should she ever decide to learn magic, would be able to cast them as well.

Age became the problem. The use of the life particles, which is what mages used to make their magic, weakened over time. That was one reason he had been pondering retirement sooner than later. If he were to die before Divi learned magic, it could potentially lead to a power struggle unlike any mage had ever seen in millennia. Neeza became ruler because the previous ruler named him the heir and treated him like a son . . . and he knew magic. It would be absurd to have a magic-less mage ruling Myyril, which made his surviving that more important. Even if it would mean his own life.

** * * * * * * * * *

The group headed out early. Neeza was still feeling the effects of the spells he cast the day before, but at least he could walk under his own power. The conditions weren't too favorable for a mage to recover here. Cooler temperatures in the morning didn't help much either.

They stayed on the coast heading north, being cautious not to come near land that the Garchai or any of the other creatures could surprise them. On their left, they remained under Mount Hrithgorn's menacing shadow. Haldirin would catch everyone taking a quick glance at the mountain from time to time. They all knew the feared mountain of legend was their next port of call. They had survived so much up to this point, but knew that they were just going from the pan into the fire. Once inside, they would never be the same.

But first things first, they had to contact Mimerck, which was proving to be a real challenge. The magic surrounding the isles caused too much interference that Neeza couldn't get through it. Short distance telepathy seemed to work, but nothing longer than a mile seemed to get through. They needed to get to a spot where the ocean could be seen again. At least there was nothing that could block his Telepathic Speak that way.

Gerran stopped and said, "Looks like in a few miles we should reach our original projected coast."

Haldirin added, "And just by looking at the way the land is set, not a damn good place to bring the boat any closer."

"At least we should be able to just stay by the coast and not worry about running into any of those creatures. They were using the forest to hide like we were," commented Joakon.

Lindaris said, "You think a little water is going to keep these things away? We can't get complacent while we're here. Stick to what we are doing. Travel quickly by day, and sleep in hiding at night."

Neeza was quite impressed with Lindaris' growth over the past days. He had begun thinking like Neeza did; taking caution in the wind and not rushing into a potential dangerous situation. He thought the same that their enemy's disappearance was nothing more than just a false security. The creatures had to drink too, and the numerous pools by the isle's edges were a freshwater source.

What was that? He could feel something coming. He had to quiet Joakon and Condarin so he could be sure. The snapping of a twig confirmed it, the other students now aware of the presence.

"Great. Something is coming!" whispered Condarin.

Neeza ordered, "Everyone ready a spell. It's coming from behind that rock. As soon as it turns the corner, hit it with whatever you got!"

The students complied, readying their most potent spell they could think of. Whatever it was, it wasn't that large. That was a positive. At least it wasn't the Garchai. The bad news was that it could be something new, something that only lived near the coast perhaps. He wouldn't doubt it in a place like that.

The students gained some distance between each other so that their spells wouldn't interfere with each other's. One thing they were going to guarantee was that whatever stepped from behind that corner was not going to get a chance to attack them. It was nearly in their view.

"Ah, there you guys are! What are you doing?"

Everyone was thankful they didn't cast on first sight. The figure that revealed itself from behind the rock was a familiar one; one Neeza was surprised to see at that point in time, to be frank.

"Mimerck!"

The mage captain replied, "Well, that's a much warmer welcome! Though, I prefer to have captain in front of my name. Was beginning to wonder! My turning the corner and seeing nearly ten spells ready to be cast on me."

Dyenarus replied, "We've experience a lot. You'll understand once we tell you."

Neeza began to evaluate their captain's appearance. His robe was dirty, his pack about half full, and his boots were caked with mud. Whatever his story was, he was not on the boat for very long after they left it.

Haldirin thankfully asked the first question, "Where have you been? We were trying to contact you!"

Mimerck laughed and said, "I was waiting at the coast you were supposed to meet at. I was getting worried when you didn't show. So, I started back down heading south. Glad to find you guys."

Neeza still had his suspicions. He could never get the captain's desire for gold to exit his mind. Was he scouting the area for an escape route if he found it? Was he going to betray them?

Neeza finally said, "We are glad to see you as well, however I am quite puzzled to see you here. You were to stay on the boat until we contacted you."

Mimerck smiled and said, "I thought you'd never ask. There is a very good reason for my leaving. Let me show you."

"This is not good."

"Now you see why I didn't stay on the boat too long."

Unbelievable. Just when he assured his own mind nothing could make their situation worse, Mimerck found something. Hundreds of row boats were coming from the north, settling on the largest atoll. From their vantage point, they could see clearly what they were. What were they doing here? How could they have possibly known?

Dyenarus observed, "By the god Bhoruhn-hi, there are hundreds of them."

From what Neeza had counted, about 1,000 to be as exact as possible. It was quite a large group of them, especially for an island that had no real army. Definitely a hundred times the size of their group, but then again, they probably didn't know they were here either. They could hear the commands being given even from their distance.

Lindaris asked, "What are they?"

Neeza said, "Ettui."

The Ettui were the main enemy of all the races of the mainland. Human, Mage, Elf, Half-elf, it didn't matter. They originated from the Barbatan continent during one of the Great Elf Wars after the Eratuu Rebellion. The elves constantly told all the races the Ettui were their brethren that changed because they destroyed the land. What they never told was why they decided to suddenly go against their nature. Elves were hard-pressed to change at all. What made a majority of their clans turn on them was an answer that Neeza would love to find out, but knew he never would.

Mimerck explained, "About an hour after you departed, a scout ship of these bastards came sailing by. I destroyed it, but not before they damaged my baby. I found a safe place to anchor it on the southernmost island. I began traveling the coast looking for materials to make repairs. When I saw that I was close to the eastern island, figured I would meet you at the meeting point."

Why did it seem like whenever the mage captain spoke, bad news was all that came out? The students realized the seriousness of the situation as well. Neeza had always assumed there might be competition for the Relic. Inno wouldn't have lied to him about that. But for the competition to be the Ettui, that was another problem. Human pirates would have been more manageable. Anything but the Ettui. On top of that, their ride home was damaged and needed repairs. It didn't sound major from how Mimerck described it, but it would still delay them a day or two at least.

Haldirin asked, "Now what? We can't defeat nearly a thousand Ettui soldiers. Not at our numbers."

Sadly, there was much truth in his statement. Neeza could take out many of the Ettui with his magic, but again, it would probably kill him. That was not a good option. Surprise guerilla attacks wouldn't work either because it would take days to wipe out this army. Fighting was not going to be a wise first choice. They were just going to need to be faster than them.

Haldirin commented, "What in our dear gods could the Ettui want with the Relic? It is the only thing here that could be of any significant value. And how is it the elves didn't bother to stop them? Fort Za must have seen this coming from Barbata."

Both questions were valid and disturbing. The elves, especially with the Ettui, liked to keep close tabs on their movement when it came to their offshore activities. Also, it would be impossible for them to not see ships coming from Fort Za. An Elf Eye would see them almost instantly. Why would they not send a ship or two to sink them? A scary answer came to him. What if these Ettui didn't come from Barbata? Where else could they come from in the north? They had no more influence there. The settlement they had long ago was destroyed, and an elf outpost survived there today to ensure it was never re-established.

Mimerck commented, "Neeza, you have done admirably here, but I think now is the time to count our blessings that we got this far and go home with our lives intact. To go against this would be madness."

Perhaps that pinch of madness was just what they needed. They couldn't leave. Not when they were so close to getting to Hrithgorn's foreboding legacy. He thought even the students would agree with him. To come away from this without trying was a failed mission. No matter the costs, they would see this through.

Neeza answered, "Perhaps. But you're missing the larger picture. The Ettuiis presence here only justifies that we must go after the Relic. I don't know what they want with it, but I'll be damned if I'm going to let them have it without a fight. We are the only ones that can stop them."

No one wanted to admit it, but he spoke accurately. The Ettuiis arrival was disturbing, indeed. But what they could do with the Relic was beyond his comprehension. He wanted it to save his dead wife. With it in their possession, the Ettui might have a tool that could see them reviving their dead almost as soon as they are killed. Its impact would be devastating on the mainland. They were the only ones who could stop them, since it appeared as though the elves turned a blind eye.

Neeza ordered, "Let's get moving. With this new piece on the board, we need to move quickly."

As Neeza and the others climbed down back toward the coast, Mimerck stayed a few seconds longer to stare at the Ettui army ahead of them. He could almost smell their foul breath. As he was about to step down a small creature flew around his head. It moved fast, but Mimerck was still able to identify it.

"Ah, a Kyroselip! What are you doing here?"

The smaller bird didn't pay much attention to him. It had to get closer to this new group that was coming. Boat to boat it weaved, breathing as it did. If a bird could smile, it would have. It had to report to its master what it could taste. His master was pleased with the latest information. If he came back with news on the new arrivals, it could only imagine the reward. After flying through the Ettui ranks undetected, it flew toward Mount Hrithgorn.

Suddenly, an arrow pierced the back of the Kyroselip, killing it instantly near the mountain base. The Ettui general growled satisfactorily. He wore heavy chest armor and a helmet with elk horns. Of course, there was an open slot for his pointed ears so he could hear well. One of the traits he kept after the transformation from Elf to Ettui was his exceptional hearing. When he heard the fast beating wings of the Kyroselip, he knew it served a master, and he wanted to get it before it could report their location.

He was also much taller than the others he led, standing slightly taller than a grown man. Still, it did nothing toward his appearance. He was still very ugly, but his muscled, green skin was impressive for Ettui standards. His curved sword, which had spilled more blood than he could remember, rested firmly in its sheath.

One of the Ettui soldiers saluted their captain and said, "Orznaii! Haasiina durin piiunt mountiia Hrithgorn."(*Orznaii! We will reach Mount Hrithgorn tomorrow at day.*)

General Orznaii, whose name in the common tongue translated to 'elf cleaver', growled and replied, "Guillimaii fuucora. Valendraii relicai cervantea!" (*Be ready to move. I want Valendri's Relic!*)

The mages traveled all day, journeying first further south from where they found Mimerck. They had to do whatever they could to stay out of the Ettuiis eyesight. When they felt comfortable enough, they began crossing over toward Mount Hrithgorn, traveling from one atoll to the next. They were less prepared for the trip than their foes were, but that was to be expected. With very little research done, Neeza tried to think of everything they might need. But alas, a small boat was not one of them. The more he thought about it, he didn't think a boat would have fit on *The Sea Dragon*. It was barely big enough to fit his party comfortably.

They hurried as fast as they could knowing the Ettui were after the prize as well. They made such great time that they reached the shores of Mount Hrithgorn while the sun still shined. The ground was a very strange, obsidian color; almost like it would glitter in the sun. It was also mixed with lightly colored rocks and minerals, which were soft to the touch. It didn't look like that from the north when they were scouting the Ettui. Gerran told him that it looked like the shiny particles might be glass, much like he had seen in previous volcanic eruptions. He didn't have any of his tools to verify his thought, of course. That didn't make wanting to camp there an easier decision. They would have to use blankets so as to not accidently breath in the fine dust. Most of the flora seemed more recent at the mountain base, as the trees were still young when compared to the ones on the outer Simorgan Chain.

Neeza wanted to continue, but Haldirin and Mimerck were able to convince him to at least take a couple hours to rest and meditate. If they were going inside, they needed to be in the best condition possible. That was the argument they used with him at least.

So they rested, that is, all but Gerran did. He wanted to try and find possible entries into the mountain while they still had natural light. It had been fabled that the entrances to Mount Hrithgorn were very difficult to find and at least from Gerran's early searches, the fables were true. Neeza was confident he would find a way. He had grown to trust his band of misfits.

When they awoke, Gerran was already sitting around a small fire, only large enough to produce heat. The sun was setting, so night would be upon them soon. They all sat around the flame to hear what he had discovered.

"Okay, judging by the sky as it is now, it looks like we will have clear skies tonight, and we are reaching a pinnacle that won't happen for another 500 years. Both moons will be full at the exact same period of time, so we will have the maximum amount of light to climb the mountain at night.

"I kept looking for entrances near the base, but the more I pondered on it, most likely those were hidden because they were secret exits. After searching for a long time I found one up there. It appears the entrances are small and they don't face outward like a normal cave. I only saw it by the way the sun was setting and casting a shadow. It's possible there are others much closer to the ground, so if you find one, use that. Otherwise, that is our point of entry. It's high, but if we take it slowly, we should be able to climb up this face.

"Once inside, your guess is as good as mine as to what we'll see in there. Most elf strongholds were mazes to throw off invaders. Fort Za is perhaps their most normal base of operations. All that matters is that we reach the center of the mountain at its lowest point. That is where I am sensing the strongest magical disturbance. That must be where the Relic is. Any questions?"

Lindaris pointed out, "You do realize that entrance of yours in near the peak, right?"

Neeza added, "Most early elf strongholds used that as a defense tactic. By the time invaders would reach the entrance, their numbers would have dwindled dramatically due to the climb as well as the elves pouring arrows and boulders at them. If that is where we must go, then so be it. The Ettui will be having the same problem as us. Great work, Gerran."

Gerran began to slowly put his papers back into his bag while the others began staring up at the entrance. It was barely visible at this point, but visible nonetheless. It was going to be a treacherous climb, but one could see where the mountain was cutaway to form a walkway of sorts leading up. Yet, after years of the weathering and shifting of Gyyerlith's earth, how safe were those paths? There was only one way to find out.

Neeza said, "Okay, everyone. Double check your supplies and get ready. As soon as the sun hides over the horizon, we make our move under the cover of darkness."

The mage students nodded and began to do as they were told. Neeza looked up the slopes of Mount Hrithgorn. The time was coming near. So far this accursed place was throwing every creature it could at them, yet they have prevailed. He was getting into that mountain, and nothing, neither Ettui nor Garchai, was going to stop him!

They were halfway up the mountain when it hit them. It started as just a set of harmless clouds, but then the wind picked up fiercely. Not long after came the rain, a heavy dousing that made visibility near impossible. Worse for them was that it made the mountain rock slick. It was too late to turn back, so the only way to go was forward.

"You said it was supposed to be a clear night!" yelled Lindaris.

Gerran replied, "I'm just your navigator and compass. If you wanted an accurate weather prediction, you should have asked Captain Mimerck."

Mimerck added, "Finally! Someone addressed me properly! Oh, and this storm is not natural! Someone seriously doesn't want us entering this place! I think Neeza has the gods scared! Bless his heart!"

Vindar looked at Gerran and said, "He is not normal!"

Condarin was staying by Neeza, daring not to stray too far from him. Even with her being extra careful, stranger things had happened. She used her staff to help provide extra balance, which was helping against the gale winds.

Dyenarus, who was next to Lindaris in the front leading the party, was having a hard time blocking the heavy rain. The winds kept changing direction and now it was blowing right into her face. She had to do something.

Dyenarus yelled, "*Sheildiia Suarra!*"

A purplish shield formed in front of her, blocking the rain for the most part. The problem now was the wind, which was making it harder to walk forward. Well, at least she tried. It wouldn't be worth having it up just to stay a little dry. She was soaked already, so it didn't matter. She negated the spell.

As she did, an extra burst of wind that was blocked as a result of the shield, hit Dyenarus with a force she wasn't expecting, driving her back and causing her to lose her footing. She tried to grab onto the rocks, but they were too slick to grab.

She was relieved when a hand grasped onto hers, stopping her free fall from the mountain. She looked up to see Lindaris struggling to get her up. The rain was making his grip hard to keep as well. Joakon helped stabilize Lindaris while he pulled her up. It took a minute, but they finally were able bring her back.

Dyenarus said, breathing heavily, "Thanks."

"Not a problem. Say, I know you're not interested in me, but I think that action at least deserves a kiss."

Dyenarus replied, "Anyone ever tell you your timing is horrible?"

Lindaris answered, "Yes, you did a couple nights ago."

She laughed as she inched forward. Although he was growing on her, she knew that a relationship could never be between them. Her situation was complicated, and her family situation was even more complex. It was for that reason that she kept her private life so secret. If anyone knew the truth, she would most likely have been expelled from the Illusions School, which she loved. Lindaris acted without any consideration of the consequences of what he said. It was a trait that was going to stay with him the rest of his life, which was why he and Guillia were perfect for each other. She would marry one day, but she knew that it would not be with a mage.

After a few more feet, despite the heavy rains, Dyenarus was able to see a crevice in the mountain ten feet higher. *Thank the gods!* It was another one of the entrances. It was still going to take some effort to get there, but it was better than having to scale to the peak.

Dyenarus yelled, "Come on! I found a way in!"

Lightning began to crack in the sky, giving them much needed light. The path was broken going toward the entrance, so they had to climb up the last ten feet. They each went one by one to make sure they all made it up safe. If one fell, at least they'd be able to catch them. Joakon was the only difficult one because of the weight of his bag. They ended up taking it separately by rope. It just wasn't working, carrying them both at the same time. Each mage made their way toward the door, with Neeza and Haldirin being the last. Neeza had a few scary moments, but he was able to pull through. Haldirin, after observing the best way to get up from the previous students, was able to make it in the fastest time.

After Neeza did a count, he said, "Okay, everyone inside!"

It felt good to get out of the rain as all the mages began to wring the water out of their robes and coverings. The water alone must have made them ten pounds heavier. That part was over now. They beat the weather and were finally inside Mount Hrithgorn. There was nothing special to the room they entered, but a hallway was seen during the lightning flashes.

Vindar cast a light spell as it hovered over his hand. Other than Neeza, Vindar was the best equipped for light spells as he could cast it longer and have many varieties of it. Divination magic relied on the power of light and utilizing it to perform at their needs. Normally mages learning White Magic would spend time in the Divination School, as the two were very close in ideology and the way they used the life particles. One needed the other or else it wouldn't work.

Gerran stepped in front and said, "Okay, follow me. Vindar, stay next to me so I can see."

When everyone was ready, they began moving down the hall. It was amazing to Neeza that they may be the first people to set foot on the mountain grounds in nearly 800 years. From the light of Vindar's spell, he could see even this miniscule hallway had designs on the wall that looked to be in the form of tree's branches intertwining with each other. To think the art was all carved from the rock of the mountain. Unburned torch holders lay empty after the years deteriorated the wood that once occupied them.

At the end of the hallway, the ceiling elevated higher. In the doorway, it was supported by an arch and two pillars with partial statues of two elves on them. The left had his hand pointed out, while the one of the right had his palm out.

As they all entered the next room, the only thing Gerran could say was, "Wow."

7

"This place is huge!"

Vindar's voice echoed through the hollowed room. It was filled with many intersecting paths and had to go near three hundred feet up and another three hundred down. To get an idea of what they were dealing with, Vindar shot his light spell up into the air and let it explode. For a few seconds, the whole area was bathed in light. The paths were actually intricate bridges . . . hundreds of them over the gaping abyss. Time had eroded the railings, leaving them broken down. On the walls were many gaps that looked like doorways. *This was not going to be easy,* thought Neeza.

As the light flickered down, Vindar summoned another light spell to replace it. The bridge on their level led to three different paths. Biverin moved forward trying to get a closer look, but he tripped over something lodged in the ground. When Neeza illuminated his staff in the general area, they saw the object he tripped over was an arrow, still cemented to the earth as it had been since it was fired.

Neeza said, "Amazing. What we are seeing is probably how things were after the Ettui originally invaded. History frozen in its last moments."

Condarin commented, "More like creepy. This place gives me bumps."

Haldirin reminded, "Just remember to try and be as respectful here as possible. We don't know what elven magic was left here when the residents disappeared."

Lindaris added, "Well, darn. I was going to carve our names in the stone walls letting everyone know we were the first here in ages."

Gerran walked out toward the beginning of the path leading to the split. He began to silence his mind, trying to find the best way to reach the Relic. He could feel its power, but it was very faint. The closer they got, in theory, the stronger the pull from the Relic should be. Strange, though, that inside the mountain its power dwindled the further they were. Outside, its pull was intoxicating. There must be a reason.

Biverin stepped up toward Gerran and Vindar and asked, "Well, where to?"

Lindaris instead asked, "You said that the Relic is down, why mess with these tunnels and halls when we can just rope ourselves to the bottom of this?"

Gerran began looking around for something until his eyes met Joakon's, "Give me one of your least important mixes."

Joakon reached into his bag and began digging through it. Hard to believe how much he fit into that little sack. It was also a little amusing seeing him try to deem what was important and what wasn't. It reminded Neeza of his late wife. Alchemy was such a hands on trade and skill that everything they made they felt was necessary. It was the main reason her shop was always overstocked. He almost thought Lindaris was going to push him over and grab one, but Joakon finally retrieved a bottle and gave it to Gerran.

Joakon started to explain, "This chemical will create a smoke screen, but I don't see how it will . . ."

Gerran grabbed the bottle and tossed it over the edge. Everyone eagerly watched as the bottle fell, fell, and then sudden hit a strange magical shield, obliterating the bottle and consuming the smoke. It took only seconds.

"Just as I feared. Haldirin was correct. This place is surrounded with elvish magic and talismans. As it didn't affect Vindar's spell, it must only be affecting the lower levels. If we want to reach the Relic, we'll need to find the correct way through this maze. Problem with that is that we still might have to go up ten stories to find the right path to take us down."

"You're kidding. It could take us days unless we split up!" exclaimed Lindaris.

Neeza quickly intervened, "We are not splitting up. In a place like this, we might never find our way back. It is obvious this part of the mountain was intended to be a defensive position. Once we get past this, getting to the Relic should be easy. There must be a way, a sign of some kind that would lead the elves down the necessary path to reach down below."

There in was the challenge. Elves liked to be mysterious and mythical; using methods only they would think of. From Vindar's spell, he could see that there was writing on the walls, but unfortunately, none of them could understand elvish. It was times like that he wished he did ask Divi to come with. She was one of the very few mages who could speak and understand their writings near fluently. It was a very difficult language to learn because of the countless dialects. Yet, she saw it more important to learn elvish rather than her god given gift of magic. That is what troubled him most.

Gerran walked up to the dividing point, now able to see each of the three entrances. They all looked similar except for one glaring difference: The statues. Each one had the same elf design, but the hands were positioned differently on all of them. Gerran fired a few light spells of his own at the ones higher up. Again, the same difference. That was how they would find their way. That must have been how they navigated. The enemy would never notice such a fine detail.

As he examined the three statue designs, only the one on the left didn't have the statue's palm facing them. Well, that was at least a start. If the plan didn't work, then they would need to improvise.

Gerran said, "This way."

Deep inside the lower portions of the mountain, a large hooded figure walked into an enormous room. A large fire burned in a pit, providing the only lighting. Ominous shadows danced around the room with the flame. He continued to move forward until he stepped in front of a throne. The figure sitting in it didn't move, appearing to be more like a statue than anything. Other than its yellowish-scaled boots, most of it was covered in the shadow.

The large figure bent down to one knee, cradling something carefully in his large hands. After a few moments, he released the object in his hands. It was the small Kyroselip, the arrow still imbedded in its chest. He muttered something softly as the hooded figure stepped back into the shadows.

The creature stirred finally, awakening at the presence of its lost friend. When it didn't return, he had worried for it. He knew there were intruders on his mountain. What he didn't know was that they could be so cruel. Whoever did the killing was going to pay and pay with their lives. The creature stepped off his throne and breathed on the dead Kyroselip. That scent, that taste. He had it before, but hundreds of years ago. That sweet, irreplaceable taste of elvish blood. *So, after all these years, they finally returned.* He knew they would. The power of the Relic was calling out, reaching to those who would listen. At last they would have revenge.

His eyeless gaze returned to his departed bird friend. His excitement at the news of the elves possible return was only surpassed by the sorrow he felt for his innocent friend who had served him dutifully for all these years. He gave out a bone chilling cry that echoed throughout the mountain.

The group paused as they heard the loud sound. It was as if all the confidence they had gained over the past few days disappeared in an instant. Neeza had to admit, even he was afraid of what caused that awful noise.

Mimerck walked back slightly and began to think. He knew all the tales associated with this place. Why was he drawing a blank on what that might be?

Vindar commented, "Tell me that was just the wind."

"Not the wind, boy," Mimerck continued as he remembered more of the tale. "There were more legends here than just the Garchai. It was said that a horrible god occupied this mountain after the elves left. He fell from the heavens to guard the Relic from all usurpers. When they were defeated, he was said to have fallen into a deep sleep. It appears between us and the Ettui being here, we have awoken that very god."

Dyenarus said, "Wait, you're saying that we're going to be doing battle with Valendri Himself?"

Biverin asked, "Who is Valendri? I know we are going after his relic, but I know very little about him."

Neeza explained, "Valendri is the elvish god of Mortality. Although Elves are technically immortal because they never age and could live forever, they still can be killed in battle or from a very rare disease that their current leader is inflicted with. So Valendri is the only god they truly fear. When they pray before battle, the last god they pray to is him because they don't want to die any more than we do. I heard of this legend as well. The Garchai might be real, but to say an elvish god is here is asinine!"

"Oh, of course. Every other legend with this place has been true so far, but this one? Truly a sham!"

Neeza didn't appreciate Mimerck's sarcasm, but he really couldn't blame him for his way of thinking. He was right. Everything in the legends with this mountain had turned out to be more fact than fiction: The Garchai, the strange magic, the Relic. It was all real. But now they were just talking crazy. Everyone knew that the only gods to ever physically step foot on Gyyerlith were their own back when they lived on the motherland before it was sunk into the ocean by the very same gods. Not even the elves believe that their gods were here. That was why they had the Wood Elves. They were the communication with their holy ones.

Haldirin finally said, "This is not a time to bicker and argue. We must be doubly cautious. If not a god, than something else, something big, is in here. We should move."

Gerran nodded as they continued out of the hallway back into the main room. They had travelled up two levels following the statue's 'directions'. He figured they would start traveling down very soon. Then the presence of the Relic would become greater. The group spread out while Gerran began examining which was the correct path. As Lindaris moved forward, a strange sound was heard, making everyone freeze.

Dyenarus commented, "What in the hell is that?"

After a few seconds the noise stopped. Lindaris chuckled and said, "Well, looks like we're letting this place mess with our heads."

Dyenarus heard the familiar sound of arrows flying through the air.

"Look out!"

She quickly grabbed Lindaris, pulling him toward her, but she was a tad bit slow.

One of the arrows nailed him in the shoulder causing him to scream in great pain. They pulled him back into the hallway as Condarin instantly went to work.

"How are you feeling? Is the pain traveling up your arm like it's on fire?"

Lindaris commented, "It hurts like hell! I just got shot with an arrow, what do you think?"

Condarin added, "Good. If you said it felt like you were burning then the arrow might have been laced with a poison. Since that is not the case, let's get to work!"

She pulled the arrow out with a great tug for his smart-alec remarks. Lindaris gave a loud scream.

"By everything holy!"

"This is going to sting a bit, but it will at least stop any infections. It might leave a scar too."

Lindaris laughed, "That's fine. Women find scars sexy."

Condarin smiled as he prepared to have the spells cast on him. Lindaris was tough, but it was never easy to take an arrow anywhere. Neeza was more concerned about where it came from. The arrow was definitely elvish, but it was too short to be fired from a bow. Neeza stood up and began walking toward Gerran. Their Black magic specialist was in good hands with Condarin.

Condarin chanted, "*Hiuelliman Cierra Donta.*"

The purplish light engulfed Lindaris' shoulder. Lindaris, in the past, had many curing spells cast on him, mainly because of his many attempts to impress Guillia. The previous times were mainly for burns due to fire spells and such. The imbedded arrow was his first deep wound and she was right, it hurt more than anything he could have imagined. In a few seconds, Condarin's spells were finished, and the skin on Lindaris' shoulder was mainly healed.

"Much obliged, my lady."

Dyenarus helped Lindaris up and said, "Well, it looks like we're even. Guess you can just forget the whole kiss idea now."

He replied, "For now. But we're far from getting out of here. Lots of time to make it up."

"You're unreal, Lindaris."

Neeza finally reached Gerran, who had Vindar fire a few balls of light in the direction the arrows came.

"What have you found?"

"It came from over there on that wall. You can see the numerous gaps," pointed out Gerran.

His sight was true. Many slots where arrows could be fired were there, but if it were the Ettui, they wouldn't have stopped after one wave. Neeza didn't think anyone fired those arrows. He began to look at the ground around where Lindaris had stood. *There!* A slight indentation was on the floor barely visible from the rocks and dust.

Neeza began to analyze, "This area . . . I don't think it was ever manned during the battles against the Ettui. This whole area is booby trapped. Why do you think they made this so complicated? They relied on these traps to take out as much of the enemy forces as possible and those that survived would feel the full strength of the elf forces below. No wonder the Ettui had issues. Their rush into the battle tactic would give them a heavy death toll. We're in the killing zone."

Gerran asked, "But wouldn't that mean we should just sit tight with the Ettui situation? The mountain would defend itself against these characters."

Haldirin, who walked into the conversation, answered, "The Ettui are probably aware of why they failed. They will be more careful this time. Besides, we are considered intruders of this mountain just like they are. What makes you think it won't turn on us?"

Another valid point. He already knew there would be no chance they could leave it up to the mountain to defend them if the Ettui and their group crossed paths. They were going to need to conquer these traps just the same as the Ettui were.

Biverin suddenly said, "I hate to interrupt this enthralling conversation, but it looks like we've got company."

They didn't have to look up. They could hear the soft grunts and whispers. Thirty stories up, the Ettui began to enter the mountain. Vindar lowered the power of his light spell. They were carrying torches and were walking in pairs, quietly down the closest bridge to the top. Haldirin was right. They learned from the fiasco that had happened there nearly nine hundred years ago.

Even though they still had the element of surprise, it would be over soon. At that point, they would be fighting both the Ettui *and* the mountain. The odds were not favorable.

Neeza got everyone together and whispered, "Gerran, get us as far as we can toward the elf's sanctuary. A clash with the Ettui will be unavoidable. The closer they get, Vindar's light will be seen more clearly. Then they will definitely know who's here."

Joakon tried to speak, "Sir? Neeza?"

Neeza only replied, "Quiet for a moment. I'm trying to think."

Joakon once again asked, "Neeza? It might be inevitable, but we might be able to delay them a bit longer."

When he looked up, he saw Joakon tossing a beaker with a reddish liquid in it. From his partially opened backpack Neeza could see that most of the bag was filled with it. Neeza and Lindaris were probably the only ones that knew what was in the bottle. *And he's only been doing this for five months?* Mierena, were she alive at that moment, would have recruited him in a heartbeat. Maybe she would still get the chance if their mission was successful. With that much firepower, bless his heart!

Neeza asked, "You are certain you know the way or can guild us?

Gerran replied, "Yes. The key lies in reading the statues on the pillars. It shows the way. Where are you going?"

Neeza grabbed Lindaris and Joakon and whispered something in both of their ears. Lindaris especially had a huge smile on his face. It perhaps wasn't the best of plans, but it was sure going to make things interesting.

"Haldirin, move the children along. We're going to make some fireworks."

****

On the top bridge of the room, Orznaii finally climbed in. The lead Ettui began sniffing around intently. He had received much intelligence from the many survivors of the original attack on this former stronghold. He wasn't going to make the same mistakes they had so long ago. The biggest issue they reported to him was stealth, and moving carefully was the best tactic. The elves were able to coax the previous Ettui army into many ambushes during the Battle of Simorgan. Although the elf defenders were gone, much still remained of their defenses. If they went in slow and steady, they would have some losses, but not as many.

One of his ranked Ettui warriors ran up to him and said, "Barunaii truccta madriia." (*The base seems empty.*)

Orznaii looked down below, which had Ettui along bridges at least ten stories down. He had heard some traps going off in the distance along with the screams of his soldiers unfortunate enough to trigger them. Acceptable losses. All that mattered was the Relic. Whatever it took to get it was fine by him.

He brought the torch to his face showing his facial features clearly. His mouth was small, but his teeth were razors. Large bumps and rashes covered his green skin. The armor he wore was stronger than the rest, made of thick steel in the chest and steel wristbands. He kept his sword at arm's length, ready to grab it if necessary.

Orznaii ordered, "Keepin driisinntuna." (*Keep moving silently.*)

The ranked Ettui nodded and ran forward to give the order. Things were going very well. When his superiors pushed for more soldiers, Orznaii convinced them otherwise. He knew the casualties would be minimal in the kill zone. That only left the eventual battle with the Valendritaii, or Valendri's minions, for him to worry about. He knew they were still around inside the deep recesses of the mountain fortress. He also knew they would not be easy to kill. Losing few forces here was key to reaching the Relic. The more he could throw at the Valendritaii as a distraction, the easier it would be to reach the prize.

Yes, if things continued as planned Valendri's treasure would be theirs by the next nightfall.

Neeza finished telepathically placing the bottles under the nearest bridge where the Ettui were. The liquid was a blend used by early mages to practice casting shields. It had other uses as well, but it was a pretty advanced mixture. It was called "Kazchum-hi's bomb" referencing the demi-god's giving of fire to the mages. When thrown, it would explode on contact. Cast a fire spell on a group of them close by, and you were looking at a firestorm.

Neeza stayed to make sure the bottles remained in position. Joakon knew the exact amount that was needed and where to place them to make sparks fly. Lindaris, well, his reason was the most obvious. Neeza would have done it himself, but even as powerful as he was, no mage has ever been able to cast two spells simultaneously.

Torchlight was seen coming from the hallway. Despite their best efforts to be silent, their armor was quite loud.

Joakon observed, "Here they come. So after we do this, how are we going to find our way back with the group?"

Neeza responded, "Gerran is leaving us a map of sorts. Just worry about the here and now. We will be fine."

Joakon was always an uneasy fellow. He didn't think this adventure would change that. *This plan was sure to work.* Not only would it slow down their enemy's advancement, but also give them the extra time they would need to reach the Relic.

The Ettui began to slowly make their way toward the center of the bridge. Lindaris was obviously ready. He had been itching for some action and now he was going to be the cause of it in a good way. Just a little bit further . . .

The Ettui were now midway across the bridge. Neeza looked over toward Lindaris and nodded. It was time.

Lindaris chanted, "*Firammii morza!*"

The fireball made a direct line toward the bottles. The Ettui on the bridge looked down, seeing nothing but three individuals. That was all they saw before the fireball connected with the beakers. The explosion rocked the entire bridge, taking out a large chunk. The piece fell along with about ten Ettui soldiers. The section damaged a few of the bridges below until it hit the point where the elf talisman was, disintegrating it to rubble. The Ettui who landed on it were instantly vaporized.

Neeza yelled, "Let's move!"

Orznaii looked below the moment he saw the explosion. Even though they were stories above it, the wake of the blast threw the ancient dust into their faces. When it was clear enough for him to see he began searching.

There was a large gap in the bridge where his lead group stood. *That would slow things down a little,* the Ettui leader grimaced. His gaze, however, shifted to the bridge a few floors down. Movement he would have never had a mind of noticing were it not for the explosion. He gazed deeper with his hawk-like eyesight.

It was definitely not an elf. They would have been able to smell them if they were. It looked human, but how could it be? The magic of Mount Hrithgorn was so powerful that it would drive the simple human mind mad. There was only one other possibility that it could be, and the robes they wore confirmed it. It was one of the last races he expected to see here.

Orznaii just said, "Maginiias." (*Mages*.)

Neeza, Joakon, and Lindaris began to run through the hallways following the breadcrumb trail left to them by Gerran. It was ingenious. He even left them clues as to what the traps were that they encountered. The first room he put pieces of cloth on sections of the floor that were safe to step on as the wrong step led to a deep chasm. Down one of the stairways, he placed the cloth on one side of the steps because stepping in the center would cause metal lances to sprout from the wall.

They finally caught up with the rest of the group, who had their spells primed and ready when they arrived. Neeza gave a quick breath of relief. *Good. If they had been the enemy, they would have taken care of the situation.*

Haldirin asked, "What happened? Is everything okay?"

Neeza said, "Well, they know we're here."

"You make it sound like that's a good thing," commented Condarin.

He didn't expect the others to understand the significance of what he was doing. He wanted the Ettui to focus on them.

Neeza explained, "The Ettui failed all those years ago because they rushed in. These knew better. Now that they know they have a little competition, I'm betting they will race through to try and beat us down. Meanwhile, the traps will be helping us to soften their ranks."

The students were impressed. Though they currently had a large lead over the Ettui, they knew it would be shrinking rapidly. The Ettui were always quick; an advantage that was always in their favor. They always won the numbers battle as well. If they wanted to beat them down below the talisman, they were going to need to hurry.

Gerran said, "We better get moving, then. The traps will only slow their ranks, not stop them. I'd rather be in the inner sanctum before they reach us."

Neeza nodded as Haldirin stepped forward. The others followed suit, although Dyenarus and Joakon brought up the rear.

She finally asked Lindaris, "So, was that explosion just as impressive as it sounded? We could hear it from here."

"It was great! You should have seen the fire and the light! It was everywhere! They never saw it coming! I take back everything I've said about you, Joakon. Is that what you do all day? Make that stuff?" exclaimed Lindaris.

Joakon answered with a smile, "Only in my spare time."

They finally joined up with the rest of the group. Neeza had never seen Lindaris so happy. Then again, the masters in the Black Magic School tended to be a little different. They enjoyed blowing things up and the art of destruction. In his experience, violence was never seen as the best first option. It did have its place just like Divination or White Magic, however. It was all perspective.

As they reached the next bridge, they could see the Ettui were only four stories away and closing in. Gerran didn't seem too concerned about the enemy positions.

"Don't worry. That way will only lead them back toward the top or worse. Let's move!"

Just as they advanced a few feet, five Ettui soldiers leapt from the bridge to the one the mages were on. Most landed on it hard, while some missed and landed on the talisman, destroying them instantly. The ones on the bridge began to charge the mages, who fired their basic stunning fireball at them. It was one of the mage's greatest spells because it didn't require an incantation. It usually disabled the enemy enough to escape or provide an opening to unleash a finishing blow. Or in this case, it knocked most of them off the bridge.

Biverin asked, "Was them jumping from their bridge to ours part of the plan?"

Neeza yelled, "No, just keep going!"

The mages made it into the next staired hallway, thankful it was not laced with traps. Gerran had hoped there was some kind of pattern to the traps being set, but the elves were probably proud of the randomness. At least they left clues. The next room was interesting. Against one wall was a pile of large boulders that an archer could easily hide behind, and in the middle of the room was a crystal ball. It was dull, as light had probably not touched it in ages.

The group was about to advance until Gerran yelled, "Hold it! This is a trap room! I need to figure it out."

Haldirin said, "Okay, but hurry. Neeza and I will keep them at bay, but we won't be able to do it forever."

Gerran nodded as him and the rest of the students began to examine the room. Neeza and Haldirin meanwhile fired at any Ettui that showed up coming down the stairs. At least they were bottlenecked so they just had to concentrate firing on one spot. Yet, just because it was a convenience, it didn't mean they could keep it up for over a thousand troops. Sooner rather than later, they would tire out.

The room was much different than the others. Those at least tried to hide the fact it was a trap. This one was proud to say it was one, which worried him. He did notice four smaller orbs in the corners as well, as he examined the room closer. All were dull like the main one. The floor had symbols on small tiles with a larger one on the tile in front of the middle orb. What could it mean?

Lindaris commented, "Come on, Gerran. This should be easy."

"I wish. These are ancient elvish tricks. These were designed to be original and tricky."

He began to look around the walls and the floors for some symbols that might help. Nothing. Not even a script of elvish writing was found. There was one thing he could try. He grabbed a rock and tossed it onto the largest tile on the floor. Again, nothing.

Neeza and Haldirin were doing their best, but more were coming down and faster than they could hold them off. One finally made it through into the room, crashing through on the tiles. Gerran watched with interest, but still nothing happened. As the Ettui stood up, he saw Haldirin aiming a spell at him and dashed for the stone shields. As he went to his right, the orbs on the corners brightly lit; Aiming toward a hidden orb in the ceiling and down onto the central orb. A beam from the central orb connected with the Ettui, causing it to shake violently. The tiles turned a light blue. After the Ettui fell dead, the lights extinguished. The other mages watched in horror, though Mimerck seemed most impressed.

Vindar asked, "How are we going to get past this?"

"That's it!" exclaimed Gerran. "Neeza, let another Ettui soldier in. We need to drive it toward the small tiles. It makes perfect sense. The purpose of this part of the mountain was to eliminate as many of the enemy with traps, right? What better trap than one that *needed* sacrifice to get through it?"

Neeza saw what he meant, "Then, while the orb is hitting the Ettui, we should be able to all reach safely across until the Ettui dies because it can only hit one at a time."

"Got to hand it to those elves. They really find some twisted new ways to kill their enemies," commented Lindaris.

"Everyone get ready!"

The other mages waited, ready to get the Ettui in position if necessary. Judging by the example, they had ten seconds to get to the next hallway. Certainly doable, but it would be close. The Ettui would have had no issues making the distance with their speed. Mages were never known as the fleetest of foot. They had no choice, though. If they stood their ground the Ettui were bound to overrun them. It appeared like everyone was ready. Neeza and Haldirin waited for the signal. Gerran nodded.

Two Ettui came rushing down the stairs. Haldirin dispatched the first one and missed on purpose for the second one. Neeza backed off out of view and got into position.

Neeza chanted, "*Iczera flirroma!*"

A sheet of ice formed on the floor. He led it all the way to the trap tiles. Because of the color of the floor, it blended in almost flawlessly. Haldirin ran in just as the Ettui did. Not seeing the ice, the Ettui slipped and slid all the way on the floor. All the mage students fired their stun spell at it to make sure it landed in the desired spot: the small tiles near the center. The orbs in the corners began to glow bright.

Gerran yelled, "Now!"

The students sprinted toward the floor. As the center orb began absorbing the Ettui's life force, the students crossed over it. Haldirin stumbled near the beginning of the tunnel and was last to reach it. Unfortunately, the stun spells killed it much faster than anticipated. After eight seconds, the Ettui was dead, but Haldirin still was on the other side. He thankfully stopped just before going on the floor.

Neeza, who just barely made it across, yelled, "Haldirin!"

He could hear a large group of Ettui coming down the stairs. Well, he always knew that he would go defending his boss, but he had always hoped it would be later in his life. Neeza had to do something. He remembered from Gerran's test that a rock did nothing when it hit the zone. Neeza began firing at the ceiling, forcing at various points large chunks to fall and hit the ground. Haldirin watched curiously, trying to figure out his boss' logic.

"Use the stones! We'll cover you while you cross!"

He finally understood what Neeza was requesting. He fired a couple stunning fireballs at the hall's entrance before jumping on the first stone. He had trouble balancing as the chunks were uneven and shifted due to his added weight. As he made his jump on the third, the first group of Ettui entered the room.

Lindaris and Dyenarus both stepped up and chanted, "*Firammii morza!*"

The fireballs each hit the group, killing all but two of them. The last was dropped just short of the tiles by Biverin, who winced after casting his defensive spell. Haldirin advanced three more stones before the next wave came. The students all fired their stun spells, doing their best to skillfully fire in between Haldirin as he moved. A few of the Ettui landed on the tiles but it was nowhere near long enough for him to stop jumping on the stones.

The next wave came as Haldirin reached the eighth stone. These were smarter. They saw what was going on as the mage struggled with his balance.

Dyenarus yelled, "Take out the stones behind him!"

The mages began casting their spells on the stones as the Ettui leapt closer to Haldirin. Their act did stop most of them, but two managed to stay in pursuit, jumping on the stone shields. He was able to make it to the last stone just as one of the Ettui jumped on his previous stone. Haldirin lost his footing and nearly fell off his rock. As he looked forward, he could see the students and Neeza urging him on, but the distance was too great for him to jump. The Ettui on the stone shields jumped toward Haldirin.

Lindaris saw it coming out of the corner of his eye and fired a spell toward the ground. He may not be a fully graduated mage yet, but he knew what would happen if he fired at the Ettui and missed. Firing on the ground caused most Black Magic spells to reflect the energy outwards, giving it more area of effect.

As the spell hit the ground, it did just as Lindaris had thought it would. The energy that kicked up hit the Ettui, knocking it off course. That same energy also knocked over the rock that Haldirin stood on. The mages held their breath as both their friend and the Ettui were falling toward the ground.

Haldirin hit the ground, expecting to feel the pulsing life-stealing light take his life force. Yet, he felt nothing. He did hear his party yelling at him profusely to hurry. He looked back to see the orb absorbing the Ettuiis life force. Time felt like it was moving slowly, but he realized he only had seconds to get off the tiles. He raised his body up and ran as hard as he could toward the mages.

The students grabbed him just as the orbs went dull. That was too close. They were all breathing heavily as they saw the next wave of Ettui make its way into the room.

Haldirin ended up being the one to say, "Let's keep going."

They all stood up and ran down the hall back toward a lower bridge.

Orznaii ordered his soldiers to keep up the work. He saw what was going on from here. The explosion was nothing but a diversion. Something meant to drive his forces to make a mistake. The earlier Ettui who first entered fell for it, but as he got the order out to continue going slow, he would only be hopefully looking at a loss of fifty soldiers.

Now, what to do about those mages? He was not expecting to see anyone else, but he supposed that with the heavy ship traffic now going this way, it wouldn't take the elves long to figure out that they would come back here. It was very clever of them to send mages. He doubted if the elves would have been able to reclaim the Relic without help because of the Valendritaii. He understood it was a risk for him and his forces as well, but the Ettui were more numerous than the elves; more now than they could have ever imagined. Lord Keth, his superior, now on a secret mission, would be pleased when he returned with the treasure. Before that, though, he needed to neutralize the mages, and he had the perfect idea.

The Ettui troops had finished rolling numerous projectiles, waiting. When the mage made their way back onto the bridges, destruction would rain upon them.

****

Dyenarus led their group along with Gerran across the bridge. It was longer than the previous ones, mainly because the room became wider the further south they traveled. Neeza and Haldirin brought up the rear. They just couldn't keep up with the younger mages. Neeza suddenly stopped midway across and looked up. Something wasn't right.

The Ettui weren't moving. They just stood on the bridge doing their infamous chant. It echoed loudly in the hollowed part of Mount Hrithgorn. Twelve stories up, he could see their leader finally as he stepped onto the bridge. Orznaii paced across among his soldiers, never taking his eyes off Neeza. Distance didn't play any factors as their eyes became locked.

It was for this reason he never saw the first of the boulders take out a small portion of the bridge to his left. The impact nearly caused Neeza to fall off, but Haldirin was there to catch him. Stones that missed fell past them, but they could tell it hit or clipped one of the bridges below them. *This was not good.* If they couldn't reach the sanctuary, they would be trapped. The Ettui could leap across, but not them. Telekinetics could only do so much. Lifting more than one person at a time left a mage strained and unfortunately, a mage couldn't telekinetically lift itself without using Dark Magic, the forbidden magic.

Vindar yelled, "We have to move!"

Gerran said, "Not this way. The passage caved in. After 1,000 years you can't expect even a well-built structure to not show signs of deterioration."

They were definitely in a bind. There was only one place for them to go and that was down. He also knew there was only one way to get there. He was going to be sore after today.

Neeza yelled, "Jump to the below path! Now!"

The mages timed their jumps so they didn't miss the bridge below them. It was a twenty foot drop, so they all landed hard. They recovered in time as the bridge above them received a bombardment of boulders, destroying a part of it as it fell toward the current one they were on. It barely missed Condarin and Biverin as the impact weakened that section.

Before he could stand up, the weakened section cracked as they dropped two bridges down. They were only a couple bridges away before the talisman. Caution had to take a high priority from here on out. Neeza leapt to the lower path, again landing hard. Instead of stopping, his momentum made him roll right over the edge. *Figures.* Of all the places he would land, it was in a section that the railing was eroded completely away. He dropped past the bridge Condarin and Biverin landed on to the one below. He was able to grab on to what little remained of the railing as he could hear the rocks being reduced to nothing underneath him from the talisman.

Joakon was now on the bridge right above where Neeza had tried to get a good angle to jump. Sadly, the best spot to leap already had a small chunk taken from it, making the jump a very dangerous one. A few boulders whizzed past them as Gerran and Lindaris joined them.

Joakon yelled, "We have to get Neeza! There isn't any bridge where he is. Just the talisman."

Gerran saw their leader's predicament, and he also knew who would be responsible for doing it. Being one of the strongest in telekinetics put him on the front. He looked to his right. The bridge leading to the sanctuary was within sight. The large arched entrance was the first sign that their goal was within reach. He began to focus on Neeza.

Neeza was trying his hardest to pull himself up, but the drops had taken a physical toll on him. The other bridge was too far away with nothing below him but the talisman. He saw what it did to the Ettui. Now that he was nearly in the same situation, he began to think that was not the way to go. At least it would be quick. Much better than Ettui torture to be sure.

His grip slipped and he began to fall. Yet, as he neared the talisman, he hit something solid. One of the boulders ricocheted off the wall and with a great stroke of luck, landed just beneath him. He could feel the talisman crushing the rock beneath him. In a matter of seconds, it would be over. *I'm so sorry, Mierena.*

When he felt the rock slip from under him, he thought he was a goner. But he could see the rocks still coming from the top. He also saw the mages using a combined effort to save him. Gerran was doing a bulk of the work with him, but the rest formed shields around him and the bridge to make sure they were all protected while they got him. Gerran finally got him over the bridge's railing, letting go of his telekinetic grip.

Mimerck walked up to Neeza to help him up and said, "You're not dying yet. Remember, you still owe me some money."

That was more like Mimerck, who was surprisingly quiet for most of the chase. Perhaps even a renegade mage captain who cared more about gold than of life did have an understanding when the situation was perilous. One wouldn't have been able to say that if they experienced the boat trip here, but that was in his arena: the sea. In a mountain, the dangers were numerously different than on the water.

Neeza stood up as the students made sure he was okay. Condarin cast a quick healing spell on him that helped with fatigue and healed minor wounds. That felt good. One could never appreciate the gratifying feeling a healing spell had unless one really needed it. The soothing, cooling effect it had rejuvenated him plenty. He was still incredibly sore. No spell existed to heal that.

He looked up once more. Orznaii was still staring at him. The look he gave him hinted that that he was impressed by Neeza and the student's defense of his attack. Mostly he was probably only angry that they survived the assault. The Ettui didn't like failure.

Gerran finally said, "Okay, this way. This next set of halls past that arched entrance should take us below the talisman and allow us to safely cross the last bridge. Just one more leap."

They all leapt down to the last bridge. It suffered some damage, but it was minimal. The direction of the current one was on the opposite side to where they were throwing the boulders. They made it to the next set of hallways, which did lead directly underneath the talisman. To slow their enemy down, Lindaris destroyed the archway to block the path. They hated damaging the historic architecture, but they had their own well-being to be worried about.

They passed through another archway and turned right into what looked like the entrance to the elvish stronghold. Even Lindaris was impressed.

"Wow."

A large door of stone and gold was ahead of them. Pillars made in a similar fashion led a trail toward it. The remains of what must have been a carpet were still evident, though most of it was destroyed. Each pillar had a lit torch on it, high in the air.

Vindar said, "Magnificent! The entrance to the Hrithgorn Stronghold, also known as The Gate of Huiilumal. It is even more beautiful than I heard it described!"

"And here we are, seeing it in the flesh," added Condarin.

Everyone began to explore except Mimerck and Neeza, the mage leader more because he wanted a few minutes of rest.

"I'm surprised. I thought if anyone would want to try and find the quickest route to your elf gold, you'd be leading the exploration."

There was no laugh or clever quip from the mage captain, just a deaf silence. That alone had Neeza feeling uneasy.

Mimerck finally commented, "Something feels wrong here. What can open a door of that size? And for that matter, you ever wonder who lit these torches? Seems like it would need to be something tall."

He hadn't considered that. Elves were the tallest of all the species. Still, there is no reason why the torches there were lit . . . that was unless . . . by the gods!

"Everyone, fall back!"

It was too late. Two trap doors opened up swallowing Biverin, Joakon, Gerran, and Lindaris, while the other got Condarin, Haldirin, and Dyenarus. Vindar tried to grab Condarin as she fell, but the door closing shortly after made that choice impossible. He banged on the hollowed floor, but to no avail.

"What's going on?" asked Vindar.

Neeza tried to explain, but as Vindar neared the floor gave out underneath Mimerck, Neeza, and Vindar. They were sliding down a smooth rock path going down. By the gods, all they could do was pray that the end of this trap didn't result in their deaths.

8
LINDARIS

The four mages seemed to go down the tunnel forever. The whole time they wondered where they were headed. Was there something dangerous at the end? They didn't want to think like that, but they couldn't deny that whatever was at the conclusion of the drop could be something that would cost them their lives. It appeared they would find out soon. Lindaris could see a light at the end or at least it was something very white.

They finally flew out, landing on some hard objects, but they were loose enough that it broke their fall.

"Wow, what a ride!"

Lindaris stood up while the other three were still trying to figure out where they were. The room wasn't very large and was empty except for the items they landed on.

Biverin commented, "You can keep your ride. I'll walk next time, thank you. Where are we? What did we land on?"

Joakon's vision finally became clear and he panicked, "Bones! Ah!"

The other three mages rushed out scared as they realized that they landed on a large pile of bones. The lighting was poor, but it looked like they mostly belonged to animals. There were some traces of other bones, though, unique to the elves and the Ettui. Lindaris chuckled as they all went by him.

"Bones never hurt anyone! Apparently we landed in a room meant to store their wastes. It's the only thing here. Gerran, you got any idea how deep we are?"

Gerran closed his eyes and said, "The power of the Relic is much closer, but it is still further below."

"And how about the others?" asked Biverin.

Gerran quieted his mind. He tried reaching out to them, but he couldn't see or feel them. That could mean anything. Worst case scenario was that their paths led to deadlier ends. Best case, perhaps the magic of this mountain was so powerful that it was blocking them from communicating.

Lindaris finally said, "Okay, well, we best continue heading toward the Relic."

"And who named you the leader?"

Lindaris was taken aback. Did he really just challenge him? Biverin stood, defiant as he stared at the others.

"What's that supposed to mean?"

Biverin winced before explaining, "I am the eldest between us and until we regroup with Neeza, I think I should be making the decisions. I have much more experience than any of us. I may not be the bravest, but I have the most life knowledge."

"I don't understand. Why can't we all just work together?" asked Joakon.

Biverin clarified, "Oh, we will work together, but when you have the threats we are facing here, we need someone who can make a decision calmly and not rush into something because they are bored. I'm not saying I want to replace Neeza, but until we find him, we need someone to guide us. I believe that should be me."

Lindaris was surprised and angered by Biverin questioning him. He knew their disdain for each other was known by the other students. He had called the farmer mage many a name on the boat trip alone. But things have changed since then. He was more mature now.

Lindaris said, "Listen, farm boy. I'm taking command because I'm in the School of Black Magic. We are born leaders, and if we run into one of these threats, I can blow them up. You won't find weeds inside the mountain here. Even these other guys look up to me. Joakon? Gerran?"

Both mages remained silent. It was obvious that neither one wanted to choose who was leading and who wasn't. They just wanted to survive.

Gerran finally said, "I think I speak for Joakon. The Relic is what is important. We just want to get there and wait for Neeza. I can show you the way. How we get there doesn't matter too much."

Biverin agreed, "He's right. We should just follow him for now. He can feel the full strength of its power."

Gerran began to move forward followed by Biverin and Joakon. Lindaris finally started going, but very hesitant. *This wasn't over, no matter how much Biverin tried to rectify the situation.* His true feelings were out there. He was going to show him and the others that he had what it took to be a leader.

As they exited out of the room, Joakon and Gerran were forced to cast light spells because it was nearly pitch black. At least the waste room was lit from an air pocket cut through the ceiling. The hallways they were walking down were numerous, as were the rooms they were passing. Old furniture was still in pretty good shape considering the years that they laid idle.

Biverin commented, "These must be old living quarters. Looks like there were numerous beds placed here."

Lindaris added, "Elves rarely sleep, so why would they need beds?"

Biverin flash him an annoyed looked, but said nothing as they moved on. The rooms were all situated the same, supporting the mage farmer's observation. These were some type of resting quarters. The rooms must be the barracks or the closest elvish equivalent of one. They obviously hadn't been used in years. Many skeletons were spread throughout the rooms.

Gerran said, "The final battle between the Ettui must have gone all the way into here. Amazing how far they had gotten. Between the traps, the outer defenses the elves must have had, the death toll for the Ettui must have been astronomical!"

Lindaris didn't really care much about the history of the place. What he was worried about was the random clicking sounds he heard from time to time. He noticed it ever since they entered the barracks. The others were too involved in the surroundings to even make mention of it. As they left the barracks, they exited into a large room with the ceiling being at least 200 feet high. Old elven sculptures were seen all around the walls and structures. The most impressive was on the northern wall located a hundred feet up it. It showed an elvish deity of some kind. It was dressed in armor with seven arrows on one hand and wheat in the other.

"How did they get it so high?"

Gerran answered, "Elves have their means. Many that we don't understand. I have heard that they . . ."

Biverin suddenly interrupted, "Do you hear something?"

Everyone was quiet. Lindaris had certainly heard it. Maybe he underestimated his rival for leadership here. Maybe he *was* just as observant as he was. At first they heard nothing. Joakon wanted to speak, but Biverin hushed him. That was when they heard the clicking sound. They all were aware of it now.

"What in Gyyerlith was that?" asked Joakon.

Gerran waited until the clicking sound was heard again, "I don't know. It sounds like its coming from the south over there based off the echoes. Sounds almost like a . . ."

Biverin and Lindaris said together, "An insect."

That would make some sense. Insects could survive under even the most traverse conditions. The Garchai wouldn't be a direct threat to them as they seemed to have other tastes. There was one thing that troubled Lindaris, which Biverin caught onto almost as quickly as he did.

"That sounds very big to be an insect. I've encountered some nasty ones in my farming, but I have never heard something like that before."

And worse enough for them, the clicking was getting louder and closer.

Gerran commented, "We should move. It's coming from the south, so let's head north. I would rather not find out what it is."

If there was one thing they could all agree on, that was it. They all ran over as fast as they could to a building that still had its door intact. When they entered, they all went silent again, listening. To be safe, each mage cancelled their light spells, opting to sit in pitch darkness. After a few seconds, the clicking could be heard much louder. Only now, they also heard a shuffling sound as well.

Gerran whispered, "It's outside."

Lindaris shushed him, but it was too late as whatever was outside scurried right up to the door. It was incredibly fast! It had taken mere seconds for it to get to where they were. A deafly silence ensued as Lindaris and the others were holding their breaths. It seemed like they were standing mute for ages.

Joakon was getting anxious. Biverin moved silently over to calm him down, casting the only spell he remembered from the School of Geomancy. He used it to calm his farm animals down, so he saw no reason it wouldn't work on one of their own. The relaxed reaction on Joakon's face proved it worked. Good thing, too, because the shuffling and clicking were loud. Every few seconds it would rub against the door. Although he hadn't seen much of it, Biverin knew what it was trying to do. It was trying to coax them into making some noise. It knew they were there, but couldn't pinpoint them. Midenbeasts were known to do the same. After a few more minutes, the creature seemed to scamper off as the clicking became softer, and the shuffling was no longer audible.

All the mages gave a sigh of relief, easing their tense bodies from the stress they just encountered.

Gerran commented, "That was close."

Joakon said, "Thanks, Biverin. If you didn't settle me down, I think I would have surely cracked."

Lindaris grunted. Just a simple act and Biverin was able to garner so much damn support. He believed that Gerran really supported him, but if Biverin was able to win him over, then who'd he be left with? He had to do something to get these two on his side.

"For the moment, it looks like whatever that thing was is gone. Let's get moving toward the Relic. Go on, Gerran. Lead the way."

Gerran nodded and began to walk through the building. The room appeared to be a church of some kind, although he had never seen elves have a structure dedicated to their deities. The world was their church. They would worship them in the middle of a dirt road if they felt compelled.

"This place is creepy," added Biverin.

Again, Lindaris had to agree with his rival for power. The statues along the walls and the shadows they cast from their light spells made them look like demons rather than the religious figures they portrayed.

"Guys, there's a passage behind this altar. Leads to another structure it seems."

Gerran led the way into the new building. It was less pleasant and even more frightful than the church, but for other reasons. The room had many rusted, but sharp tools lying on stone tables and benches. The floor was littered with ancient red splotches all over the floor. One thing was for certain, it wasn't paint.

Gerran was about to tell them about the room, but Biverin said, "No worries. I think we know what happened in here. Must have been won by the Ettui and the elves captured were tortured to death."

Part of that was probably true, but Lindaris saw more than that. The Ettui were savages, this much was true, but there was still some elf in them from what he heard. They wouldn't ravage their victim on the floor unless they were starved. They would rather torture, then like an elf obsessed with cleanliness, do their consuming on a table of sorts. Whatever caused these bloodstains, it wasn't the Ettui.

They moved through a few more rooms littered with bones and weapons. Strange, of all the dead remains they have seen, not one of the skulls looked like they belonged to an Ettui. He found it hard to believe that a hard battle was fought here and not one of them was killed.

"This isn't good."

Gerran stopped and looked forward, disappointed. Ahead of them were three paths. As far as he could tell, there were no telltale marks like in the bridge room.

Biverin asked, "Is the power of the Relic stronger down either of them?"

"Not that I can feel. It seems the same in either direction."

He was waiting for his chance and now he had it. Time to prove to Biverin and the others that he knew how to make the right decision.

"We should take the right most path."

Biverin looked at Lindaris curiously, folding his arms, "And why is that?"

Lindaris continued, "Judging by the way we fell, it was leading us toward the edge of the mountain. Gerran eve said it must be toward the center when we were outside. So, the path to the right is the most logical place to go."

"Charming theory. But the elves are cleverer than they are logical. They would be expecting the simple minded to take the obvious route. I suggest we take the left route. Much like the bridge room, it probably takes us further away before it takes us closer," analyzed Biverin.

His calm nature was beginning to annoy Lindaris. He didn't know what he was talking about. The bridge room was designed to confuse the enemy. This was their stronghold. They would have wanted the quickest routes to get to the desired destination. Why would they want trickery in their own stronghold?

"You know I'm right, Gerran. Go ahead and check it out."

Biverin signaled for him to not go, but Gerran went anyway. Lindaris scared the map-smart Gerran plenty. All members of the Black Magic School did for that matter. They usually had very short tempers, which when it came to military service, were usually given the glorified life because they were the bread and butter of a strong mage attack. Anyone could fight, but the mages that trained in that school were considered the elite. Being so young, he had hoped their representative would be different. Yet, it appeared as if the lifestyle of the Black Mage had already corrupted him. Oh well, what could go wrong? He would walk down the path a short while and then be able to decide whether it's the right way or not.

As he walked under the arch, he could have sworn he felt a heavy breeze. He stopped to fire his light spell out toward the hall. It looked pretty straightforward at least up to the point where the spell died. Maybe Lindaris was right. He was agreeing with Biverin, but based off what he saw there wasn't any reason it would change course. He took a couple more steps in.

Suddenly, a stone block jutted from the floor, blocking Gerran into the path. Biverin yelled, "Gerran!"

They tried pounding on the stone, but they could hear nothing on the other side. Lindaris was just as surprised.

Biverin turned to him angrily and said, "Seems you have chosen poorly. Let's go my way and pray that the path meets up with the one Gerran is stuck on."

Lindaris, trying to cover for his mistake, suggested, "Why aren't we trying to blast him out of there? Get out of the way. *Firammii morza!*"

Biverin yelled, "Wait! Don't . . ."

The fireball ricocheted off the hidden door and nearly hit them. The spell negated after hitting the ceiling, causing rubble to fall over them. Why didn't it work? It was just stone! It always exploded when he cast the spell on rocks at home.

"The wall is protected by an elvish magic! You know what your problem is? You think everything can be solved by destroying it. Some things in this world can't be answered with a fireball or an ice spell. Some things require more knowledge and reasoning, which at this point you lack both!"

Biverin would have continued, but he grimaced and grabbed his side. Joakon rushed to him for support.

"Are you okay? You're grabbing that same side you injured a couple days ago. It should be somewhat healed by now."

Should be. Lindaris was able to figure it out, though. He was more injured than he was leading everyone to believe; maybe even seriously injured. Instead, he opted to stay mum. Biverin looked at both of them.

"I'm fine. Let's just go down the left path and see what happens."

Joakon nodded and took the lead. Lindaris walked up to the farmer mage, a blank stare on his face.

Biverin said, "I can see it on your face. Thank you for not telling Joakon. He already has too much on his mind."

"If you don't take it easy, you're not going to make it. The wood punctured your lung, didn't it? You wouldn't be wheezing like you are if it didn't."

Biverin replied, "I'm not a doctor, but I do believe so. Nothing we can do for it here. Let's get to the Relic and then get home so I might be able to make it home for treatment."

He began to join Joakon, who was waiting at the path's entrance. Lindaris stood still a while longer. Maybe he was taking this Biverin hate too strong. After all, the man could very well be dying in front of him. If the lung was punctured as seriously as he believed, than Mount Hrithgorn might be claiming another life. He didn't want that to happen. He didn't care much for Biverin, but he didn't want him to die either. He even respected him more knowing that he was giving everything for the success of the mission. Lindaris finally reunited with the group.

Joakon had the lead as they turned left for most of the way. But just when it appeared they reached a dead end, the path made a sharp turn right . . . toward the center of the mountain. *I'll be damned*, Lindaris thought. *He was right this whole time.*

At the end of the hall they entered what looked to be former quarters for blacksmiths and clothiers. The ceiling was elevated, or rather hacked off to make it larger. More disturbing was most of the blacksmith pits were still burning with hot coals and a few torches were still lit. Joakon negated his spell.

"I don't like the looks of this," commented Joakon.

Neither did Lindaris and Biverin. What this proved to them was that this mountain was certainly occupied by someone, and they had a pretty good idea by whom. Just the size of the weapons and tools lying around were a dead giveaway.

Lindaris suggested, "We should go. Go now."

Before they could move, however, a familiar clicking sound was heard. It was scurrying closer. The shadows cast by the torchlight and blacksmith pits gave eerie profiles across the walls. It was their first glimpse of the creature: Its deranged shadow spilled across the wall. It looked to have at least twelve legs and a head, but they could tell nothing else from the silhouette.

They began to wonder how it could have followed them without them hearing it. Then again, there were probably hundreds of secret passages. The creature didn't move for a long time, just as the mages hadn't. Lindaris readied his spell. If it came toward him, he would be prepared to blast it to oblivion. The creature, like before, instead turned around. The mages didn't ease up until the shadow was completely off the wall.

Lindaris said, "That thing is beginning to annoy me. Wish it would just go away."

"We're probably the freshest food it's seen in years. Think it's going to let us off that easy?" commented Biverin.

"If it can even see us. Nothing seems to have eyes in this place."

The attack happened so fast, that the only warning they had was the shadow rapidly reappearing on the wall. Going off the clicking and shuffling noises were not enough. It pounced toward Biverin, who was just able to move out of the way.

As it stepped into the torchlight, they were able to see the creature clearly. It was about ten feet long and had at least twenty hands or feet on each side of it, the clicking came from how its hands and feet were cupped, while the shuffling was from the legs rubbing against each other. Its body was sleek and its head resembled that of the Garchai, except it had no helmet. The pale skin seemed to overtake the eyes. The head was bald and the teeth were sharp. It looked like a deformed Garchai centipede, making Lindaris want to refer to it as a Garchipede. But those ears . . .

The Garchipede moved quickly toward Biverin as he hacked away at it with his staff. It certainly knew which one was the weakest of the group. It must have been able to smell Biverin's injury from the moment they began exploring. *Let's see how hungry it would be after he blasted it with his fireball.*

Lindaris chanted, "*Firammii morza!*"

The fireball made a direct hit with the Garchipede which was pushed back to the other end of the room as Lindaris celebrated. That was easy.

As quickly as he thought that, from underneath one of the benches, the Garchipede crawled out slowly. It was glowing a bright red. The creature first looked at Biverin before facing her attacker. It suddenly shot a flame out of its mouth that nearly hit Lindaris. He used a bench for cover until the flame was finished.

Lindaris yelled, "What the hell did it do?"

Biverin explained, "Blast it! The thing absorbs magic! Anything you cast on it, it can absorb it and shoot it right back at us!"

That certainly complicated things. Magic was going to be useless against the beast. The weapons lying around were made for the Garchai, so there was no chance at him being able to wield one. They were simply too big.

The Garchipede instantly went after Biverin again as he tried to maintain a high ground by staying on the benches or blacksmithing surfaces. It moved unlike anything he had seen on Gyyerlith. Lindaris began to look around as there had to be something they could use against it. His attention fell on the still burning coals of the used blacksmith forge. It could absorb magical fire, but let's see how it handled the real deal.

"Biverin! Head toward the forge! Get it into the fire!"

He nodded and tried to get to where Lindaris instructed. The Garchipede kept pace, not giving him room to relax. Biverin was finally a couple steps away from the burning forges.

The Garchipede sprouted its head up in front of him just a few feet before the forges. Biverin backed up as the creature was getting ready to strike. A glass beacon suddenly hit the demented Garchai in the head, causing an instant smoke screen. Thank goodness Joakon had good aim. Biverin leapt through the smoke and onto the edge of the forge, barely escaping its sharp teeth and maintaining his balance enough, so he didn't fall into the flames too.

Once balanced, he tried to coax the creature to leap after him, "Come on! I'm right here! Fresh meat! Come get me!"

The creature was at first hesitant, but once Biverin started talking about meat, it must have gotten its hunger driven. It leapt forward as the mage moved to his left and out of the way. The Garchipede landed in the coals as flames began to cover its body. It pushed itself out and began to roll around the floor as Biverin joined Lindaris.

Lindaris celebrated, "Got him this time!"

After a few seconds of rolling, the flames just magically extinguished. The Garchipede returned to its many arms and legs to confront the two mages, making a sound that resembled laughing. Lindaris gave a heavy sigh, slumping his shoulders in disbelief.

"Oh, this thing is going down," stated the Black magic mage.

But how were they going to do it? It was resistant to magic. It definitely didn't mind being on fire, so that wouldn't work. He didn't get his answer until he looked up. The ceiling was littered with racks of weapons. If he timed it right, he could knock the rack down on top of it. The chains, even from their vantage point, looked extremely rusted.

The Garchipede slowly began to make its move as Lindaris fired a fireball at the chain. The spell obliterated the chain holding the rack, causing it to free fall. The creature leapt, stopping inches in front of them. A Garchai sword had pierced it firmly to the ground. Biverin and Lindaris moved out of the way. Joakon, who had had managed to climb on top of a bookshelf, climbed down to join the other two mages.

Lindaris asked, "Please tell me you have something that can finish this thing off in that bag of wonders?"

Joakon pulled two yellowish liquid beakers out of his nearly empty bag, "I might have something. Throw them at the neck."

He gave Lindarus one as they walked toward the creature. Biverin walked to the other side so it drew the Garchipede's attention, and thus exposing its neck to them. It fell for the bait instantly, smelling the scent of the injured mage. Once it was in clear view, Lindaris threw his beaker. It broke and a terrible hissing sound could be heard. Joakon threw it at the bottom part as the strong acid began to eat away quickly at the Garchipede's neck. It was clawing at the floor, trying to free itself, but to no avail. It was sickening to watch, but the students realized if they didn't kill it, it would have killed them. In about a minute, the creature was decapitated. Its body was still trying to figure out what happened, but that too finally went silent.

Lindaris finally celebrated, "That's what you get for messing with mages! Good work, gentleman!"

Biverin finally added, "That was very ingenious of you, using that weapons rack to our advantage. How did you think of it?"

Lindaris admitted, "Well, I saw how everything I could think of didn't work, so I decided to think how you'd think. You would look to take something from the room and make it our weapon."

Biverin laughed and responded, "There might be hope for you yet."

The two mages shook hands to show how serious their recent bond had become. Joakon was happy as well to see those two made amends. It was going to make things easier for the rest of this journey.

Lindaris finally said, "Okay, if this path goes this way, the one I sent Gerran on must intersect at some point. We should keep going in case . . ."

Lindaris stopped talking when they all heard large footsteps coming from the north. They all knew what was causing the noise; though he was a little surprised they were being so obvious. In the forest on the other island, you almost wouldn't have known they were there.

Joakon said, "Well, I think we're done here. Let's say we move? Fast."

Lindaris and Biverin nodded as a second roar was heard. The three mages sprinted down the nearest hallway, hoping and praying this was the route that would reunite them with their friends.

9
DYENARUS

Dyenarus began examining the ground. Definitely footprints and definitely not Human or Mage. Condarin and Haldirin fell with her, but it wasn't a long drop. They were also thankful that they had a soft landing. A large pile of hay awaited them at the end of their fall. She could only pray that the others had a similar fate. Since then, they had been seemingly wandering aimlessly. Traveling through unfinished pathways there seemed to be no end to and nothing to see. That was until they saw the footprints.

"Do they belong to the Ettui?" asked Condarin.

Haldirin examined the tracks closer and said, "Not unless they decided to walk like men and have a severe limp. Judging by that print something was being dragged. Ettui tend to have a slight leap, digging their claws into the ground to get that extra distance."

Dyenarus suggested, "Maybe it's injured?"

Haldirin replied, "Possible, but unlikely. There are many strange things inside this mountain. The Garchai are just the tip of the iceberg. The Kyroselips, the wolves are just pawns. There is something dangerous here, something we haven't seen yet. I fear we will end up meeting it before we reach the end."

That was very comforting. However, that didn't stop him from being completely right. All of the beings, the Garchai especially, didn't seem like the kind that worked independently. They served *someone*, but whom? She felt this just like he had. This whole mountain was filled with illusions.

Haldirin finally suggested, "We should get a move on. Neeza and the others can't be far."

He moved ahead while Dyenarus and Condarin followed. The White Mage looked at her, trying to be discreet about it, knowing full well she was getting caught. She played the game for a while, but finally couldn't stand it anymore.

"What's on your mind? You're acting like I have some obvious mark on my face."

Condarin laughed and said, "Oh, it's not that. Well, I just wanted to ask you something. You know, girl to girl."

Dyenarus smiled and said, "If it's about what Vindar likes, you're asking the wrong mage. I barely knew him before this trip."

"Actually, I was curious about you and Lindaris."

Dyenarus became silent. She was hoping their conversations would have gone unnoticed, especially with the two lovebirds. With the way Lindaris went about it though, she wouldn't be surprised if even the Ettui were aware of it.

"There is nothing between him and me. We're just trying to work together to survive this place. That's all."

Condarin replied, "That's not the way I see it. I see how you look at each other. I can tell when early love is beginning to bloom. Very similar to how Vindar and I met."

Dyenarus liked Condarin, but she was getting quite annoyed with her right now. Couldn't she take the hint that she didn't want to talk about it?

She finally spoke sternly, "I'm going to say this just once. There is *nothing* between me and Lindaris. There will *never* be something between us. I would appreciate it if you never bring it up again. Okay?"

Condarin was taken aback by her reaction. She was always so collected until that moment. It was probably best that she leave it be. Haldirin also overheard them talking, curious about what Dyenarus said. He would have to inquire about it with her when they had a free moment.

They moved in silence throughout the plain caverns. Calling it plain was being generous. Dyenarus was trying hard to figure out what these halls were used for. They were much too wide to be used just for casual use. It must have been where the elves had transported things. The room they fell out of most likely was once a stable with all the hay. To her, that meant one thing: there must have been an exit somewhere nearby. *Good to know if they needed a quick escape.*

Haldirin opted to not follow the footprints, which seemed to scare them. It was not one of their own, that much he could be sure of. As they continued, they eventually came upon an extravagant entrance. It had a large mural of what appeared to be one of their gods smiting their adversaries; very elegant, yet also very horrifying. Haldirin hated elvish art. Much of it was so lifelike one could almost feel like it would reach out and grab you. This was no exception.

Condarin asked, "So what do we do? Continue down the path or go in here?"

Haldirin wished his telekinetic senses were stronger like Gerran's. The Relic's power was strong enough to where they could all feel it's pull. Just because they could feel it, didn't mean they could track it. It took strong practice in the telekinetic arts to be able to track powerful magic. He was pretty certain even Divi would have been helpful because she was stronger than Gerran could ever be. Not bad for barely attending a day of school.

Haldirin's curiosity finally bested him, and he replied, "Let's go inside. We might find an exit out here, but we won't get any closer to the others or the Relic."

He slowly pushed the doors open. The light they were getting from the air pockets flooded only three feet into the large room. Haldirin cast a light spell and fired it into the room, exploding about a hundred feet in front of them.

As it did, a colony of bats flew furiously out into the hall. Dyenarus and Condarin covered their hair as Haldirin dropped to a knee and remained still. If they were Viampere Bats, then he knew they were more likely to attack a person high and in motion. They got alarmed very easily and were almost impossible to outrun on foot. Although a single bite was not harmful, numerous bites with the toxin they injected had been known to instantly stop the beating of one's heart. Thankfully the two ladies realized this too because other than Condarin's initial scream, they remained still and silent.

When the bats were safely gone, they got up and brought up their light spells. The room was in the shape of a dome and what looked to be a stage on the far end. Stone tables were on the edges still with goblets and wooden plates as they were when they were deserted.

Haldirin commented, "This was a ballroom. I wonder how many elvish performances were given here before hell broke free."

He was always a lover of elvish music. It was relaxing and could calm even the wildest of souls. Almost hypnotizing in a sense, but in a good way. Divi actually knew how to play their flute, an instrument called the Fiiacava. Its sound was unique as it would travel with the wind, changing as it did. Everyone heard something different, but there was never a negative thing said about it. She was supposed to show him one day, but normally Neeza would do something that put her in her now infamous foul moods. One day he'd learn. One day.

When they exited the ballroom, they entered another set of hallways to a bunch of random rooms. All of them had the minimal furniture and were of different sizes. There were many more skeletal remains of both Ettui and Elf.

Condarin said, "I'm still trying to figure out how they organized this place. Why all these rooms right next to the ballroom?"

Dyenarus commented, "Would it surprise you if the elves had a type of brothel?"

It did . . . sort of. Haldirin knew the elves had had them back in Barbata, but not in the way they were known today. It was supposed to be a beautiful experience where nature and ecstasy were combined into one glorious moment. It was a practice they no longer continued on the mainland. Their Fall Festival supposedly replaced this activity, being *much* tamer than the actions on Barbata. Divi had convinced her father to let her go during one of these. He might have decided differently if she had told him what it was really about. He wasn't going to tell him. No one would have done anything to her because of who she was, and plus, she had needed a few days to completely unwind.

They finally reached a hallway that led to an open area. It reminded him of the bridge room, but only a lot smaller and none of them apparently had ever had railings. A cool wind hit them immediately as they entered. There must have been a hole dug out to the edge of the mountain.

That wasn't the only thing that almost hit them. An arrow whizzed by Haldirin's head, missing by mere inches. He looked up to see four Ettui archers on a bridge above them. Damn, they got past the talisman. He had hoped they would be long gone before that happened. Then again, the floor traps that separated their group didn't help at all.

"Take cover!"

The other Ettui archers fired as the two female mages moved back toward the hall. The arrows missed as their attackers began barking orders. Haldirin tried to fire a spell at them, but every time he tried, there was always an Ettui archer there to fire at them. These guys were good or at least their commanding officer was. He set them up in such a way that it made it hard to fight back.

Dyenarus asked, "Any ideas?"

He had one. He just needed a moment. After a few more waves, he finally saw his opening. They had to reload on arrows. Haldirin fired a couple projectiles toward the ceiling, just above the where the Ettui fired, breaking a large chunk off. As the Ettui came out to fire, the rock landed in it, pinning it to the ground, unable to move.

"Move now! Fire constantly at them with your weakest fireball toward the entrance!"

All three ran forward firing at the hallway entrance by the Ettui. Smoke and rock flew everywhere as they didn't let up until they were on the other side. Then they waited . . . waited to see if they had taken care of the rest of them. Haldirin didn't believe so because they were just firing blind at them with their weakest spell. After a few minutes and no return arrow fire, though, he began to think otherwise. They slowly made their way forward, trying to find a way up to see what happened. They eventually reached a set of stairs that went in their desired direction.

Haldirin led them, checking around the corner at the top. It looked clear, but he didn't take anything for granted. He made a left and slowly advanced toward where the Ettui were. He had his hand ready to cast a spell if needed. As he turned the corner, he leapt out with a fireball ready to shoot. With the exception of the Ettui trapped under the rock, the other three were gone . . . literally. There was no sign of them.

Dyenarus said, "Haldirin, look at this."

He turned around and walked toward the two students, who were focused on the ground just east of the stairwell they walked up. There were the strange footprints again. That wasn't the only thing. A trail of black blood smeared across the ground going back toward the corner.

"Am I seeing this right? Did our mystery being take out three Ettui and we didn't even hear him?" asked Condarin.

Haldirin said, "I think we got them all from our magical barrage. This thing probably just took the corpses."

He wanted to believe that, too. The truth was the spells they had cast would only kill the Ettui if the rocks had collapsed on them. Looking toward the west, that was obviously not the case.

He suggested, "Well, being as our friend went that way, I suggest we go the opposite way."

Both females were in agreement as they followed Haldirin over the higher bridge. He considered helping the Ettui that was pinned down earlier, but he wasn't moving by the time they passed him. He was either knocked out or dead. Whatever the case, he wasn't going to take the time to find out at the risk of their lives. They moved across without incident.

The next rooms were a little disturbing. The beautiful statues were broken in the most unusual ways. Some had a spider web look as if something had punched them. Others were even stranger, almost like something had melted the stone. The stone tables were shattered in half. Skeletons were still hanging on the wall, the only thing holding them up being the weapon that killed them so long ago.

The smell was a mixture between rotten food and decomposing corpses. There was nothing evident to justify the hideous scent. They covered their noses as they moved to the next room.

They froze at the sudden noise behind them. It was definitely footsteps and they were coming their way. Haldirin signaled for the students to be ready, pointing down the hall. The footsteps grew closer.

Once again, the three mages were very glad they hadn't cast their spells. Control was one of the first things taught in a mage school, right after the first fireball. Each mage cancelled their spells, relieved to see a familiar face among the dark crevices of the mountain.

"Gerran!"

"That's what I know before we got separated."

Gerran told them all about what happened from the drop up until the wall as well as his uneventful journey in the dark until he found them. Haldirin listened attentively as Gerran explained the events, not showing any emotion. Dyenarus had to shake her head when she heard about Lindaris' actions. She knew he hadn't completely grown up yet. Even after all those talks, he still didn't understand.

Haldirin finally commented, "I'm glad to hear you guys were safe. It is quite disturbing to hear of this dissention. I would have hoped that with our experiences it would have matured everyone."

Dyenarus commented, "Obviously, not all of us have."

She stood up and walked toward the other side of the cylinder room. Haldirin watched her until she sat down before he excused himself. Staring at the wall, it was obvious to him she had much on her mind.

"Mind if I join you?"

She looked up as Haldirin didn't even wait until she answered. He sat down next to her just as if he had been invited to do so. The prized pupil from the School of Illusions was hiding things from them. It was something he noticed the moment he met her back on the dock of Myyril. He was certain Neeza had felt it too, but with the mission deep on his mind he didn't think to ask her more about it.

She shrugged and said, "Go ahead, I guess."

He could tell she was trying to avoid him. What sort of secret could she be covering? If he was going to figure it out, he was going to have to be tactful. Dyenarus was a strong woman who didn't let people dictate what she was supposed to do.

Haldirin, instead of inquiring about what happened back with Gerran, asked, "I'm sorry to pry, but I overheard your earlier conversation with Condarin about Lindaris. Believe me, I realize he has many shortcomings at this point in his life, but I'm still puzzled. Why would you never even consider him to be an option for possible further relations? To have a Black magic user such as Lindaris, and his potential, would be the dream of mostly every female mage. He also comes from a fairly respectable family."

A long way for him to ask the simple question it was, but it got a smile out of her. Not being direct was sometimes the best way to go.

"Well, I'm not your typical female mage, as I'm sure you've noticed."

Haldirin continued, "Yes, you are very skilled at your craft. Something tells me that there is more to you than just that. You can tell me."

Dyenarus gave a quick look over to Condarin and Gerran. They were too engulfed in their own conversations to care with what they were talking about.

She said, "There is, but how can I trust you?"

It must have been quite the secret if she even doubted his trust. His curiosity was never higher. There was only one way he saw that would get him the answers he sought.

Haldirin stated, "I promise on the life force of my wife and child, that I will keep your secret safe, and this conversation will not go beyond us unless you want it to."

Dyenarus took one more look at the other mages before saying, "I would never go out with a guy like Lindaris because we are too different."

That was it? That was her secret? That she just felt they weren't compatible? No, there was more to it. He began to think about what she said and look beyond what it could mean. After what seemed like minutes, his eyes opened wide. *No, it couldn't be.*

Haldirin asked, "Dyenarus, you're a half-mage, aren't you?"

Her silence was all the answer he needed. Incredible!

"This is most shocking, but also enlightening. How did you get your birth past the Kittara?"

"You know my mother, right?"

Haldirin knew her very well. Her name was Fionna. She was a superstar in terms of Illusion magic. She was even a finalist to go to the last Elvish Games 24 years ago. She didn't end up competing because Neeza felt it necessary that the ones representing Myyril should come from the Black Magic School. She was quite beautiful and unbelievably skilled.

Dyenarus continued, "My mother, when she was visiting in the border towns, met a human male who she grew smitten with. One night, she had snuck out and made love with this man. When she found out she was pregnant, she knew it was the human's child, so she spoke to Dinermar. Afraid that his greatest pupil would lose the one thing she loved most, she and him cast a potent Illusion spell, making the birth, my birth, seem like that of a regular mage. As you know, if the Kittara don't take the child at birth, they won't know unless the secret is made public. That is another reason why Dinermar suggested I volunteer for this journey. If I can graduate with a signed acceptance of the highest honor by our leader, then I would be untouchable by the Kittara. To answer your question, I can't ever date a mage because they would find out, if not during our relations, then when I gave birth to child. It wouldn't be fair to me or to them."

That was most interesting. It went all the way up to Dinermar. It was just incredible that they were able to outsmart the Kittara. Previous to the knowledge he just gained, there had been many attempts to mask the birth of a half-mage by their parents. They all failed, of course. But they never had to deal with two extremely powerful mages doing it. Neeza would be interested. If this was true, perhaps he could use it against the Kittara to demoralize them and weaken their power.

Haldirin asked, "But how did your mother help? Females temporarily lose their ability to use magic during childbirth."

She was reluctant to answer, but seeing as she had already gone that far with him, might as well tell him about her other dark secret.

"They discovered there was a Dark Magic ability that allowed a woman to use her spells even when bearing a child. She loved me so much that she was willing to dabble in Dark Magic to protect me. That is why I have an interest in it. I want to know if their using it at my birth might have some . . . side effects on me later."

Haldirin couldn't believe it. Why would Dinemar risk so much for one person? If anyone discovered that they performed Dark Magic, he would have been expelled from the council and Fionna with him. He understood why Fionna would do it. A mother would do anything to protect her child, but what did Dinemar have to gain?

Dyenarus gave a heavy-hearted plea, "Please don't tell anyone. I love the School of Illusions. If the other schools found out I would be exiled. The same with my mom. And who knows what they would do to the Honorable Dinermar."

He smiled and said, "I promise. Your secret is safe with me."

He patted her on the shoulder as she smiled. He wasn't sure how he would keep this secret away from Neeza. He had been looking forever for a way to consolidate the Kittara's power. If he could use her to prove that the Kittara are becoming ineffective, then he could convince the public to possibly even disband them entirely. When the time came, he would need to ask her for her permission to tell Neeza what she told him. Until then, he was a mage of his word. He would keep her secret as long as she would allow him to.

Suddenly, they heard a soft chanting coming from the distance. Condarin and Gerran heard it too because they stood up and joined their friends.

Condarin asked, "It's the Ettui, isn't it? That accursed chant?"

"Yes, and they're coming from that direction. The direction we need to go."

Haldirin asked, "Why do you say that, Gerran?"

"Because the power of the Relic is stronger going this way. That is what was leading me this way until I found you."

That wasn't good. That meant that the Ettui were ahead of them. Haldirin figured they were at an advantage because they most likely knew where it was located. They were primarily relying on Gerran to lead them because none of them could sense its power as strongly as he did.

Haldirin said, "If that is the case, then we have already fallen behind. We must find a way to regain our lead on them. Can you lead us to them so we can see what we are dealing with?"

"I wouldn't be any good at my work if I couldn't. Let's go," said Gerran.

They travelled for about thirty minutes through winding hallways and empty rooms before finally coming to a large room that had makeshift tents made. The mages hid behind a fallen rock pile and began to observe the situation.

"That's not good," commented Condarin.

No, it definitely was not. There had to be at least three hundred Ettui soldiers camped out, apparently working on a sealed door to the north. Just by the bluish glow it emitted, he assumed it had an elvish spell attached to it. As this was close to half his force, it must have been one of the most direct routes toward the Relic. How they were going to get through, that was going to be a challenge.

"No, but at least we now know a potential path to the Relic."

Dyenarus asked, "What good is it if we can't get that door open? It looks like they are having trouble."

Haldirin added, "It has an elvish seal. We won't be able to open it. That path next to it might lead us somewhere, but how we are going to get to it is beyond me."

Condarin asked, "Dyenarus, can't you cast an invisibility spell on us? You are advanced enough to do it at your class, right?"

She replied, "Group invisibility is tricky because it would require me to get internal life particles from every person I'm making invisible, which makes the act borderline into the entry of Dark Magic. The longer the invisibility lasts, the more desire the caster would get. I could kill you all if we stayed invisible long enough, not to mention I'd be going down a path I don't want to even step foot on."

Invisibility was always considered the most dangerous spells a student in the School of Illusions could perform. It wasn't so bad when you had to cast it on yourself because the internal life particles are borrowed then returned, never fully used. When having to cast it on others, she was correct. If she did it wrong or for too long, she could unwittingly kill them because it involved constantly using another person's life particles. Why they haven't banished it yet like most of the Dark Magic spells was beyond him. Spells that dangerous shouldn't be taught in their schools. Being what he just learned about her birth, he didn't want her casting anything that might sway her affiliation toward their God of Death.

Haldirin replied, "I won't force you to do it, either. There has to be another way. This place is full of paths to get to the same location. We just have to find the right one. Let's go."

The mages began to go back the way they came. Condarin, when she moved, knocked a piece of rock off accidently. It bounced toward the Ettui camp. The other mages turned around and froze. The nearby Ettui noticed the stone and stared at them.

"Maginiias. Maginiias!" (*Mages. Mages!*)

Haldirin commented, "That's our cue. Run!"

Everyone followed his advice. Haldirin cast a spell on a pile of rocks nearby hoping to slow them down for a few seconds. Other than causing some ancient dust to fly in the air, it did nothing to slow the enemy's progress. They began to sprint down the halls as fast as they could. Their staves were rocking on their back holster, hitting the back of their boots. He couldn't tell how many were following. He thought he counted twenty, but it was probably triple that knowing the Ettui.

Finding Gerran had been a godsend. He seemed to know which way to go while also using tricks to throw off their scent. Telekinesis was a powerful tool to mages who could master it. Neeza may have condemned his daughter for not continuing her studies, but there were few stronger than her in it. When they reached the bridges, he instead went to a hall facing north.

Gerran explained, "This way! This leads to the edge of the caverns. Might be able to find another route toward the Relic."

Dyenarus and the group listened as they followed. She felt they could have taken that small group that was pursing them. In those halls, their superior numbers would mean nothing. They could just fire their spells at them, and they would eventually be destroyed. Haldirin, as she was learning, was a cautious man by nature. He would rather evade and run than fight to the death. She was like that before the trip. That's what she got for spending too much time around Lindaris.

Just as Gerran had said, they were back in the recognizable plain and unfinished halls of the outer layer. These service tunnels were much darker than the other ones because there were fewer air pockets. It took a few minutes, but they finally reached the lighter edges of the tunnels. Gerran headed east, believing their pursuers would continue to track them to the west. They could hear the Ettui behind them, but still they had a considerable distance on them. Passing a northern outlet, they continued east.

Gerran stopped suddenly, almost getting bowled over by the rest of the mages.

Dyenarus shouted, "Better warning next time!"

It was then they noticed the Ettui pack coming toward them. Either they knew a different path to get that far or it was yet another group that they had the unfortunate luck to run into.

"Go toward that northern outlet. Fast!"

Dyenarus led the charge as they turned around and sprinted back. The Ettui pack, ten in number, noticed them and began to give chase. As they turned down the north path, they could feel the strong breeze hitting their face. Although it felt good, Dyenarus also knew what that meant: This was an exit to the mountain.

At the end of the path, her theory was correct. There was a large hole in the wall, probably one of the few made this obvious. When they reached the edge, she could see why. Nothing laid before them but a steep and dangerous hundred foot drop to the forested base of Mount Hrithgorn. One had a great view overlooking the northern island of the Simorgan Chain from here, but that was all it could serve.

Dyenarus yelled, "Damn it! Dead end!"

The Ettui could be heard coming from the entrance of the northern path. In less than a minute, they would be on them and they had no place to go but down.

Condarin asked, "Now what? No place for us to hide here."

Hide . . . that was it! She looked to her right and saw the smallest of floor. It was going to take casting a spell that she hadn't tried with a group before, but at least it was safer than casting invisibility on everyone.

"I need you to go to that sliver and look scared."

Gerran commented, "Look scared? No problem there."

Haldirin asked, "What's you plan?"

"No time to explain. Just do as I say. Trust me."

The Ettui were nearly on them. They were so close that they could see the scared looks on their faces and the tears flowing off Condarin's cheeks. They could almost taste their blood as they began to sprint harder toward them. At ten feet away, they leapt to tackle their prey.

To their surprise, they passed right through them and began to fall out of the mountain. When the tenth Ettui was sent plunging to the ground below, Dyenarus negated the copies she made of them.

The mages stepped out from their hiding spot amazed at what just happened.

Condarin said, "That was weird. When they passed through us, I could almost feel them."

Dyenarus explained, "Because technically they were passing through you. I made life particle copies of you by using your internal life particles. Unlike invisibility, where I need to absorb other life particles, copies allow me to borrow your internal life particles and return them once the spell is done. It's much safer. Good work acting scared."

Gerran added, "Who said anything about acting?"

They laughed as they waited a few moments to be sure no other Ettui were coming.

When they confirmed it clear, Haldirin finally said, "Okay, let's go. I don't think those were part of the ones chasing us originally, which means there is another entrance somewhere. So let's move."

They returned back to the main tunnel and continued going the way they intended to before the Ettui interrupted them. It looked like there was another path, but that wasn't what caught their attention. About fifteen Ettui were lying dead on the ground, nearly all of them with their skin melted on the floor. The smell was horrible.

Dyenarus bent down and once again saw strange footprints. Whatever that thing was, she didn't like. Luckily for them it was finding the Ettui first, but she knew that it was only time before it would discover them.

Dyenarus evaluated, "Tracks go that way, continuing down the outer tunnels."

Haldirin looked down the path. They could see the trail all the way down until it went around the curve. He looked over at Dyenarus and the others.

"Well, as the footsteps go that way, let's go inside this path here."

10
MIMERCK

Mimerck seemed to be wandering for hours. Despite falling down the same hole as Vindar and Neeza, he ended up falling down a separate hole that split off during the drop. It wasn't a soft landing, either. The only reason he was alive was because the end was only a few feet from the floor. It was also completely dark, so for the first thirty minutes he laid on the ground cursing and unable to see anything. When he came more to his senses, he composed his thoughts and cast a light spell. The rooms he dropped in were frightening, and he had been to some of the scariest taverns on all of Gyyerlith.

It was slow going, walking for hours alone in silence. He considered calling out to see if anyone responded, but decided against it. He had no way of knowing how close or far anyone else was. He was close. Oh, so close. He could feel its power. He didn't need Gerran's strong telekinetic abilities to know it.

He let the power guide him, only really needing the light to make sure he didn't fall into another trap like before. He knew there was something funny about the room, and if they would have listened to him, they might still be together as a group. But alas, as a result there he was, alone in person and in thought.

He began to rub his arms through his robe. Was it getting cold suddenly or was it just him? He really didn't even know how long he had been wandering. It was so easy to forget one's self down there, especially by yourself. Yeah, it was definitely getting cold.

Despite that, he moved on. He might not be able to find Neeza and company, but at least he could find the Relic. Then he could claim that he had found one of the greatest undiscovered treasures on Gyyerlith. The ultimate treasure, as every mage knew, was the Tear of Kazcum-hi, but he began to believe that one as myth. At least this artifact was associated to a place that still existed. Mount Hrithgorn was visible every day of the year. The Tear was fabled to be on the mage's homeland, a continent that supposedly sunk thousands of years ago.

As he walked, he swore he could hear shuffling. The echoes made it difficult to tell the distance between himself and the sound. Then again, his mind could have been playing tricks on him. This place was known well for that. That was for humans and elves, though. Mages were far too in tune with the life particles to be influenced by this dark magic.

As he turned the corner, he came across two paths lit by torch fire. At last he could negate the troublesome light spell. Now, time to figure out the right path. As a sailor, he tended to have great know-how about directions. But as many have told him, navigating on land is much different than the sea. He failed to see the difference. Both were deserts, one was wet and the other dry. As long as one could read the stars, moons, and suns, it didn't matter.

He decided to go down the right path, or rather the 'feeling' led him down that path. He had a hard time describing it. He felt in control with what he was doing, yet not in control as well. It had given him a strong sense of confidence, but also frightened him. One thing he knew was that he was not going to let it do to him what it did to the other sailors.

When he finally returned to his senses, he stopped. The shuffling was much closer. He didn't think it was his imagination. It was the second time he heard it. He had to double check his own steps to be sure it wasn't him, which it wasn't. He scratched his beard as he moved forward.

He stopped once again when he heard a different strange noise. It almost sounded like someone was choking or coughing something up. It was a sickening sound, to say the least. It almost made him want to vomit and he hadn't eaten anything since they were at the base of Mount Hrithgorn.

A shadow appeared on the wall, causing Mimerck to freeze. It looked humanoid, but he doubted that it was. The head seemed to constantly be hanging limp on a stiff neck. Its movements were hectic and violent. He was afraid of the shadow, yet he couldn't look away. Even when it brought its head back and spewed something out of its mouth, he couldn't do anything but stare. He had to move. He didn't want to wait around long enough to see what this thing was.

He found a passage to his left. He wasn't sure if it was leading him away from the being, but anything was better that watching that shadow. He believed that strange feeling was leading him again. It hadn't led him into eminent danger yet, so he just let it slide. Besides, the power of the Relic was getting closer with every step.

He would find himself looking back, as if he expected the creature to be following him. He didn't know what even gave him the idea that it may have seen or heard him. He began to travel quickly from room to room, trying not to trip over the numerous bones on the ground.

As he turned the corner, he froze. There was the creature! It didn't move and didn't seem to notice him yet. Was it possible that he had gone in a circle? The creature spewed more of the strange liquid onto what looked like an Ettui soldier. A loud hissing sound was heard as it connected with their dead rival. A part of him felt pity, but the other half was just glad it wasn't him.

The strange abomination suddenly turned around and just stared at Mimerck. *No, it couldn't stare. It had no eyes like the rest of the god forsaken species on this rock.* It was listening, however. Ever so carefully it was listening. Mimerck didn't make a sound, even holding his breath. The creature didn't fall for it as it continued to face in his direction, softly hissing occasionally. The mage captain hoped being still would be enough for it to go away. Yet, it still knew he was there.

It moved ever so slowly into the torchlight, issuing his first clear look at it. Its skin was smooth and and plain like it was sun-dried. Its head was seemingly just hanging at its neck. Lips . . . it had no lips. He didn't even see any teeth. *How did it chew?*

He was so enthralled in the physical appearance of the creature that he barely noticed it whip its head back and begin making that disgusting sound. As it brought its head forward, it spewed out a strange liquid toward Mimerck. It was sheer luck that he raised his arm so his robe sleeve covered his face.

The liquid began to eat away at his sleeve rapidly. He could feel the heat as it soaked ever closer to his skin. He quickly began to tear the sleeve off, not an easy task. The robes were meant to outlast fire and most other destructive forces. Whatever it used, it was more potent than a mage's spell.

He finally ripped the sleeve off just as the acid neared his skin, throwing it on the floor. The sleeve was nearly nothing by that time. He looked at the creature, one he would call a Spitter. It seemed agitated that his prey wasn't on the ground. The Spitter threw its head back. Mimerck could hear the bones of it's back cracking followed immediately by the gross gurgling. *Damn,* it was preparing to spit more of that acidic liquid at him.

Mimerck said, "Don't you know it's rude to spit at others? *Viriman Xerpharon!*"

He fired a pulsing ball of light at the Spitter. It hit the target dead on, not that it was difficult to hit a slow moving object from his distance. His smile turned to a frown when he saw that not only did the monster seem to absorb it, but he also seemed to grow in size! *What sort of devilry was this?*

The Spitter didn't move toward him, but just seemed to blow up larger. It had to have tripled in girth since he hit it with the spell. It was then that he realized his use of the term 'blow up'. That's what it was doing. And if its saliva acted like acid, what did the rest of it do? He didn't want to find out. He hid behind a rock just as the creature exploded. He could hear sizzling everywhere near him as the acid of the creature was attempting to destroy everything it came in contact with.

When he thought it was safe, he stood up from his hiding place. The torches that had been hit by the Spitter's blood barely held a flame after being melted from the wall. The Ettui was now just a melted piece of armor and flesh. He wouldn't have been able to identify it, if he had just come across it. Stone seemed to be the only material impervious to the blood. He found a decent sheet of rock that was about the length of his arm. Using a leather strap he had in his bag, he tied it to the rock and around his exposed arm. Now equipped with a shield, he felt more confident.

In the midst of the fallen torches and those still standing in their holders, he saw another figure coming his way, moving with a limp. Then another . . . and then another. It had to be more Spitters. *Just his luck; these creatures travelled in packs.* He quickly turned around and left through a different passage. His shield gave him confidence, that didn't mean it made him stupid.

He again began walking rapidly in the dark. He could hear the shuffling of the Spitters, but the echoes left him unable to judge where they were coming from. It was maddening. He decided to let the feeling guide him again. Maybe if he thought of the one thing he wanted most, it would drive him toward it. He silenced his fears and let the power of the Relic guide him.

Many, many rooms later the shuffling finally stopped. He must have lost them at last! His mind was really starting to play some nasty tricks on him. When he found Neeza again, he had to convince him to leave the mountain. Mount Hrithgorn was always a place of death, even when it was controlled by the elves. They had been fortunate to make it as far as they had without a fatality. The longer they stayed, the greater the chance the mountain would add them to its body count.

As he returned to his senses, he appeared to be in a gigantic lobby with two tall doors. One of them was slightly cracked open with a bright light seeping through it. He was yelling in his mind to keep going. Whatever was inside that room was not worth the trouble. The lure was too strong, though. He had to take just a peek.

The door opened easily as he pushed it open a few feet. He shielded his eyes as the bright light engulfed him. As his eyes began to adjust, they opened wide with awe and wonder.

"By the gods!"

It was real! By the gods, the legends were true! He stood at the foot of the greatest treasure room in all of Gyyerlith. Golden coins littered the floor hundreds of feet high. Statues of pure gold and silver were piled everywhere. Weapons of the finest skill hung on the walls. Chandeliers of gold dangled from the ceilings, glistening from the torch light.

He moved deeper into the room. Jewels and jewelry were also cluttered amongst the gold. *Oh, there was so much to take home!* He was going to be rich! No more going on these worthless trips to make ends meet. Just a bagful of the wonderful treasure would be enough for him to live a comfortable life for hundreds of years!

He ran deeper into the treasure room. It was beyond his wildest dreams! He ran to a shorter pile and began to rummage through, finding some of the most valuable jewels and statues he could find. The gold coins would be last to fill all the gaps. He began admiring the sapphires and the rubies. The emerald necklace, he discovered he examined with glee. His bag was halfway full when he noticed the pile of gold in the near distance seemed to move.

Mimerck stared at the pile as a few coins near the top fell to ground. *Were his eyes playing tricks on him?* Maybe the earth had shifted. They were in a mountain after all. He was told by a few explorers that one was more prone to feeling the movements of the earth when inside caverns. Same story here, only he was in a room full of glorious gold and riches.

He suddenly heard more coins dropping, this time from behind him. Now he was starting to worry. The room was extremely large and the noise coming from different directions was disturbing. More coins fell, this time in front of him.

"I know someone's here! Show yourself!"

His voice echoed in the room. Instead of an answer, he was greeted only with the sound of more coins falling as it echoed in the room. He stayed silent for a little while longer until he began to laugh. He had to just be paranoid. *This place, this damned mountain!*

"It's okay. You're in here by yourself, talking to yourself. Totally normal. Just grab the rest of the gold and get out of here."

He bent down to grab whatever gold he could get his hands on, not being picky this time. As he did, he suddenly heard a large wave of coins hit the ground behind him, causing him to freeze. That wasn't the only thing that he heard: A loud grunt followed by a soft roar. To his right, another mountain of gold disappeared as a large beast emerged. No, not a beast. How could he have forgotten the legend? They both had golden scales and red eyes. They were smaller than most he had heard about, but they were at least a hundred times his size. They were the fabled Twin Dragons, Jujikui and Vuldiima.

The two dragons began to circle Mimerck, who stood paralyzed. He completely forgot that back in the day, every elvish fortress had the assistance of a dragon. Because of Mount Hrithgorn's importance, the Dragonians allowed them two to protect this facility. He had thought them long gone, having returned to their homeland.

Jujikui spoke in the common tongue, *"Who is it that disturbs our slumber?"*

Vuldiima, the female between the two, continued, *"For generations we slept. Why have you come here? You should not be here."*

Mimerck was going to answer, but Jujikui spoke instead, "*I think he comes for our gold, Vuldiima. Why else would he risk battling through the cursed ones? It is the only reason to be here.*"

He again tried to answer, but the dragons didn't seem very interested in his reasoning.

"*Our gold? He is foolish! We let no one leave with our gold!*"

He knew he had to try and simmer the situation because there was no way he was going to be able to defeat one dragon, let alone two!

Mimerck said, "Oh, wise and merciful dragons of the Mount. You have me mistaken. I haven't come for your gold! Why would I want to steal from you! I am here with my friends. We seek out the sacred relic of Hrithgorn. If you could point me in the correct direction, I shall let you back with your gold."

The dragons gave off their best attempt at a laugh before Jujikui answered, "*You are even more foolish then we thought then. Valendri's Relic is a power you can't understand. It corrupted the people of this fortress just as it corrupts you now. It must stay here.*"

Vuldiima yelled, "*Foolish mortal! You will not survive here!*"

Mimerck asked, "If everyone here is corrupted, then why aren't you? The power of the Relic is the strongest I've felt?"

"*Who says we haven't been? The gold protects us from the full power it possesses. For every piece taken from here, our power would weaken, and we too would become a cursed one.*"

"But if it protects you, then why have the door open? The Garch . . . the cursed ones could enter then."

Vuldiima answered, "*Because that is how we feed. Too dangerous it is to leave. When they wander in, we strike and sleep until we must feed again.*"

Mimerck didn't like the sound of that at all. It had been a trap, and he walked right into it. Neeza had warned him that the lure of the gold would be his undoing, but he had been too proud to listen.

"You don't want to eat me. I'm stringy and old. There isn't much meat on this old mage I can tell you that."

Jujikiui's eyes opened wide, "*Maginiias! We have never tasted a mage before. The elves used to speak highly of their ability.*"

"*Let us sneak a taste then, shall we?*"

"*We shall, Vuldiima. Any last words, Maginiia?*"

Mimerck took his pack off his shoulder filled with gold and said, "Look, if it's about this on my shoulder, then you can just take it. Actually, I was just seeing how much it weighed."

The dragons weren't buying it, "*Submit, meat! Escape is futile!*"

Mimerck replied, "But still, I insist. Catch!"

He threw the bag of gold in the air as he chanted a weak fireball at the bag. It exploded. Gold and jewels flew in every direction. It did what he had hoped it would do. It took them by surprise, offering him a chance to escape. All he had to do was get back into the dreary hallway. Based off what they said, they wouldn't follow him outside of this room. It was so far away, nearing two hundred yards. He didn't even realize he had gotten that deep within the cavern of false hope. Even though the room was filled with riches, in truth, it was filled with nothing.

The dragons roared, "*This is unwise. You cannot defeat us!*"

Exactly. That was why he was running. He purposely aimed for his bag of gold so that his spell wouldn't hit the dragon. According to elvish tales, the dragons had an aversion to being touched, unless they initiated the act. It was a risk. If he missed the bag it would have hit one of them. That would have made the situation much worse. They may have chased him outside of the room for that insult.

As he maneuvered past the gold piles, Jujikui was in hot pursuit. Vuldiima was to his left, trying her best to get ahead of the mage and block the door. He had to slow her down as there was little chance he could outrun them on speed alone. He fired a fireball at the chandeliers in front of the dragon's path. The two fell just in front of Vuldiima, slowing her progress significantly. He just had to worry about Jujikui.

Nothing seemed to be getting in his way. Gold piles were just pushed aside and large statues of gold and silver were knocked down after staying in the same position for years. Jujikui even tried throwing statues at Mimerck to slow him down. It wasn't going to work. He wasn't going to slow down for anything. Despite that, he wasn't going to make it if things continued on their present course. He was still a decent distance from the door and the male dragon was drawing ever nearer.

As he looked up, he saw his answer. A large net, most likely to protect against falling stones, was loosely hanging. As he ran he telekinetically yanked the loose net off, letting it fall toward the ground. Jujikui was so focused on catching Mimerck that he didn't even see the shadow as it neared the ground.

Vuldiima tried to warn him, but it was too late. The net fell on Jujikui, entangling him to a full stop. He roared with anger as Mimerck made for the door.

Jujikui yelled, "*Your kind will not survive here! It is only time before Zondiir finds you. Then your taste will be familiar among us all!*"

Mimerck closed the door shut, reactivating the elvish seal. He breathed a sigh of relief as he leaned against the door. It was amazing that he couldn't even hear the dragon's roars. He knew they were upset about letting a potential dinner escape. It must have something to do with the seal.

A gurgling sound caused Mimerck to freeze and open his eyes. Not one gurgling sound, but many. As he fully opened his eyes, he saw at least seven Spitters, all facing his direction. The worst of it was all of them had their heads cocked back, ready to fire their life taking acid at him. Mimerck adjusted his rock-shield as he took a deep breath.

Telepathically, Mimerck said, "Neeza, don't know if you can hear me. But if I should fall, good luck to you."

The Spitters brought their heads forward, releasing their venomous acid saliva.

11
NEEZA

"Neeza!"

What was that? Who was that? He recognized the voice, but his vision was still faded. All he knew for certain was that he felt cold, very cold.

"Neeza!"

He really couldn't remember anything past the end of the fall. Did he break something that killed him? No, if he was dead, he most likely wouldn't have felt cold. That was a relief at least. He tried to open his eyes, but they stung whenever he tried. He suddenly felt the cool, icy hand of cold water being splashed across his face. It felt good, but the temperature was much too chilled for his liking. As far as he knew, there was no way to control that aspect of the spell. His vision became clearer.

"Neeza! Wake up!"

He could now see that he was with Vindar. At least he wasn't in the clutches of the enemy. His vision finally returned.

"Neeza, thank the gods you are alive!"

Vindar helped the Myyrilian leader up. He was still a little dizzy from the fall. As he reached up to wipe something from his forehead, he winced at the sting. He looked at his hand and saw a red mark. That would explain the stinging sensation. He was definitely bleeding, but it felt mostly dried up.

"How long was I out?"

Vindar explained, "Over an hour or two. I'm not sure how long. I tried casting a healing spell on you, but I'm not sure how much it helped. Condarin's would have been more powerful."

He did feel some pain in his right ankle as he tried to stand on it, but that was all. He must have landed on it when he hit the floor. All in all, he should have felt lucky that it was only a sore ankle he suffered. It could have been much worse.

As he looked to see where they were, he was most surprised, "Are we in a cage?"

Vindar answered, "Yes, and it's magically protected. I tried casting a light spell on it to test it and it bounced back. If no one finds us, we might be here for a long time."

As he looked past Vindar, he noticed there was another cage. An Ettui soldier sat in it. It was still knocked out as well, but looked like he was beginning to stir. Vindar noticed what Neeza was staring at.

"He fell in about forty minutes ago. They must have reached the gate, but fell under a different trap. I had been making sure none fell in here, and if they did, I was ready to take care of them."

Neeza leaned against the bars and asked, "Do you know about any of the others?"

"I'm sorry. This magical barrier doesn't allow me to communicate with them. I don't know if they are safe."

He was frustrated, but understood. He truly hoped they were safe. The only reason they were there was because of him and his quest to save his departed wife. He had never lost anyone on his adventures before. He hoped he would not have to feel the regret of losing one for the sake of saving one.

Neeza said, "They must be safe. Haldirin will make sure they are all right. Still, I've caused so much pain for our group."

Vindar stopped him and said, "I have no regrets, Honorable Neeza. Neither do any of the other students, I can guarantee you. Don't have any for yourself."

Neeza smiled as he looked at Vindar. The Ettui, who was fully awake, noticed the mages and charged. He was stopped by the cage bars though, never putting them in any danger. They both looked at the soldier, who stopped eventually after seeing it was futile.

Neeza said, "Kind of wish I could speak Ettui so we can at least know what he thinks of this."

"He thinks only of seeing you bleed. Other than that, it would be quite a boring conversation."

All three looked ahead of them, surprised at what they were seeing. *How could this be?*

Vindar commented, "An elf? Are you one of the original defenders of this fort?"

The elf walked in slowly, his hands behind his back. He stood well over six feet tall. His pointed elf ears were easily noticeable, uncovered by his long yellowish hair. His clothes were ragged, like old armor that never saw repair after a lifetime of battle.

"No, sadly the defenders had met a fate more horrible than death. My name is Higalmos, former Elf Eye of *The Forthcoming Sun*. A grand vessel she was. Sad to see how she met her fate."

Neeza remembered the name, "That was the ship famous for trying to find a westerly route to Cordca from Formia. Believe she was under contract to deliver goods to an elf stronghold when she disappeared."

Higalmos nodded and said, "That is correct. You are well versed in the ways of history."

Neeza added, "That happened nearly four hundred years ago."

"If you say so. I have no way of telling time here, and honestly, down here time is unimportant. The ship was sank, but not in the way you were probably told. Our captain was drawn to this island, saying it would be wise to get more supplies. I advised him not to, but he was unwilling to listen to reason. The ship took too much damage, sinking near the northern island and marooning us here."

Neeza found it truly amazing! There was a survivor of that incident and he ironically was able to find shelter in one of the most dangerous places on Gyyerlith. But how did he survive all this time with the Garchai? Did he know something about them that allowed him to last as long as he did?

Higalmos said, "I do find it curious how you know about that incident. It was supposed to be a secretive one that few knew about. I know you aren't an elf either, yet you have a long enough lifespan to remember it. You wouldn't have made it this far if you were. The Valendritaii would have made sure of that."

Valendritaii? They must have been what the elves called the Garchai. What else could they have been talking about? Vindar was about to answer, but Neeza stopped him. He didn't trust Higalmos one bit. Was he telling them the truth about his history? He was pretty certain that he was. But what was to say he was on their side? Maybe he struck a deal with the Garchai to help them lure food for a safe life. He needed to find out more about their new 'friend' before he would tell them what they were. Plus, it seemed like keeping the identity of their race had kept them alive longer.

Neeza asked, "Since you mention them, how have you been able to survive the Valendritaii? As you said, an elf would not survive this place with them here."

He could tell the question took the elf by surprise. He looked at Neeza giving a sheepish smile. He now realized he was dealing with someone who had a lot of sense. Anyone else would have just given their secret without even asking.

Higalmos replied, "A very tactful question, my friend. Sacrifices had to be made, but my safety here is secured."

A very tactful answer. He knew how to play the game as well. He was telling them the facts, but with the vaguest of answers.

Higalmos continued, "Personally, I have no hatred of you, but you did trespass Mount Hrithgorn."

Vindar exclaimed, "Then let us go! If you have no ill-will toward us, then free us at once! We will leave as you say."

Higalmos laughed and said, "It doesn't work that way, I'm afraid. Now are you going to tell me what you are, or am I going to have to ask your friend over here?"

He looked at the Ettui, who looked back at the elf. Neeza had a bad feeling. The Ettui could tell Higalmos what they were. And with the magical shield, there was nothing they could do to silence him. The former Elf Eye walked dangerously close to the Ettui cage. The soldier seemed ready to pounce.

Higalmos suddenly asked, "Huii frumon otraii?" *(Who are they?)*

The Ettui seemed surprised. It could actually speak their language. Except for high leadership of the elves, the Eratuu language was not known by many.

Higalmos asked again, "Onmuaii morta timmta, huii frumon otraii?" *(I ask one more time, who are they?)*

The Ettui answered, "Nuntaii. Unakaii ninta."*(I don't know them. I have never seen them.)*

Neeza could see the disgusted look on his face as he said, "How disappointing. So you're nothing but a stupid soldier. So be it."

The Ettui gave a quick glance. Just by the look on his face, he could tell that the Ettui lied to him as well. He knew they were mages, but the Ettui probably were the only other race that didn't trust the elves more than he did.

Higalmos stopped when he reached the far wall in front of them and said, "This is your last chance to tell. If you will not tell me, then I will be forced to bring you before Commander Zondiir. And I promise you, he will make you tell whether you want to or not."

All three stayed mum. Neeza was certain that he wasn't joking when he said that, but one thing he learned over time was that they would be apt to find out more by remaining silent then spilling their life story now. Higalmos kept looking at one then the other, trying to get an answer, but getting none.

He finally said, "Very well. I suppose I have no choice but to inform Zondiir of your unwillingness to cooperate. Farewell."

Neeza yelled, "Wait!"

"Ah, so one finally wishes to talk now? I could hardly blame you with the choices you have."

Neeza explained, "I just have one question. You have been here for four hundred years. Why hasn't the power of the Relic overtaken you?"

He didn't want to give him a hint as to why they were there, but it was important to know. If it had such a strong magical force that drove the elves mad, it would be good to know what he had done to be able to resist its power. It was a five day trip back at least, one that he didn't want to spend worrying every minute if the relic would cause one of their own to betray them.

Higalmos replied, "Ah, so it is the relic you seek. You are more foolish than I originally imagined. Most come here for our gold. You, however, have come for the greatest prize left here. It is not leaving this mountain. Zondiir has it well protected, and even if you happen to reach it, the relic has a spirit to it, one that these people here feed from. They crave it. They will not allow you to leave here with it alive.

"To answer your question, no one can live here and not be influenced by its power. This amulet, however, makes it tolerable. A gift from Commander Zondiir to me so I may complete the task I was chosen for."

The amulet was nothing elaborate, but it did have a large orange jewel that had a dull glow to it. How something so small could defend against a powerful magic like one the Relic exhumed was amazing. He was going to ask him more about this 'task' he did, but Higalmos had already left. An eerie silence filled the room.

Vindar asked, "What do you think they will do to us?"

Suddenly the ceiling above them rose. Standing above them were three Garchai in a very well lit room. Torchlight was seen from everywhere. The Garchai grabbed the cages and began dragging them past the rock alcove Higalmos exited from. As they cleared it, the sight shocked him. There had to be a hundred of them lined up, leaving a pathway toward a large throne. The Ettui soldier even knew it was not a good situation and was racing around the cage for an escape.

The Garchai were chanting something in a foreign language that he was not aware of as they dragged them forward. All of them looked the same with exception of the remaining armor some had. As they neared the throne, he once again looked at the Ettui. He wasn't sure if what he was about to do was the right thing, but there was an old saying in Myyril: The enemy of my enemy is my ally.

Neeza yelled, "Ettui! I don't know if you can understand me. Whatever you do, don't move and be silent! They can't see you if you don't move!"

The Ettui did hear him and instantly stopped. The cages were brought to an open area in front of the throne and dropped roughly, causing all three to fall. That didn't help his ankle any as he stood up wincing. The Garchai went silent as well, expecting what Neeza could only imagine was their leader. Instead, the only person to come up front was Higalmos. He had to use his elf jumping skills to reach the large steps leading to the throne.

Higalmos faced the crowd and yelled clicking his throat, "Hua'gwu nu, frie la'juantwai solantuman. Oola'hiu Commndrai Zondiir!"

The elf leapt down the steps as the Garchai screamed and cheered. Some were mashing their maces and swords on the ground, causing the mountain to shake. Some had lances designed the same way as the maces, with blades that retracted at the user's demand. Where did these creatures learn to make these horrible weapons of death? As Higalmos walked near the cages he looked all three in the eyes.

"If I were you all, I would kneel when he arrives. It is a small gesture, but you would be surprised how even the tiniest of respect can save your life."

The elf took his position toward the base of the stairs. They began to feel the ground shake as Zondiir made his grand appearance. He was much different than the rest. He was taller than the normal Garchai, and his helmet was more elaborate than the others. Again, there were no eye slots in it, so like the others he must have moved based on smell and sound. He also had a large scepter that reminded Neeza of an over-glorified staff but without the jewel. Unlike the others, he also wore metal boots and chainmail leggings.

Neeza signaled for Vindar to kneel, the Ettui following suit. He didn't know what good it would do them because they couldn't see them anyway. Though, he supposed Higalmos could tell him what they were doing.

The elf jumped on a special platform near Zondiir's ear. He began whispering, and Neeza wished he could hear what they were saying. If only they could be taken out of these cages so he could use his abilities to the fullest.

Zondiir quietly spoke to his elf contact as they continued to converse. Higalmos finally stepped forward. Before he spoke, Zondiir barked an order out, causing the Garchai who dragged the cages out to move toward the gates.

Higalmos said, "The great and powerful Zondiir appreciates your respectful gesture. He wishes you to move forward so he can examine you personally and speak to you in your native tongues."

Well, at least Neeza was able to figure out Higalmos' role and its importance. He was more or less a chancellor. He sometimes sent Haldirin to do the very same tasks. His first task was to meet and ascertain if the person was a threat. To a point, he could also act as the Voice of the Chair, which allowed him to issue decrees should he be unable to.

The gates opened and they all walked out, stopping ten feet in front of their cage. He could instantly sense the strong magical properties. They must have been very close to the Relic. He considered perhaps making a run for it and fighting their way through, but there was no place to go. All the exits were covered by the Garchai. Another solution would have to present itself.

Zondiir stood up and began to slowly advance toward them. Neeza could tell the Ettui was afraid knowing full well what the Garchai were, and wanted to bolt. He signaled for him to stay. The Ettui were fast, but so were these creatures. He might make it near an exit, but not before they would get to him. In the open, it might have been a different story, but in this enclosed space, it was a recipe for failure.

Zondiir moved down majestically. He may have only been a commander, but he was being treated like a king. As he reached them, he sniffed around and bent down in front of them. He opened his mouth and breathed on the two mages, much more powerful than the normal Garchai's. He then began to sniff at the area before giving a grunt.

He moved toward the Ettui next, who remained still and silent too. Seeing it worked for Neeza and his companion, the Ettui seemed less afraid. Its eyes told a different story, not ready to believe it was that easy to elude these creatures. Zondiir did the same, breathing on him and then sniffing at him. He began to lift his head when suddenly the Garchai leader's hand quickly wrapped the Ettui up. It tried its best to escape, but the grip was too tight. Neeza considered helping it, but a spell wouldn't have done much except get them all killed. Zondiir brought the Ettui to its mouth and ripped off the top half of its body. Neeza and Vindar had to close their eyes. They may have been their mortal enemies, but that was not the way to die.

After Zondiir finished the Ettui off, he headed back to his throne. Higalmos never took his eyes off the mages, strangely enjoying their reaction.

"Any Ettui or Elf would have met the same fate. It is not so horrible after a while. Now listen. Zondiir will speak to you. Answer wisely, or you may end up like that simple-minded soldier."

Great. No pressure. He wasn't even sure how they were going to talk to this creature. They spoke a language unlike anything he had known. He was convinced that Higalmos would be translating for their leader, but that was not going to be the case.

"What are you doing here? What are you?"

The voice in his head surprised Neeza. Was that really their leader? He looked at Higalmos, whose nodding head confirmed it. There were only two races in the world that could do it, and he was very certain this creature wasn't a mage. It couldn't be possible! It must be the power of the Relic that caused this. Yeah, that must be it.

Neeza replied telepathically, "Oh, great and merciful Zondiir. We are but simple travelers who were investigating the disappearances of many lost ships recently. We believed the sacred Relic to be its cause."

A long silence came between them as Zondiir stared in his direction. Maybe his use of telepathy was his eyes. If that was the case, then it was very easy to see how he could have vision without the use of eyes. He mentioned the Relic because he believed Higalmos informed him of why they were there. If he lied, they would end up like the Ettui soldier.

"No one will take the relic. This is its eternal home. My question is still unanswered. What are you? Your taste is unfamiliar to us."

Neeza replied, "What do you mean my taste? I don't understand."

He truly didn't. Just when he believed he understood what these creatures were all about, they threw more cryptic jargon his way. One of the benefits, though, was that it allowed him to stall as he desperately looked for an escape. His first idea was to blast their way through with magic. He might be able to surprise them enough with the first spell, but that would be it.

"My patience wears thin. Tell me!"

Neeza decided to try and be bold. It was actually bothering the Garchai leader that he wouldn't tell him anything. He had to know.

"What is it about me that has you curious, all wisest Zondiir? Is it that I have knowledge of the magical properties around you that normally only elves can feel? Do I scare you?"

"*I fear nothing!*"

Zondiir stood up smashing the bottom of his scepter on the ground. Higalmos, who had approved of everything up to this point, shook his head.

"Why do you provoke him as such when you know he will kill you for it?" asked Higalmos.

Neeza answered, "I was under the impression that we were going to die whether we were respectful or not."

"That much is true, but at least it would have spared you a few more minutes of life. That is only when we truly appreciate how our lives are, at that moment when death is certain."

"And is this how you plan to live the rest of your days? Help us escape and I swear to you I will lead you back to your people so you can live the rest of your life like a normal elf should," asked Neeza.

Higalmos stood up near the angry Zondiir and chuckled. The mage leader began to wonder what was so funny.

He finally explained, "An enticing offer. But even if I were to escape, the call of the relic would drive me back. It is . . . too late for me. As far as help, there is nothing I can do for you. You have chosen a quicker death over a much delayed one. It is in Zondiir's hands now."

The Garchai leader smashed his scepter on the ground once more, causing the rest of the Garchai to become restless.

Vindar said, "Neeza, if you have a plan, you better start it with much haste. The natives are growing restless."

That was an understatement if he ever heard one. Twelve Garchai advanced toward them slowly, all equipped with maces, spears, and swords. Unfortunately, he didn't find a way out of here. They were stuck.

In Neeza's mind, Zondiir yelled, "*We shall feast on your blood! When we do, your taste will become one with ours. Get them, my followers!*"

The Garchai gave a blood chilling screech. He truly didn't want to do it, but he might have to perform one of the forbidden spells. If he was going to die here, he was going to take as many of the hell beasts with him. He was certain the gods would find it a just cause to use it. If for no other reason than to wipe that sadistic smirk off of Higalmos' face would make it worth it.

Thankfully, an answer presented itself before that became an option. About half the Ettui force came charging in, pouncing on the nearest Garchai. It was trying to shake them off by reaching over his back, but they proved elusive. By the gods, he never thought he would see the day when he would be happy to see the Ettui.

Zondiir yelled, "Nui'gwa llala'jhi sufara! Mor'kui Ettui!"

The other Garchai began to charge at the incoming Ettui ranks. Neeza quickly grabbed Vindar as they began to run toward the wall and away from the fight. He had seen enough combat to know when it wasn't his battle. The Ettui were providing the perfect distraction.

"Where do you think you're going?"

Higalmos jumped in front of them with a sword in his hand pointed at them. The elf looked mad; the craziest stare he had ever seen one give, followed by a demented giggle that matched it. *This must be what he meant when he talked about the Relic influencing him.*

Neeza ordered, "Step aside."

Higalmos laughed and said, "I told you that you wouldn't leave here alive. Zondiir will be upset that he won't get your taste, but order must be restored. Prepare yourselves!"

The elf charged forward as Neeza yelled, "Vindar, now!"

Vindar chanted, "*Lightima Ghorma!*"

A bright light stopped Higalmos as he had to cover his eyes. Neeza took this chance to disarm the elf with a spell of his own. He kicked the loose sword out of the way as the elf fell to the ground. Neeza walked over quickly to retrieve the amulet before Higalmos could recover from the spell. When the light spell dissipated, he stood up.

Neeza said, "You are right. You cannot be saved. You were wondering who we are? We are mages and damn proud of it. *Firammii morza!*"

The spell hit Higalmos right back into the middle of the skirmish between the Ettui and the Garchai. Ettui bodies were lying everywhere, but amazingly they had been able to take down some of the Valendritaii as well. He tried to stand up. He had to tell his master what they were dealing with. He only made it a few steps when he felt cold all of a sudden. He looked down to see a blade sticking out of his chest. So, death was finally coming to him. At last he was free. The relic could control him no longer.

Neeza and Vindar stayed only long enough to see Higalmos' death. The Ettui who slayed him went on to battle the Garchai. He did hate to do that to the elf. On the inside, he knew he was being led against his own will. But the power of the Relic had corrupted him too greatly. If anything, it proved that they had a strict time where they could examine it. After that, it had to be disposed of.

Vindar finally said, "We should hurry, the Ettui forces are dwindling. Won't take them long to notice we are missing."

He was right. They had their path of escape, so they had to take it. Once this Ettui force was defeated, it would be only time before they were found. Neeza nodded and led them down a hall that was too small for the Garchai to travel. He had to find the Relic. He could feel it. It was closer than it ever was before. They just needed a little more time.

As the last of the Ettui forces were defeated, Zondiir turned his head down at the scene, letting a long breath out. He could taste the blood of the Ettui as well as a few of his own kind. He also tasted another anomaly. This was elf blood, and there was only one elf that was allowed to live on this rock. Those spawns of hell! They kill his pet Kyroselip and now the only connection to what they used to be. All the invaders would be found and their blood spilled from their bodies until they were dry.

Zondiir yelled in the common tongue so that even their captives would hear them, "*Find the blasphemers! Kill them! Kill them all!*"

12

Neeza led Vindar down the various hallways; trying his best to let the power of the Relic guide him. They could hear voices behind them, but they knew that the Garchai were too small to fit in the halls. Granted he was certain that they had ways to get to almost anywhere in the mountain, at least in the tight halls they would be safe.

Vindar asked, "How much further? The echoes make it sound like they are nearby."

Neeza honestly didn't know. It was amazing to him that the Relic seemed to be pulling from every direction the closer they inched toward it. It made it that much harder to know what the right way was. The big disadvantage they had was that the enemy knew their target. The Garchai could very well be waiting for them there. Then again, maybe the Ettui's involvement made them more enticing targets rather than the mages. Zondiir did go after the Ettui first after all when he could have eaten any of the three.

As they advanced forward, they both noticed they were going downward. They were moving in the correct direction, but how much further down would they have to go?

They proceeded deeper, both growing more worried as the rooms were getting noticeably bigger. The rooms were almost large enough to hold a solitary Garchai in it. It made sense, though. If what Higalmos said was true, the location of the treasure would be heavily guarded. In order to do that, the rooms would have to be large enough to accommodate its defenders.

Hallway after hallway, room after room they travelled. He felt like they were going in circles. Despite that, the power of the Relic was growing stronger. Oh yes, it was. He could feel it begin to tickle at his nose. A strange sensation, but one he was beginning to enjoy.

Vindar commented, "By the gods, these rooms look all alike. Are we lost?"

No, my dear boy. They weren't lost. He had a guide leading them straight to the prize. It wanted him to find it. He was destined to be the one to take the blessed artifact from its resting place after all these years. How else could he explain surviving the experiences he had? *It was destiny, my friend. It was destiny.*

He snapped out of his trance when they heard movement coming from a side hallway. The room they were in was like the others, but had pillars and statues of unidentified elves on the top if them. At least they had hiding spots in here. Most of the rooms were wide open. He grabbed Vindar, and they concealed themselves behind two pillars. The footsteps were getting closer and he was certain he heard voices.

Vindar asked, "What should we do?"

Neeza said, "Do the same as we did with Higalmos. Whatever is walking down here must have eyes. You blind them, and I'll finish the rest."

Vindar nodded as they waited. That was the hard part, the waiting. They could definitely hear voices, more than one. It was spoken softly, so it was hard to determine what was being said. It had to be the Ettui. That was the same strategy they were employing earlier. Vindar began to prepare his spell, but Neeza stopped him.

"Not yet. They'll see your spell from behind the pillar. Wait until they are in the room, and then fire."

Vindar negated his spell and continued to listen. The voices were getting closer and much clearer. It almost sounded like the common language, but just because of that he knew he couldn't assume they were friends. He knew the Ettui understood the language and even a few of them could speak it fluently. A light could be seen coming from the hallway.

Neeza whispered, "Count to five and then go."

Vindar gave a deep breath,

One.

His hands began to sweat. Even though he shouldn't be nervous with what they experienced, the reality that death could occur at any time was enough to keep that feeling strong.

Two.

The light was getting closer in the hallway. They could almost make figures out of the shadows splashed against the wall. Definitely humanoid, but again, the Ettui could walk bipedal as well.

Three.

Vindar tried to relieve the stress by moving his fingers to keep them loose. That wasn't working, either. His thoughts then returned to Condarin. She was somewhere in here. He wanted badly to be with her again. He didn't know if any of the mages fell with her, but he knew at least for the moment she was safe as he could feel her life force. Neeza had said he wasn't going to leave without the Relic. For Vindar, he wasn't going to leave this mountain without Condarin.

Four.

The voices were very audible now. He almost believed there was a female voice mixed into the chatter. Despite that, Neeza began to gather the life particles to cast a fireball spell.

Five.

Vindar leapt out and was prepared to fire a light spell into the air. His spell thankfully never left his hand as it was friend, not foe that walked from that hallway.

"Gerran!"

Neeza had already negated his spell. He had to hand it to these kids. Their spell control and decision-making was incredible. All of them. It seems that added curriculum he passed over a hundred years ago was beginning to reap its rewards. At least three times on this mission alone did their control avoid friendly fire.

"Vindar! Neeza! By the gods you're safe! Guys, come here!"

Out of the hallway stepped Dyenarus, Condarin, and Haldirin. Vindar instantly ran to Condarin as they embraced. Knowing she was safe put much ease to his heart. Haldirin and Dyenarus walked up to Neeza and they shook hands.

"Well done. Glad to see you all in one piece."

Haldirin commented, "We could say the same for you."

Neeza laughed as he asked, "Do you know of the others?"

Haldirin and Dyenarus explained to Neeza what Gerran had told them about Lindaris and the group. Neeza shook his head, but said nothing. Not that he needed to. His action spoke louder than any words.

Haldirin asked, "What about Captain Mimerck?"

By this time, Vindar and Condarin had rejoined their group. Neeza had no idea about the fate of their captain. He knew he fell down the same hole as them, but Vindar made no mention of him when he woke up.

Vindar explained, "I'm not too certain. As we fell, there was a split in the paths. Neeza and I fell down the right, Mimerck must have fallen down the left. He wasn't in the cage when we exited the tunnels."

Haldirin asked, "Cage?"

Neeza put a hand on his protector's shoulder and said, "We have much to catch up on."

Neeza and the group travelled together again, with Gerran back in the lead. He told them how he followed the Relic's power to the location they'd met. That eased Neeza's heart that he was indeed going the right way. Why he doubted it was another thing. The feeling was not going to lead him astray. As he always believed, it wanted them to find it and rescue it from its Garchai captors.

Likewise, Neeza and Vindar told them about Higalmos and Zondiir and what happened before the Ettui interfered. They were shocked to hear that an elf had survived in the mountain that long, but not so surprised when they told them that it was willing to die for the Garchai and the Relic in the end.

Dyenarus, the more she heard about their target, the more she hoped they didn't find it. She couldn't tell for sure, but she was becoming more convinced that the object was pure evil. It seemed all who went near it eventually succumbed to its strong urges. She hoped no one in their group would be so unlucky. She decided then and there to keep a close watch on everyone. If she noticed a change in behavior, she was going to have to take matters into her own hands.

The person she was most worried about was Gerran. He had been allowing his senses to follow the strongest urges of the Relic so that he could lead them to it since they landed on these islands. The closer they got, would the influence it had on him be strong enough for him to betray them? She thought he understood the risk he was taking, but it didn't seem to bother him. He had a job to do, and he was going to see it through to the end.

Condarin and Vindar were hanging around Neeza, mainly because he had begun to limp. When he told her about the ankle, Condarin jumped into her role as the medic. That was a funny thing she noticed about mages, purebloods at least. When they chose a role, it became their life's work. Condarin was most likely talented in other things. But when a situation arose, she would instantly put on her White Mage cap and get to work efficiently and with excellent results. She even displayed a sense of humor, as was evident when she worked on Lindaris earlier.

She guessed that was true of all mages, including Lindaris. It was something she would never experience as a half-mage in hiding. She was toying around with a suggestion Haldirin had for her moments before they re-connected with Neeza. He suggested she tell Neeza her secret because he would not be angry, but thrilled to learn of what she had accomplished. He joked that he would probably coronate her before they even left the mountain, he would be so impressed and thankful. But could she trust even him with that information? Haldirin made what the mages called a blood promise. It was when one swears on the blood of their kin that they will keep a secret or else the gods could very well take those very relatives he swore on. It was nothing to take lightly. If Neeza made that same promise with her, then maybe she would consider it. She doubted he would do it with his only daughter, though. Then again, with what she heard about him encouraging her peers to make fun of her just so she would learn magic, anything was possible. She trusted Divi more and she had never met her.

Gerran suddenly stopped everyone, saying, "Hold on. Something seems strange."

Their navigator began to slowly move forward. Dyenarus tried to see what was ahead, but the only odd thing she could see was a large metallic object lying on the floor. After a moment, Gerran signaled them over, but refused to enter the room. As they arrived, they could see why.

The room was filled with fallen Garchai, so freshly killed that their blood was still seeping on the floor from their wounds. From what Dyenarus could count, there had to be at least twelve of them. Haldirin moved forward and began to examine the room, looking up and down the walls and ground.

Neeza asked, "Gerran, please tell me you had something to do with this on the way to finding us."

"If I did, would you be impressed enough for me to get your instant recommendation?"

If it were true, that would have been a guaranteed recommendation. However, it was not even close to being accurate and both knew it. They were never even near that part of the mountain. Haldirin knelt down examining a wire and some footprints. Dyenarus began to look around curiously when she noticed something strange hanging from their leader's robe pocket.

"Neeza, what is that?"

He saw her point to the amulet that he had grabbed off of Higalmos. He had forgotten he had it. Not that it appeared he needed it. No one here seemed remotely affected by the Relic's power.

Neeza said, "It was something we found. You can have it."

He tossed it to Dyenarus, who barely caught it not expecting the throw. Vindar gave a concerned look as he moved over to her. Condarin joined them out of curiousity.

Vindar whispered, "We didn't just find it. That amulet is supposed to suppress the power of the Relic so that one could tolerate it and not be driven mad. That elf, Higalmos, wore it."

Dyenarus replied, "And he just gave it to me without an explanation or anything. Vindar, Condarin. I hate to have to say this, but I think we need to keep an eye on those three up ahead. I want to be wrong, but don't you see that as odd behavior?"

Both couldn't have agreed more with her. As much as they hated to have to keep a watchful eye on their own, Neeza's willingness to pass the amulet on knowing what it can do was enough. Condarin was the last to agree, but did so under Vindar's reassurance. Dyenarus put the amulet on and walked toward Haldirin.

"What have you found out?"

Haldirin saw her and said, "Mostly theory, but one thing I know for sure is that the Ettui are responsible for all twelve of their deaths. I'm seeing thin, but strong metal wire everywhere that was broken. These are made in the classic Ettui design. I think these Garchai stepped into a trap."

Dyenarus asked, "How could the Ettui take out twelve of these things? We have more power than they do and we couldn't even take one out yet."

Neeza stepped forward, "Vindar and I alone had witnessed the Garchai take out at least three hundred Ettui with only minor wounds to show for it. Yet, this Ettui leader of theirs is very well versed in this place and its residents. Perhaps they knew they would come this way eventually and set these wires to snap."

Haldirin finished his thought, "Because a broken metal wire if strung tight enough could rip through any known metal known to man. It would have cut through the Garchai like hot butter."

They all looked toward the beheaded Garchai at the large puddle of green blood near both his head and the rest of the body. As they moved deeper into the room, they saw more dismembered Garchai and their bodies. The smell was starting to take form as they neared the end of the room. Haldirin looked up to see many places on top that seem to be platforms of some kind. That must have been where they had it set up the wires.

The room looked very incomplete as well, like they were in the middle of molding it when something happened. Gerran overcautiously took them through the remainder of it until they reached the hall. He didn't want to happen to them what happened to the Garchai. In the hall, they began to hear sounds faintly coming from the other side. When they found the end, they entered a large and cavernous room. It was pitch black where they were, but they could see the torchlight ahead illuminating the entire area. The mages carefully advanced until they came to a set of stones that overlooked the area.

It was huge! The ceiling was at least eight hundred feet high and a large double door could be seen to the left. A large camp had been set up by the nearly seven hundred Ettui that cluttered the area. The most curious ones were holding a bluish veil across the great set of doors, which were being pounded on the other end. They were pretty sure they knew who was on the other side. Whatever that veil was must have been strengthening it. Beyond the area was dark on the other side, but every once and a while a torch could be seen going or coming back.

Vindar exclaimed, "Wow! This place is amazing!"

Condarin commented, "That it is, but I'm more concerned about how we are going to get past the rest of these Ettui."

For once the woman said something that would actually make them think instead of sugar-coating the problem, Dyenarus almost said aloud. This group of Ettui seemed different than the others. Their armor looked stronger and they seemed more disciplined.

Neeza said, "We know we are going in the right direction because I think this is an elite squad. The ones thrown at Zondiir was a ruse; something to keep the masses busy while these made their way to the Relic. Smart . . . too smart for my liking."

Gerran asked, "How are we going to get past them? The walls are too smooth for us to climb."

Neeza began to look around the area as he said, "The good thing about this place is that there always seems to be another way to get to where you are going. The problem lies in trying to find out where they are going. If they know so much about this place and how to dispatch the Garchai quickly, then they certainly know exactly where it is."

"And judging by the strength of it, we are getting very, very close to it," added Gerran.

Haldirin asked, "How are we going to find out? None of us can understand elvish to even try to listen in on their conversations."

There was a way, however it was going to be dangerous and unfortunately, he would need someone else to do it. He wasn't going to be sneaking in on anyone soon with his ankle hurting like it did. Healing spells could only do so much sometimes. He had his preference of course, but that would be only be if she was willing.

Neeza explained his plan, "We might not be able to understand what they say, but I'm quite certain they have a map. Maps, like music, are pretty standard. As it so happens, we have a mapping expert. I believe it would be in the command hut, in the far distance over there."

They all looked in that direction. It was only about two hundred feet away, but with the Ettui soldiers everywhere, it might as well been two thousand feet.

Haldirin commented, "Well, unless someone learns how to make an area effect sleep spell, that isn't happening. We'd be seen the moment we hit the torchlight."

Neeza smiled as Haldirin used the key word he was looking for, "The key is to make ourselves unseen."

At this point, everyone looked in Dyenarus' direction. Other than Neeza, she was the only one who knew how to make him or herself invisible. It sure sounded to her that he was suggesting that they use group invisibility to get them there.

"No, I won't use group invisibility on us!"

Even Haldirin showed a concern look on his face, "I have to agree with Dyenarus. It's too risky, for us and for her."

Neeza clarified, "That is why I am asking only her to go. She will sneak into the camp under the cloak of invisibility, steal the maps, and return here so we can figure out where we can get ahead of them. Believe me; I would do it if not for my ankle. I believe in you."

Dyenarus looked around at everyone's faces, but stopped mainly on Haldirin's. His face said it all. She was the only other one who could do it. She didn't want to admit it, but she was scared. Staying invisible, like any spell that wasn't instant like a fireball, would be physically draining on her. If she stayed invisible too long on the trip there, she might not have the strength to make the trip back. But if it was the only way they were going to get out of here, what choice did she have?

Dyenarus finally said, "Okay. I'll do it."

"How is she doing?"
"She's about halfway there."

"Where?"

"By that crate. Can't you see . . . just believe me."

"Would all of you please be quiet? It's hard concentrating on staying invisible. Having all of you chatter in my mind isn't helping!" telekinetically scolded Dyenarus.

She hated to use her Telekinetic Speak while she was invisible because that was more physically draining on her, but she had to keep them quiet. She allowed the other mages access to her mind so they could let her know if any of the Ettui discovered her fast. Invisibility was nice, but on surfaces like this, she still made easily traceable footprints. She also had to be cautious not to knock anything down as that would give her position away.

She could see the command hut about fifty feet away, but there seemed to be a constant stream of Ettui soldiers coming from that direction. Their leader must have been in there. That was going to make things tough, if he was. One thing she knew was that she was going to have to take a different route. There were too many chances that she could walk into one of these soldiers. She turned right, between a couple of huts.

"Careful, Dyenarus. We are losing a visual of you and the quarters seem tight."

Thanks for the concern Haldirin, she wanted to say, but kept silent. She knew this was risky as well. Not many Ettui seemed to come from this direction, but if one did, there was not much room to avoid a collision. She looked back. She could see her footprint trail as plain as day. She hated this sandy material. This room must have been quarried to the point that the stones were grinded so fine they became a nice granule.

She moved slowly, hoping to minimize the risk of someone hearing her. She tried her best to control her breathing because that could be seen as well. She didn't realize how cold it had gotten the further down they got. The Ettui didn't need to worry much about temperature. Unless it was below zero, their tough skin made them adaptable to the environment. The huts were quickly made out of animal leathers and pre-made sticks. As these materials were easy to come by, they could set this up and leave it without regret of leaving anything valuable behind in terms of housing material.

She froze when she heard movement from inside the huts next to her. That was the other factor that made this route more difficult. There could be a number of Ettui soldiers in the tents that could pop out at any time. She finally began moving again around the nearest hut.

Suddenly three Ettui raced past her. She had to make evasive maneuvers to get out of the way without landing on the hut. Sand kicked up as she did. The first two continued on their way. The last one, however, stopped and turned around. *No, no, no, no, no, please turn around!* She closed her eyes and took a deep breath. The Ettui moved to her direction, stopping about three feet in front of her. She remained silent, but it was difficult. It looked around the area. All he had to do was reach his arm out and his hand would have hit her. Luckily, it must have assumed they had done the strange sand kick as they raced by. He finally moved forward. Dyenarus breathed a heavy sigh of relief as she tried to catch her breath.

As she turned the corner, the command hut was only forty feet away, and with very little traffic going that way. She began to quicken her pace as she wanted to get it over with. About halfway, one soldier stepped out of its tent, not more than two feet in front of her. If it turned right, it would have walked right into her. By the good grace of the gods, it turned left toward the hut.

She decided to follow right behind it. When she was within five feet from the side of the command hut, she sprinted to her left. The Ettui she trailed looked back, but seeing nothing, it continued on its course. Dyenarus found a window and a group of crates that provided great cover. As she stepped behind the crates, she cancelled out her invisibility spell.

"Okay, I'm near a window. Going to look in and see what it's like inside."

Partly on the side of caution, and partly the need for a rest from the spell, she decided it best she scouted the room before entering it. She didn't want to walk in and discover more Ettui than she'd be able to handle. As it turned out, there were only four inside, one of whom was the one she had trailed behind. They were speaking in their language, so she couldn't understand a word they were saying.

She did recognize one of them. The leader, who she noticed back in the bridge room, was dictating to his lesser officers most likely. He had a commanding voice for an Ettui. Four was not many, but it was probably wise that she didn't jump in as the leader would probably be more than she could handle. She began to describe the scene to the mages telepathically.

"Okay, the leader is here. He's having a small meeting. There are various papers and scrolls, but I can't see what they are from here. There is a table that has a map of some kind, so I will check that out as soon as I can."

Orznaii began to gesture with his hand toward the door. The other Ettui in the room began to leave. Wow, was she fortunate. Now all she had to worry about was the leader and if push came to shove, she should be able to get out.

"The leader just sent everyone out. Getting ready to make a move."

She readied her invisibility spell as soon as the last Ettui exited the hut. It was going to take some skill, but she was confident in her abilities to do it.

She stopped herself as her vision zoned in on Orznaii. He reached into his armor and pulled out a pouch as he walked toward a weak flame in the center. She couldn't tell what was in it, but it was some kind of powder.

"Dyenarus, you have an update?"

"Shhh! Something is about to happen."

He threw it on the flame, causing it to grow nearly to the top. She was afraid the hut would catch fire. The flame soon turned to a dull blue, but that wasn't what shocked her. It looked as if there was a man in the fire!

"What have you to report, General Orznaii?" asked the man.

Orznaii spoke in the common tongue, "We advance on Valendraii's Relic. It is just down the tunnels past here. One way in, so we will not be disturbed."

As surprised as she was that they were actually talking in the common language, she was more relieved than anything. That meant that she didn't have to sneak in. All she had to do was listen.

The man said, "Good. Have you met any opposition while in the Mount?"

Orznaii replied, "The Valendritaii guarding went down easy. Thank Lord Ulcinar for that recommendation. They fell right into the trap like he foresaw they would. However, we also ran into a group of mages."

The man in the flame went silent. This news was obviously very concerning. She tried to memorize every feature of the man that she could. She didn't know his name, but he did have long white hair, and seemed to wear all black. He was actually quite handsome from what she could see. She did have one name, though. Lord Ulcinar.

The man said, "Dispose of them if you see them, but I am quite certain the Valendritaii will save you the trouble. Their leader is the most important mage. I doubt that he would be there. His name is Neeza."

Orznaii said, "I don't know what Neeza looks like or if he's here, but if he is, he would be in charge of the group. I will kill him for certain."

That wasn't good. What was so important about Neeza that they knew him by name? How was he considered the most important mage? This situation was starting to become much grander than she could have imagined.

The man continued, "That would be most pleasing. When you do, bring his head to me when you drop the Relic off and we will see. Fortune would smile upon us if he's there because it would save us much trouble. The shield my master gave you is working as well?"

"Yes, my four strongest Ettui are holding it up. The Valendritaii won't be getting in with that up." answered Orznaii.

Dyenarus telepathically spoke, "Good news, the leader . . . sounds like his name is Orznaii, is speaking with a man through a flame. Spilling out everything!"

"What do you mean, talking through a flame?" asked Neeza.

She continued, "That's not important. That bluish light in front of the door is a shield. It is keeping the Garchai out of this room. That's the rhythmic pounding you hear on the other side. And the Relic is just ahead, but there is no other known way to get there. We are running out of time."

Haldirin said, "Come back, Dyenarus. We'll discuss how to get there even if we have to fight our way through."

"Hold on. They are speaking about other things. I want to hear them out."

She could hear their displeasure, urging her to go back, but she zoned them out. She felt it was important to learn more about this man if she could. He was the driving force behind why the Ettui were there in the first place. All she had was one name.

The man said, "Once you have recovered it, take it to the eastern coast of Dyyros. Either myself or General Alcatar will recover it from you."

As the man shifted, she could see what looked to be a long, black blade sheathed at his side. Even though he looked handsome, he was probably very dangerous. Come on! Say your name!

Orznaii said, "It shall be done. When does the main operation happen?"

"Soon enough. The Ettui are ready on the northern front, I assume?"

"They are, master swordsman. They are just awaiting orders from Lord Ulcinar to proceed. They shall have no problems. The alliances for the enemy are fragile and will fall quickly."

The swordsman in the fire could hear it in the tone of his voice, "I know your thirst for revenge against the elves is strong, but Lord Ulcinar needs you to curb your thirst until he has completed his objectives," answered the man.

Orznaii seemed upset, but also willing to do what he had been told. *Okay, so this guy is actually working for someone else, someone powerful who lives on Dyyros.* She began to think. That had to be one of the human lands, but not on the mainland. She wished she knew more about the human kingdoms. Mage schools refused to recognize the existence of the Worlds of Man as they were called, and only seemed to focus on the elves and everything to the west. Humans are only mentioned because of their treachery at the end of The Great War so many years ago.

Haldirin in her mind yelled, "Dyenarus, you need to leave now! The Ettui are doing something."

Orznaii answered, "I understand. Revenge will be at hand."

The man replied, "Very good. Just be sure to get the Relic. Very soon, you as well as the rest of Gyyerlith will get to see the world bleed."

Very soon! What were they planning? She wanted to find out more, but the flame was beginning to die down. The image of the man was no longer there.

Dyenarus finally said, "Okay, heading back. And do I have some information to tell you guys."

She turned around to cast her invisibility spell, but as she did, she was greeted with three swords pointed at her. The Ettui who found her gave a sickening smile as they growled at her.

All she could muster was, "Uh oh."

13

"Damn it!"

The mages watched as the Ettui dragged Dyenarus toward the center of their camp where a large fire was set. The pounding of the door could be heard louder as the Ettui made their celebratory chant to signify an important capture. The Garchai wanted in too, but for other reasons.

Two Ettui held her arms as they awaited Orznaii's arrival. Condarin ran over to Haldirin and Neeza, panic written all over her face.

"She's in trouble! We have to help her!"

Haldirin nodded, "We can't stop them all, but we have to at least try and divert their attention so we can get enough off her."

Neeza was trying to think of a way, but the harder he tried, the more he thought about forgetting her. Why would that idea ever enter his mind? He made a promise to everyone that he would bring them home alive. *Promises . . . promises were made to be broken.* Neeza covered his ears, trying to silence the other voice in his mind.

Haldirin asked, "Are you okay?"

Neeza quickly said, "Yes, I'm just trying to think of a way to save her."

Haldirin could see his leader and friend had changed somehow. While he was staring forward, from time to time, he almost believed he caught a sinister look on his face. *Was the power of the Relic doing this?*

Vindar said, "I'm going to cast my most powerful Light spell. It will give you about thirty seconds of cover without any resistance. I pray one of you is fast enough to reach her and get her back."

Vindar started to work on his spell. As it was a potent one, he needed a few minutes to maintain the proper focus to enchant it just right. Condarin and Haldirin both got ready to make a dash over to her. It was going to be close, but it was the best idea they had. They wished Lindaris were here as he was the fastest of them all.

The Ettui held Dyenarus still as Orznaii finally stepped in view from the command hut. He looked her in the eyes, and she looked at him back. They never broke their stare until they were five feet apart. One of the original Ettui who discovered her ran to his side.

"Orznaii! Fuondas ouncia commndraii hutta."*(Orznaii! We found her outside the command hut.)*

He looked back at Dyenarus curiously. She wasn't normally good at reading people, but she almost thought she saw a genuine look of him being impressed with her.

The Ettui soldier asked, "Muriaii ohta?" *(Shall we kill her?)*

Orznaii responded, "Nuntaya." *(Not yet.)*

He once again stared at Dyenarus, who refused to back down her gaze even when they stood only a foot apart. She wished she had a better position to cast a spell, but without being able to center the life particles with her hands, it wouldn't work. The spells learned in Illusions were much different than most schools in form and what was required to cast them.

Orznaii finally asked, "Where is your leader?"

She refused to answer. She knew that telling him where he was would probably kill him. There was something different about this beast apart from him being able to speak the common tongue.

Orznaii asked again, "Where is your leader? Is his name Neeza?"

Again she stayed silent. Orznaii was bred and taught about the mage race and how they thought in order to be a more efficient weapon against them. From his studies, the differences between them and humans were not comparable. Normally the threat of torture was enough to make a human spill his guts out, first by giving out information and second by slicing their bellies open after they've divulged said info. Mages, he heard, were much tougher to crack, but he had ideas and theories . . . and he now had a means to test them. He would find how tough they truly were.

"It was very clever of you, listening to my conversation. Where are the rest of your peers?"

Dyenarus figured she would try and throw him off, "With any luck, they've already gotten the Relic and are heading back to the ship."

Orznaii laughed and said, "If they had, why send you to spy? I wouldn't be surprised if they were somewhere in here as well. They are, aren't they?"

Dyenarus tried to deny it, but Orznaii was much better at reading her emotions than she was at hiding them. He stepped back and began to examine the room.

"Where could they be? Are they in one of my tents? Or maybe they are hiding behind some rocks? Shall I have my soldiers find them? I promise you, they will not be as merciful as they have been with you."

Dyenarus said no words, instead she spit in Orznaii's face. It hit him straight in the eyes. The nearby Ettui growled with anger at her actions, but their leader motioned them to hold still as he wiped her saliva off him. No, he wouldn't get anything from this mage . . . directly at least.

Orznaii stated, "I was going to spare you, but for the actions you caused, you must be executed. Before you are, I want to state some truths. We will find the Relic. We will find your friends. And we will be sure that not one of them returns home. Taka ghoron! Executaii herra!" *(Take her away! Execute her!)*

As they began to drag her away, she had an idea that they were going to be giving her a very public execution. She had to stall for some time, hoping Neeza and the others would find a way to save her.

"What is this plan you were talking about? Why do you need Neeza? I'll think about it if you tell me more!"

Orznaii had the Ettui stop for the moment as he moved closer to her again. He gave a small chuckle.

"You heard that far, hmm? That is the one thing I cannot give. Know that beginning here, on Mount Hrithgorn, set the wheels in motion of a force you can't stop. Neeza will die and there will be nothing you can do about it. There is no safe place for him, not even at home."

What did he mean by all that? She never got the chance as he nodded for them to take her to the chopping block. A large Ettui soldier was already there with an axe nearly twice his size. The blade was caked with dry blood from its previous kills. As they walked her over, the soldiers binded her hands together with rope. *So much for getting yourself out of this mess.*

Condarin watched with great concern. Dyenarus had done a great job of stalling, but she knew the moment that she got captured this would be their plan. She checked back with Vindar. He appeared to be almost ready to go, but still needed a few more moments. For whatever reason, Neeza was only staring at the large doors, not even offering any suggestions. Was Dyenarus right when she said they had to watch for their leader? In her heart of hearts she didn't want to believe it, but the more she saw, she just didn't know.

Dyenarus was roughly put to her knees on the hardened surface. They stung as the sand rubbed against the fresh wounds. If she somehow survived, she was not going to be in a very good mood. She had been trying to free her hands the entire time they dragged her, but the knot was too tight.

The executioner harshly forced her head down. She wanted to laugh out loud. Yeah, like she was going to stay put while she just *let* him cut her head off. The moment he stood up to leave, she tried to get up and move, but the Ettui were too many and too quick. She barely made it to the edge of the platform. The soldiers began punching her in the stomach and face. They could have easily run her through, but they wanted a show. When she was too weak to stand on her own power, they dragged her back to the execution block.

They dropped her down in front of the block again, this time two Ettui held her down while another was holding her head by her hair so she wouldn't be getting up. At least she didn't go down without a fight. They had to earn their entertainment.

Condarin was getting ready to go as the Ettui lined up the axe. She only had seconds left to live unless they were ready. *Please, Vindar! Please hurry!*

The way they positioned Dyenarus' head, she was looking right at the executioner. Not the prettiest option for her last sight. She would have rather been looking at the northern skies by Formia where at night during certain seasons the sky became a rainbow show of light. Or watching the people walk down the street at a busy city corner. Or see an exotic island at sunrise. Not here. She closed her eyes and began to imagine sitting on the beach as the axe was raised.

Yet, the axe never came. She opened her eyes to see his arms were wrapped up in some kind of green bind. A voice she could hear in the distance yelled a familiar spell.

"*Firammii morza!*"

The fireball hit the executioner, driving it past Dyenarus. It clipped her as it did, knocking her off the block. Thank the gods! She may not have liked many things about him, but he always had a knack to be at the right place at the right time.

From a higher entrance just to the north of the door, Lindaris, Joakon, and Biverin stood as the Ettui were still trying to figure out what was going on.

Lindaris finally yelled, "Hey, you sure act brave against one woman. Let's see how you like it when the competition fires back!"

Typical Lindaris; cocky, bull-headed, but there was no one happier to see him than her. The Ettui seemed to forget all about Dyenarus, instead focusing on the three new arrivals.

Condarin yelled, "Now, Vindar!"

She began to sprint forward as Vindar chanted, "*Sevinarrai Guthorom Hujiva Lieforem!*"

A ball of light headed toward the center of the room and stopped. It suddenly began to absorb any life particles around as it grew to ten times its original size. When it got large enough, it exploded into an epicenter of light. The Ettui were blinded and most fell to shield their eyes. Condarin covered her eyes, only looking through the slits of her fingers. It wasn't the easiest way to get there, but it was the safest way to navigate with this spell active.

Haldirin was about to join her when Neeza grabbed his arm, "What are you doing? I need to help Condarin!"

Neeza answered, "We have to take out those Ettui holding the shield!"

"Are you mad? If we take them out, the Garchai will be in here!"

"Indeed they will be. But if the Ettui are too busy dealing with the Garchai . . ."

Haldirin finished his sentence, "That means they aren't going after the Relic, leaving us a clear path."

Now he was getting the picture. There was no way they would be able to battle through this Ettui force. He also knew that there was no way that the Ettui could beat the Garchai unprepared. That also meant that they had to leave the room as fast as they could. The Ettui wouldn't last long against them and once they were gone, the mages were most likely next.

Neeza yelled, "When the light dies down, we'll take out the holders! Then make a dash toward that path!"

Haldirin nodded as they both waited. Condarin meanwhile was near Dyenarus, who had shut her eyes and covered them with her arm. She wished there were less Ettui around as she nearly tripped over a dozen of them on the way. She knew she only had about fifteen seconds to go before the spell fizzled out. She stepped up the platform. Dyenarus gave a little fight as Condarin tugged her arm.

Condarin yelled, "It's me! Come on! Cover your eyes!"

She did exactly that, but getting up was a challenge. She was still feeling the effects of the Ettui beat down she received. Condarin realized there was no chance of them getting back to Neeza before the light would extinguish, so she decided to get as close to the hall where Dyenarus had told them the Relic was.

The light finally began to lessen until it was nothing more than a dull ball hanging in the sky, which also dissipated. Lindaris uncovered his eyes trying to regain his senses after that spell took them by surprise.

"Damn it, Vindar! More of a warning next time!"

The Ettui were beginning to regain their composure as well. Neeza saw it as their best chance.

"Now!"

Haldirin started to run, but saw Vindar was very weak from the spell. He slung his arm over his shoulder and began to pursue Neeza. Once close enough, he fired a fireball at the top left Ettui. It nailed its target, dropping the soldier immediately. Haldirin tried a couple fireballs, but both missed as he was having a difficult time aiming while holding Vindar. Gerran eventually came to take Vindar off him, but the element of surprise was gone. The Ettui found the source of the magic, making hitting him that much more difficult.

Lindaris observed what Haldirin was trying to do. That Ettui was being quite elusive, especially for as little ground as he had to work with. He had to help him. That door must be a way to the Relic if he was making the effort to bust through it. He looked at Biverin and Joakon, who were behind him.

Lindaris said, "Guys, make sure Dyenarus and Condarin are okay. Vindar looks in bad shape, but at least he has Gerran there."

The two mages nodded and moved down the stone steps, firing a volley of fireballs at any Ettui that got in their way. Lindaris aimed carefully as Haldirin continued to miss.

"*Firammii morza!*"

The fireball hit the bottom left Ettui as the bluish shield dropped to the ground. Lindaris began to celebrate the hit, and instantly stopped when the first wave of Garchai crashed through the door. Why in hell would they want those demented creatures here? Did they know they were behind there?

Orznaii looked forward as the Garchai, about five of them, stormed into the room. The Ettui leader showed no fear and neither did his forces.

"Chiiargjia!" *(Charge them!)*

The Ettui forces began to swarm toward the Garchai. Neeza was amazed. These were much more disciplined troops. The cursed ones were having a very difficult time grabbing a hold of them. Even when they did, they put a fierce fight to the end. They might be able to take out a quite a few of them before the battle was over.

Biverin and Joakon reached Dyenarus and Condarin, who made it all the way past the commander's tent, thanks to the distraction. They had just taken out one Ettui soldier that decided they were an easier target than the Garchai.

Biverin commented, "Hello ladies! How can we be of assistance?"

Condarin yelled, "Keep them off me! I want to see if I can cure her wounds enough so she can move on her own at least."

Joakon grabbed a couple jars, tossing them in the air. Biverin saluted her and moved to the other possible point of entry for the enemy. He grabbed his side and grimaced when he finished, but he didn't let it slow him down. She would have to check on him after this was through. Unless her memory betrayed her, she thought Neeza took care of him during the immediate injury. Something was obviously still bothering him with it. That would have to wait. She began casting spells on Dyenarus, praying they would allow her to help in the battle.

Orznaii tried maneuvering through the huts when a Garchai crashed through them, taking out two of his soldiers. He could have run away, but Orznaii stood his ground. The beast looked in the Ettui's direction, knowing he was there by his taste. As the Garchai charged, Orznaii leapt onto its back, thrusting his blade deep into its spine. He let momentum bring him down, his sword destroying the rest of the Garchai's backbone down to his pelvis. The Garchai tried to stand up, but Orznaii knew it was already dead. He didn't even bother turning around when the body of his enemy went limp.

Neeza and Haldirin were battling through the Ettui they ran into, but their main concern was to stay out of the Garchai's path. They were extremely angry, and he believed that he was a major reason for it. He just wanted to be sure he was out of there when Zondiir arrived, and he knew he would soon.

Lindaris stayed on the elevated ground trying to keep order from above, but since the Garchai arrived, he was just trying to make sure he could keep tabs on his party members and ensure they were safe. Dyenarus and the majority of the others were holding well against light opposition. Gerran led Vindar through the huts trying to reach her, mostly underneath the noses of the Garchai and Ettui. It was Neeza and Haldirin that worried him. They were right in the thick of the battle. Exchanging blows with each Ettui they crossed. A Garchai suddenly stepped in his path, but Neeza was too focused on the Ettui to notice. He had to warn him!

Lindaris yelled, "Neeza!"

Dyenarus' eyes opened wide as she heard him all the way from their position.

"No."

She ran toward the battle as Condarin yelled, "Come back here! I'm not finished!"

Dyenarus ran as fast as she could. She had to shut him up!

"Neeza!"

"Lindaris! Shut up! Don't say his name! By the gods, don't say his name!"

He finally did stop yelling, but it was too late. Orznaii heard him, too, and noticed how the old man of their group answered his call. *So, that man from the bridge is the one called Neeza. Perfect!*

Neeza was so confused why Lindaris was calling him that he never did see the Garchai as it was ready to bring its mace down.

"Look out!" yelled Haldirin.

Using a telekinetic ability, he pushed Neeza out of the way, separating the two mages. The mace just barely missed the mage leader as the ground shook violently. He landed on some Ettui bodies as he began to stand up. As he did, coming toward him was Orznaii with sword in hand and a vengeful look on his face. Neeza remembered him from the bridge room. Back then he thought it destiny that they would meet in combat before they left the mountain. Now, here they were. Neeza grabbed his staff and tightened his grip. He might be old, but he was one of the best mages when it came to close-combat fighting. Orznaii took an overhead swipe, and he blocked it with ease.

Condarin and Joakon ran over to Dyenarus, stopping her short of the killing field. She felt weak and disoriented; the drawback of interrupting a cure spell in mid-cast. It was a necessary risk. She had to try and stop Lindaris. Seeing Orznaii and Neeza locked in combat, she realized she failed.

Lindaris finally joined her as he asked, "What was the deal? Why didn't you want me to warn him?"

Dyenarus explained, "Because Neeza's survival is the most important thing right now, even more important than the Relic. All of this is part of something larger, and Neeza living can throw the whole thing into shambles! No time to explain! We have to help him!"

Joakon looked at Lindaris before saying, "Okay, Lindaris and I will go. You keep healing. We got this."

Before they left, Dyenarus stopped him, "Lindaris, wait. Come here for a second."

He walked quickly over to her, "What? You said yourself time is of . . ."

His sentence was interrupted as she kissed him hard on the lips. He was shocked at first, but accepted it not before long.

Condarin smiled, even if she knew it wasn't because she loved Lindaris. That was a kiss of thanks. A kiss of love was much sweeter and gentler, like the ones she and Vindar experience. Still, it was nice to see Dyenarus do something 'girly' for a change. She slowly let go of her embrace.

Lindaris finished his sentence, ". . . the essence. What was that for?"

Dyenarus explained, "Because you won. I don't think I'll be able to top saving your life like you have just done for mine. Just don't get the wrong ideas. This was strictly your reward for winning this little bet of ours."

"I wouldn't think of it. Stay here."

She didn't want to, but knew she was no good to anyone yet in this condition. In a few more minutes her wounds would be tended to mostly. Then she could help them fight. She only hoped Neeza could hold up that long.

Neeza was exchanging blows with the aggressive Ettui leader. He tried every tactic he could think of, but Orznaii was different. He seemed to know how a mage fought. For every attack he made, he had a counter. Every time, he was certain that he would hit him with a spell up close to faze him, he'd quickly move to the opposite side.

His thoughts of a perfect defense fell as he tripped over a dead Ettui soldier. Orznaii could smell blood as he looked to take advantage. Neeza moved away just in time as the blade crashed down on the dead Ettui below him. He swung so hard that it broke through each bone of his fallen comrade. The blade halting only when it hit the sand underneath. Neeza quickly tried to gain some distance, as Orznaii pursued him calmly and cool. Even with all the death and the Garchai, the Ettui leader was poised.

After getting a good ten feet in front of him, Neeza chanted, "*Firamma krusantra!*"

A long flame snaked its way toward the nearest enemy heat source. Orznaii quickly grabbed one of his troops behind him, using him as a shield. The spell hit the soldier with an electrifying jolt of fire as it killed the creature instantly, throwing the body with the rest of the dead.

He didn't like this at all. This Ettui was too smart. How could he have known what that spell did? That was one of the spells that was unique to the sacred-bloods and usually only people on the council knew of them.

Orznaii spoke in the common tongue, "Don't fight it. You will die here. Why try and stop the inevitable?"

"That is where you are wrong. I'm not going to die here. I have too much to live for. You have nothing!"

Orznaii retorted, "I remember a human prisoner saying before we killed him, that a man with nothing to lose is more dangerous than one that has everything. I am more dangerous than you can ever imagine!"

The Ettui charged after him, attacking aggressively. Neeza was struggling to block them all. Forget trying to cast a spell. That wasn't going to happen. After a couple near misses, Orznaii hit his staff from below so hard that it flew about fifty feet behind the leader. Had Neeza not tripped again over the Ettui bodies, he would have tasted his blade for certain. As he stood up, he knew he had only one thing he had to do. Get his staff back.

Neeza began firing a barrage of weak spells toward Orznaii, hoping that some would hit, and he would be stunned. Yet, it looked like they all missed. *How was this possible? What sort of trickery was he pulling?* He was still about forty feet from his staff, but Orznaii's resistance was not going to make it an easy forty feet.

Just then a Garchai mace nearly hit Neeza causing him to fall backwards. It was trying to attack the mage while it had four Ettui stabbing its back. It looked to be in some serious pain, and for good reason: It was dying. The Garchai fell limp right in between Orznaii and Neeza. This would be his chance. Instead of running the closer path to his staff, he ran in the other direction taking the long way. The injured ankle wasn't going to help matters, but he was going to need to push through the pain somehow.

His decision was correct as Orznaii was trying to trick attack him. At last he finally outsmarted the damn creature. He sprinted as hard as he could. The staff was only a few feet away. Orznaii suddenly leapt in front of him. *Damn! And he was so close!* He looked and found a loose piece of Ettui armor just underneath his attacker. He telekinetically hit him in the face, giving him the space to get past him and retrieve his staff.

Both looked at each other before Orznaii commented, "Your staff will not help you. Nothing can. You are mine!"

The two once again began to exchange blows.

Lindaris and Joakon tried to maneuver through the carnage. The battle between the Garchai and the Ettui was growing outwards. The Ettui were fighting valiantly, but the Garchai's sheer power would eventually win out, he believed. The bad news was that it also made it difficult to reach Neeza.

He had to give the Ettui credit; they had taken down at least twelve Garchai compared to the one hundred fifty they lost. It was the way they acted against them. They didn't seem surprised or scared about them. If he didn't know any better, he would have assumed these Ettui had trained for them.

A new wave of Garchai arrived from the door, looking for targets. Lindaris couldn't be concerned about them at the moment. A group of Ettui began running their way.

Lindaris asked, "Is there ever an end to these guys?"

Joakon answered, "I don't know and don't want to find out. Let's get Neeza and Haldirin and get out of here."

Two of the Ettui stood to fight the mages. The rest scampered off to find the next Garchai target. Good. The least they had to worry about was fine by him. Lindaris finished his mark quickly using a fire spell. Joakon used a prismatic solution that seemed to disorient his target, and he began to attack another Ettui.

Lindaris commented, "Well, that wasn't so bad. Thought that would be harder."

A more heavily armored Garchai charged in and growled in their direction from the door.

"You need to learn to keep silent. Every time you comment on something it gets worse," added Joakon.

Unlike the others, a crack in its helmet allowed them to see their enemy's eye for the first time. It had a plain white eye, but one could make out the vague outline of where the pupil would have been.

Joakon observed, "These creatures are blind! They use the helmets to hide this!"

"Blind or not, these things know how to hunt regardless. That still makes them a problem in my book."

The Garchai looked directly at them hearing their voices. It gave a roar before charging toward them.

Lindaris stepped up and yelled, "*Firammiyan trigutra!*"

A group of fireballs formed on the ground and rained on the Garchai in an arc. The extreme confidence he felt just moments before casting the spell hurtled down in flames as he saw his spell had no effect on it. That was one of the more potent spells he knew. Any spell that cast more than one of it (fire, water, lightning, etc.) always packed an extra punch, sort of like an after effect. For fire spells, he should have felt a burning sensation throughout his entire body and thus disabling him for precious minutes. On the Garchai, though, it seemed like the regular rules didn't apply.

"Damn it! What does it take to kill these things?"

Joakon stepped in front of Lindaris holding two beakers of yellowish liquid. He had an idea what could kill them, and it wasn't going to be magic that a mage would normally think of. It worked against the Garchipede, so why not the Garchai?

As the Valendritaii roared, Joakon tossed the first bottle of acid into the creature's mouth. He heard it break as well as the burning sound it made. The Garchai was panicking, not very sure why it was in such extreme pain. Joakon ran a little further forward and tossed his second beaker. That one broke at its neck as its skin instantly began to eat away. Within seconds, between the acid burning through its throat from inside and out, it fell dead as blood seeped out from its wounds.

Lindaris patted him on the shoulder and said, "That was amazing! Remind me to not make fun of what you do again."

"You mean even after the bridges you were still making fun of me?"

Lindaris commented, "What can I say? I'm hard to please."

They gradually moved through the battlefield. They were getting closer to Neeza, who was once again engaging Orznaii in combat, but still had some distance to close. They only hoped they wouldn't be too late.

He was going to need help, and fast! Haldirin was not the best at up close fighting. It wasn't exactly the way mages were bred to fight. He felt he was decent enough at it, but he needed to be better. Neeza needed him, and he couldn't reach him fast enough because he couldn't beat his Ettui opponents with great speed. He was the closest to his leader, but he felt like the furthest. He did notice Lindaris and Joakon coming, but they would never make it in time.

There was another reason they had to hurry. He felt the ensuing arrival of another Garchai, one that was bigger and angrier. It allowed its emotions to be felt with anyone strong enough to feel it. He didn't want to be anywhere near there when it arrived. Let the Ettui deal with him. Their journey was so close to being finished. By the gods, please help him!

Neeza could feel himself becoming weary. It was obvious that Orznaii was impressed with how well he fought and for how long he did, but that wasn't going to save him. It became clearly obvious to him as this fight went on: One of them wasn't leaving the mountain alive. His opponent was like no other Ettui he had ever faced, and he had fought many in his lifetime. These battles ranged to light as they were in The Torgeetra Valley encampment or heavy as they were in the Battle of the Four Forks, which ended in disaster and the reason why he believed any more allied assaults on Barbata would never happen. Orznaii was in a class above the rest.

Orznaii become more aggressive in his attacks. Neeza sensed his aging legs were beginning to tire as his arms struggled to keep his staff up for much of the blows. He had to do something to change the fortunes of the fight, or else he would have failed this mission. He had one card that he hadn't used yet, but he hadn't done it since the Four Forks battle, and he had been much younger then. He didn't have much of a choice as he saw it, regardless the potential dangers to his own health.

As soon as Neeza found the slightest of openings in the attack, he casted, *"Hastergila Bumari!"*

He was surrounded by a yellowish light which threw Orznaii on the defense. It was not going to be easy because this required the casting of many short spells in between attacks. It also required an excess use of life particles at the same time. He might not be able to walk by his own power after he was done. When he was younger and did this, it saved his life, but it also cost him seven months of recovery time. The mage body was just not equipped to use so much of the life particles all at one time like this.

The movement speed spell made his attacks more frequent as Orznaii was even having trouble keeping up.

Neeza chanted, *"Hujiyamon Guirondom Firammii!"*

Four white fireballs ejected from his hand. The two in the center went straight forward, while the other two arced to the side. All four hit Orznaii, as he grimaced.

Before that attack was even done, Neeza was already casting the next spell, *"Earotha Vindarra!"*

Two large stone spikes ejected from the ground when the tip of Neeza's staff touched it. The spikes barely missed Orznaii as his quick reflexes were the only thing that saved him.

Neeza next cast after a quick two blows, *"Littara Guivantta!"*

A lightning bolt encased Orznaii as he was in too close of quarters to evade it.

"Iczera Nuikolone!"

A small group of icy needles began piercing the Ettui leader. All but one of the attacks had hit its mark so far, and he was halfway done. When he was done, if Orznaii wasn't dead before, he'll at least be weak enough to finish off.

"Aiga Hufriiga!"

A weak tornado surrounded Orznaii as he tried his hardest to escape it, but the winds forced him in.

"Watera Dicotta!"

Six water 'bubbles' formed and rushed at Orznaii with such force Neeza was certain he heard a rib break on the Ettui leader as they hit him in the mid-section.

"Drikontra Vuumartin!"

A dark cloud formed around Orznaii's head. It followed him wherever he went, making his vision obscured. Time for Neeza to try and finish him as his haste spell was about to wear off. His staff jewel began to glow as he swung it up toward the Ettui leader's head. His blow hit Orznaii at least twenty feet in the air and another twenty feet away.

That was it. Neeza held the staff in the ground just in case he couldn't hold his body up. The adrenaline from the battle was probably delaying the effects, but for the moment felt good. And it was a good thing, too, because Orznaii survived. His breathing was heavy, and he looked like perhaps the injury to the ribs might have been the blow that did it. However, he knew he couldn't leave him alive. Even if he was injured, the Ettui could mend him, and he could come back later to haunt them. Neeza slowly walked up to Orznaii and raised the pointy tip of his staff toward the Ettui leader's neck.

In a quick motion, Orznaii grabbed his sword and drove it into Neeza's chest.

Dyenarus, Haldirin, Joakon, and Lindaris collectively screamed, "No!"

The Ettui leader stood up, his display of pain a farce. Neeza's spells may have hurt him, but this Ettui was bred to not mind whatever was hurt. He knew he was an experiment, a test to see whether the Ettui could be made to be stronger. He was the only one to survive the tests and now it was time to prove to his masters that he was the future of their race. Orznaii smiled as he pulled his sword out of Neeza, who fell to the ground hard.

The Ettui leader gloated, "I told you that you had no chance of beating me. I'm different. Now it is time to make Lord Ulcinar proud!"

Orznaii brought the sword up ready to strike at his neck as Neeza continued to stand on his knees, fresh blood pouring down his leg. It hurt so damn much. In all his years that he had seen combat, he had never been stabbed. Sadly, his first time might also be his last.

Just as Orznaii was about to swing his blade, a large fireball connected at the Ettui leader's feet, causing him to be driven back nearly fifty yards. He felt pain rush through his arm as he hit a large boulder hard. He was taught to not let pain bother him, but he knew when he might have broken a bone. Although he was confident he could kill Neeza with one arm, the Garchai were another matter. Plus, as important as the Relic was, his survival was even more paramount to the greater mission; words spoken by Lord Ulcinar himself. He grabbed his sword with his good arm and ran through a small opening, away from the battle. It was not over between him and the mages, he was quite certain of that. Soon, Gyyerlith would see that this was only the beginning.

Haldirin and Joakon reached Neeza, grabbing him before he slumped to the ground. His breathing was quick and the bleeding was still not subduing.

"We have to get to a safe place so we can try and heal him. I don't know if he stabbed an organ or not," Haldirin observed.

Mages were complicated to kill. They could survive most wounds that would instantly kill a human. Not to say those wouldn't kill one of their race, but it would have to go untreated for that to happen. The one sure fire way to kill a mage quickly was to hit one of its major organs. Heart and lungs were the most common, but damage to the liver and brain would also do the trick. The half-elves discovered through organ replacement, a mage could be saved if an organ was hit, but there were risks there, too. Neeza's wound was much too close to the heart for him to tell if it was one that a simple healing spell combination could cure or if they needed more.

As they began to head toward the others, the next wave of Garchai entered, and the first one to enter caused even the mages to hesitate.

"By the gods!"

Zondiir gave a blood chilling yell as the Garchai began to charge into the room. The remaining Ettui, unaware their leader had abandoned them, continued to fight. They had to believe that the situation seemed hopeless. The Garchai leader was now here. Despite their ability to take out the whole first wave and most of the second, Zondiir was different than the rest. Not because of the armor he wore either.

Haldirin yelled, "Get moving!"

The other mages began to run toward the place where Dyenarus directed them to go for the Relic. As they headed down the ramp, there were a few Ettui, but most had heard what was going on and withdrew. The few that remained, Dyenarus and Gerran took care of. Biverin was struggling to keep his breath as he held his side. It felt quite moist to the touch. As he moved his hand, he saw fresh blood on it. *Damn, this was not good. This was not good at all.*

"Biverin! Move!"

Lindaris and the others began to come down the ramp carrying Neeza. *Believe me*, he thought. *I want to.* The pain on his side was getting greater and greater. It felt like he was on fire. Lindaris grabbed his arm and dragged him down the rest of the ramp when the first couple Garchai tried to pursue. The size of the ramp would delay them slightly, but not for long. They needed to find a safe place and fast.

As they moved through another large room, only slightly smaller, Condarin and Dyenarus found a niche that was compact enough that the Garchai wouldn't be able to fit in, but they were still at risk. The room wasn't nearly as deep enough as they liked. One sword stab could take them out. But time wouldn't wait. They had to see how serious Neeza's injury was and if they could heal him.

Condarin was trying to figure out every possible combination of spells that would be needed to cure Neeza. Minor injuries usually only needed one; major ones like the one Neeza sustained needed a little more extra, which required planning. One spell cast in the wrong order could be disastrous. Closing one layer of the wound before it was healed properly would do nothing to save the recipient. White Magic was not as easy as everyone made it out to be.

Haldirin laid Neeza out on his back as he began to examine the wound. He was praying that it didn't pierce his heart in anyway. They had nothing to transplant it with, which meant certain death. Even after looking at the location of the wound, he still couldn't determine without a lengthy evaluation, which they had no time for.

Haldirin said, "I'm pretty sure it missed his heart, but the way his blade was crafted it might have severed a main blood line. If that's the case, normal healing magic won't help him."

Condarin stepped up with a face full of focus and conviction, "Then we do it unconventionally. I think I can heal him, but I need all of you to help me. I don't have the strength or power to do it alone."

Haldirin finally understood what she meant to do. It was a very risky spell and one that she was correct in evaluating that she alone was not ready to perform. It was a spell that even the head of the White Magic School wasn't proud to know of. It allowed the White Mage to borrow energy from other mages to make an extremely potent heal spell that was believed to heal almost all physical injuries. Doing it temporarily would disable their ability to cast magic because of the sheer power drained. And by including themselves in the spell with the Garchai around, she could jeopardize all of them as they would lose their magical advantage.

Haldirin ordered, "I can't let you do that! If you're wrong, we could all die!"

Lindaris asked, "What is she planning to do?"

"A spell called the Angel's Gavel. It *might* save him, but will disable our use of magic for a few hours," Haldirin explained.

Lindaris commented, "Whoa! Okay, we can't do that with the Garchai out there. No way!"

Condarin yelled with a conviction none of the students had seen before, "I will not just sit here and let him die! You said yourself you're not sure it hit his heart. Please! I need you!"

The room was silent as Neeza began to breathe heavier. In the distance, the sound of stone crashing down on the ground and the rumble of feet could be heard. Damn, the Garchai were coming and they hadn't even begun to try and save Neeza.

Biverin finally said, "I'll keep the Garchai at bay. You and the rest work on him."

Haldirin walked up to the farmer mage and said, "You can't. Not in your condition. Don't think I don't know about it."

"You stop worrying about my condition. I won't let you down. The Garchai will not get past me."

Condarin wanted to stop him, but she knew someone had to do what he was doing otherwise the Garchai would be upon them before they finished.

Lindaris walked to him and said, "I know we have had our rough edges on this adventure, but one thing I can never question is your courage. Let those pieces of Midenbeast fodder know who they are messing with."

Biverin smiled and said, "You know I will."

Everyone sat down next to Condarin. Before Dyenarus did, she walked over to Biverin and placed her hand on his shoulder.

She finally said, "This is not goodbye. Once we save Neeza, I will come back for you. You got that?"

Biverin smiled, and said, "Okay. Go on ahead. Neeza needs you all."

She nodded and sat down next to the others. Biverin walked out of the hallway and grabbed his bag of seeds. Using a wind spell, he blew the seeds out everywhere in the room, even around the doorway where the rest of his party sat. The Garchai were getting closer.

"Okay, Biverin, my boy. You can do this. Those Garchai bastards are going to rue the day they messed with us."

Images of his wife and children popped in his head . . . well, child and soon-to-be child. Oh, how much he wanted to see them again. He knew, though, that even if he survived the mountain, he wouldn't be coming home alive. All he could think about standing alone and about to encounter their enemy was to make his son and daughter proud. That was the real reason he wouldn't let them get to Neeza and his friends.

In the room, Condarin began the spell. Neeza's breathing was getting shallower. Time was running out. Reaching what mages called the *craterta*, or the first part of the incantation, her body began to glow a bright white light. The others were slowly engulfed by it as well. Condarin placed her hands on the wound waiting for it to work.

The first Garchai turned the corner as Biverin chanted a silent spell. He made a few of the seeds grow into vines and they grabbed the Garchai's arms and legs. He did the same for the second one that came. Every time he did it he could feel the pain in his side as the blood continued to drip. He hoped they would hurry. He was going to give it everything he had to stop them, but he only had so long.

A purplish light began to emit from her hands as the group began to feel disoriented. Haldirin knew this was the part of the spell where Condarin was absorbing their powers. It felt like a pulsing headache, but thankfully didn't last very long. The spell was almost done. And when it was, they had to hope that it would be enough to save him.

Biverin was having his hands full with the Garchai. The ones entering the room saw what was happening to their kin and were either freeing them or doing their best to avoid his vines. He took a quick look back. They were almost finished. Good. When they were, he knew what to do. He had about seven Garchai captured in his vines, five of which he felt confident would stay there for a while. That was when Zondiir entered. At that moment, Biverin knew which of those damned creatures he had to focus on. That was the one he had to stop.

He unleashed as many vines as he could at Zondiir. All these wrapped around the arms and legs tightly. After struggling initially, he ripped the vines easily off the walls and floor that bound him. *Yep, this guy was going to be a challenge.* He shot more vines toward Zondiir, but once again, after initially struggling, he broke through with no trouble. He knew what was happening. He was breaking free because he wasn't holding it. The more he held it, the more his side would bleed.

He took a quick glance at his friends. Condarin was nearing completion of the spell. He promised he wouldn't let them down, let his family down. He had never broken a promise before and he didn't intend to start. Using every seed he could find in front of him he made the vines wrap around Zondiir's arms, legs, neck and torso. He could feel every struggle as he held the vines on him. This wasn't going to be able to last forever. *Go Condarin. I have faith in you.*

Condarin said the last lines of the incantation as the white light in her hands illuminated brightly. Neeza winced in pain as the once damaging wound began to mend in front of their eyes. Never had any of them seen a wound heal so fast. Even under these circumstances, it was quite amazing. When the wound was healed, the spell negated, and the room went dark again. Now came the moment of truth.

Haldirin went over to his boss and asked, "Neeza? Neeza, how are you feeling?"

After a short silence, a voice finally exited his lips, "Like a million Magari. A little weak, but other than that, quite good. Thank you, Condarin. That was a quite a reckless risk for one so young, but I'm glad you took it."

Haldirin smiled and said, "Lay down. You lost a lot of blood and need to replenish. Take a few moments."

There were no complaints from Neeza. Dyenarus, seeing he was okay and breathing a sigh of relief, ran over to the doorway. Biverin was holding Zondiir with the vines, but was obviously struggling. She could see the fresh puddle of blood that formed at his feet. She couldn't see his face, but his arms were already going pale.

Dyenarus yelled, "Biverin! Come on! Neeza's alive! He's okay! We have to get out of here!"

Biverin gave a weak chuckle and said, "Glad to hear that. Now go. I can't let go of him otherwise he'll kill me then you guys. I am not going to let that happen."

Haldirin yelled, "Come on, Biverin! We can get out of here."

"You will, but not me. This is where my journey ends."

Haldirin noticed the puddle of blood by his feet now. It was the same side that was punctured during the fall of the Kyroselip chase. Their worst fears were coming true. When he saw him struggling to run, he assumed he had broken a rib. That was sadly not the case. The wood did pierce him in his lung. It was forcing the magically repaired wound to reopen. That was something they'd have to watch with Neeza, but he was quite sure he would be okay. Biverin was doing a brave thing. He was going to give the ultimate sacrifice.

Condarin and the others all joined them and she yelled, "Come on, Biverin! Hurry! Why are you not coming?"

He wanted to say something to her, but knew it best he be silent. Condarin was a very emotional person, and he didn't need her taking any more risks, especially now that none of them could cast magic for a short time. They needed to go and now.

Biverin instead turned to Haldirin and said, "Can you promise me something? Can you tell my wife and kids that their father says he's sorry he won't be coming home, but that my last thoughts were of them and their mother?"

Haldirin unleashed a tear as he replied, "Of course. They will know that their father died a hero."

Condarin yelled, "Biverin! Don't do this! We can still get out of here!"

Biverin replied, "Good luck all of you. Find the Relic and return home. I was very proud to see you all grow before my eyes. You will all make wonderful mages, and I was honored to call you family for the days we were together. Be strong all of you. If you will forgive me, I don't think you'll want to see what happens next."

Biverin made weeds grow in front of the doorway. Condarin was doing her best to try and break through them, but it was too late. He imbedded his will into those weeds, so it was going to take a lot of effort to break through it, even for the Garchai. And with none of them able to use magic for a short time, they couldn't even magically burn through it. Condarin, realizing there was nothing that could be done, fell to her knees crying.

On the other side, Biverin looked at Zondiir and yelled, "I won't leave here, but at least I can go with the peace of mind knowing you won't kill my friends. Do what you will to me, but you will never get them. You have failed, Your Highness!"

Biverin finally let go of the vines as Zondiir broke through them easily. He was tangled slightly because there was so many, but once free, he grabbed his scepter and lifted it high.

Biverin spread his arms opened wide and lifted his head. Closing his eyes, he fully intended on fulfilling his promise. The last thing he remembered was sitting at the dock of Myyril's capital with his wife, the son he never met, and his daughter watching the stars on a clear night, in peace.

14

The journey through the tunnels was quiet. Not a word had been said since they decided to continue moving forward. While Neeza rested, Haldirin was able to find a secret passage, which Gerran confirmed was on the correct path toward the Relic. When Neeza felt stable enough to walk, they kept going.

Everyone was silent because of the loss of Biverin. For some, he was the first person close to them to have died. No matter if it was their first or if they had seen numerous before, Biverin's death hit them all hard. It hit Neeza the hardest, however. He had promised that he would send them all home. That was unfortunately not going to happen. Had he not been disoriented, he might have been able to help him. He was currently the only one of them who could still cast magic for the next few hours at least.

All the mages learned a valuable lesson: Life should be cherished because it can end at any time. For Biverin, he decided to give up his life for the lives of his company . . . no, his second family. For Neeza, there could be no better definition of a hero in his book than one who dies to protect the ones he cares about. When they returned to Myyril, he would be certain that Biverin's family were fairly compensated for their tragic loss.

As hard as his death was, they still had a mission to finish. Even one of Biverin's last requests was to find the Relic. And based off its power, it felt like one should be able to touch it. The hallways were small enough that the Garchai couldn't pursue, so they didn't have to worry about them.

Neeza began to sweat the closer they got. He didn't know why. He didn't feel any ill effects from the spell. And the temperature of the cave was actually quite cool. Why was he feeling this? Maybe it was that intuition the Relic had given him before; talking to him, leading him, directing him on what needed to happen. *Yeah, that was it.* It must be making him hotter because they were so close. One thing he knew was that he had to keep this to himself. They would never understand.

Gerran finally broke the silence, "We are very close. The great power it radiates is beaming through here. I can't believe how strong it is."

Believe it, my friend. You can't even begin to comprehend its power. He could. It entrusted him to be the bearer. The elves proved to be unreliable enough to be the deliverer of its might. But he was different. It trusted him and him alone. If the others tried to stop him, they would find it to be a mistake.

Neeza had to shake his head. Why was he beginning to think these things? It was getting worse, too. He first felt it vaguely on the boat as they neared the Simorgon Chain and now that they were so close, he was feeling it more frequently. Was the Relic really doing this to him?

Dyenarus suddenly said, "Someone's coming."

"I feel it, too," added Gerran.

The mages grabbed their staves, ready to pounce on whoever was trying to make their way toward them. They couldn't cast magic for the time being, but at least they didn't lose their telekinetic senses. Neeza almost joked that his party was reduced to his daughter's level, and she would have been the most powerful of them all then. The footsteps were getting closer and closer.

Lindaris commented, "Man, you don't realize how much you rely on magic until you lose it."

For students of the Black Magic School, that was a very true statement. Their 'fire first, ask later' policy meant that he was probably the one of their group missing it the most, but he was sure they were all feeling the same.

Dyenarus commented, "Don't be a baby. Women lose their magic power temporarily every time they give birth. Why do you think it's so easy for the Kittara to take the children of parents having a half-mage baby? Mothers would do anything to protect their children."

Haldirin was surprised she used that as an example, given her situation. Thankfully no one tried to inquire further. The stranger slowly making his way toward them likely helped halt any further questions. Maybe she was much smarter than he realized.

The figure's shadow could be seen on the wall. It seemed to be dragging a foot based on its movements. Haldirin and the two girls had seen way too much of that before reuniting with Neeza. They, thankfully, never met up with the creature that made those footprints. It looked like they were now, but this time they didn't have the magic to defend themselves with.

Neeza said, "Everyone stay behind me. I'll take care of whatever is down that hall."

The figure was just about to emerge as Neeza jumped out. As soon as he did, he negated his spell. By the gods, he was alive!

"Mimerck!"

The mage captain responded, "Can't we ever meet without you guys pointing some spell at me?"

The mages were relieved to see the seafarer, if not only for the reason that he was their ticket home. No one knew how to sail a ship, and the only safe refuge, if one could call it that, was way to the south and east in the elf territories.

Neeza asked, "Glad to see you are all right. What happened when you separated from us?"

Mimerck stared blankly at Neeza, "What happened when our paths diverted?"

His mind began to think back as he pondered about how to explain it . . .

The acid flew through the air as the Spitters were hell bent on destroying their target. Mimerck raised his stone shield. He was able to duck under or block most of them, but one landed on his wrist and a drop landed on his cheek from the splash of it hitting his shield. He had never felt pain like he did with that acid. He could smell his own skin burning. He splashed his cheek with a water spell, which soothed the pain a little, but not entirely.

Hitting these things with a spell wouldn't help either. Killing one would set up a domino effect, causing each to explode. Unlike the first time, there were even less places for him to hide in this room. Entering the gold room wasn't a good idea either with the Twin Dragons still in there, freshly awoken from a long slumber. The Spitters prepared to fire another volley when they suddenly froze and looked to their right. He looked there too, but saw nothing. The Spitters quickly scattered, running over each other in an attempt to make a quick getaway. Were they . . . afraid? Of what? There was nothing there.

"You have come for great riches."

Mimerck asked, "Who is there?"

Was he just imagining it? Who else here had proven enough to speak the common tongue other than the dragons? He knew that would have been enough to scare the Spitters, but they said they never left their room because it was dangerous.

"You won't find them in there."

"Then where? Where are these great riches?" asked Mimerck as his question echoed in the room.

He almost felt silly. He had to have been just talking to himself. Maybe the Spitters were just his imagination as well. He touched his cheek, and it stung horribly. Okay, they were real. This voice, though, had to be his imagination.

"The Relic is the greatest treasure. The wealth you will gain from it would know no bounds. I will show you the way."

Mimerck looked as excited as back when he was in school, "Yes, show me the way! The Relic is the real prize!"

Mimerck didn't feel like normal. Something suddenly changed. Why did he out of the blue want the Relic? No, not just want it . . . desire it. He wanted gold more. Who would want to buy something that is priceless?

A door made of stone opened up to his left as he walked toward it.

"Follow this path. When you return to your ship, bring it to the city of Canta. Someone willing to pay handsomely will be there."

Good idea! He had never heard of Canta, but oddly he knew exactly where it was. No one was going to take away his riches from him. No one! He began to walk with a limp because he knelt down in the acid accidentally. The pain didn't bother him. He was about to go find that which has never been found.

He scurried as fast as he could down the hall.

. . . No, he couldn't tell them that. There had to be a better way to say it. That's it! He got it!

Mimerck answered, "I . . . escaped, escaped barely with my life."

The delay it took him to answer was quite odd, but at what point since meeting him did he think the mage captain to be normal?

Neeza answered, "We're glad we ran into you. The Relic is really close."

"I know it is. I just came from it."

Everyone looked at Mimerck strangely or shocked. Neeza was the only excited one.

Neeza asked, "Where is it? Is it far?"

Mimerck said, "Not at all. Follow me. I would have grabbed it, but it is far too heavy for one man to carry. Come quickly! We should be out of here before nightfall."

The mages began to follow with exception to Vindar, Condarin, and Dyenarus, who walked toward the back. The White Mage was beginning to read her quite well now since they had been on the mountain.

"You seem uncomfortable."

Dyenarus explained, "It's a feeling. Something doesn't feel right. Isn't Mimerck acting strange to you?"

Vindar commented, "Well, I always thought him crazy, but you're right. There is something odd with the way he's speaking, moving around. I didn't know he wanted the Relic as much as Neeza."

That was another thing worrying her too. What did he mean by when he said that he would have grabbed it if not for its weight being more than he could handle? Was he going to grab it and leave? She overheard him say that he was here for gold, but to be as bold as to find it and then betray them would have been foolish.

Now that she looked around, everyone was seemingly acting odd the closer they got. Lindaris became incredibly silent, something not in his character. Joakon began whispering and laughing every few minutes. Gerran seemed to be losing his senses, taking him twice as long to find the Relic's path despite admitting its power was growing. Even Haldirin began to show signs of overprotectiveness for Neeza. The only ones not affect were her, Vindar, and Condarin. The one thing they shared in common: they were wearing or standing near the amulet.

Dyenarus suggested, "I want you two to stay close to me. Don't wander too far ahead. I think we've all underestimated the power this Relic has."

Condarin asked, "But what good can we do? We still can't cast magic for a while longer."

She didn't know. She just didn't know. But she would find a way. She didn't come all this way to die. When they reached the it, the answers would hopefully come to her. If not, then may the gods have mercy on their souls.

They finally reached a long corridor leading to a partially opened door. Everything about the hallway was frightening. It was completely dark, meaning Neeza and Mimerck were the only ones who could light the way. The relic room appeared to be lit somehow from where they were.

Mimerck urged on, "Come! It's just ahead. It's magnificent!"

Dyenarus highly doubted it, but the other mages seemed excited, like they were seeing a city made of gold. Condarin and Vindar were more uneasy, not experiencing the strange euphoria, being as close as they were to the amulet.

The door was foreboding enough. A skull surrounded by vines was engraved on the ancient doorway. The elves liked to post what was inside a room on their doors or archways so as to warn the person entering what they might face. Is this what they really were saying with this door? If so, she wasn't too sure she wanted to enter.

At last they were in the room that had housed Valendri's Relic. The light was coming from a large number of air pockets too high to get to and too small to climb out of. At least that meant that they were near the edge of the mountain. By the time Dyenarus and her small group of trusted allies entered the room, the others were staring ahead in marvel.

Mimerck said, "There it is! The Relic, the mechanism of Power!"

Condarin examined it closer, unbelieving to what she was seeing, "So, the Relic is . . . is . . ."

Vindar finished her sentence, "It's a coffin."

So that was what the line in the song referred to. The Relic was actually a coffin, Valendri's Coffin. It was that artifact that brought about the destruction of the defenders and settlers of the once proud elvish stronghold. It wasn't a disease of the body, but a disease of the mind. She wasn't certain, but she had a feeling it had something to do with the appearance of the Garchai as well.

Neeza walked slowly toward it. The Coffin was very intimidating. The top was sunken in and was covered in dried red liquid. The design on the side was beautiful. It was a combination of language, drawings of ancient battles, and vines etched into the stone. It was partially made of stone, but mostly it was made from an unfamiliar black metal. Strangest thing he had seen.

As he ran his fingers over the metal, Neeza said, "At last. The Relic. I have the tool to save you."

Mimerck moved carefully over toward Neeza, causing Haldirin to react, "You see? We must carry it out. Needs four people to lift. Telekinetics won't work. Tried, I did."

"We should open it."

Everyone looked in Lindaris' direction. His face was dark, and he had an angry smirk on his face. Nothing was right about this. Opening it was just as bad an idea as was taking it with them.

Lindaris continued, "We discovered it. We should be the first to gaze on its glory."

Joakon and Gerran joined in agreement. Condarin and Vindar watched in disbelief and horror. The people who showed excellent judgment the whole trip were now suddenly going on whims and assumptions. Their careful natures were being overtaken by desire.

Mimerck stopped in front of them and said, "No! We must leave with it! When we return we can open it. Then we can see its glories!"

The two sides began arguing against opening it now or later. The jewel in the amulet began to shine bright. That was it! The amulet was the answer. If she could get close enough to the Coffin and place it on top, it should block the Coffin's power. Getting to it was going to be the challenge. There were three who wanted to open the Coffin here at all costs and three who wanted to take it with, two of which could still cast magic at this point. It was going to have to take some guile.

Neeza finally decided, "I'm the leader here! And young Lindaris has a mighty fine idea. Let us see what the Relic holds! Better here where we can claim as being the only ones to lay eyes on it!"

Eyes . . . maybe that was the reason the Garchai and everything else suffered from ailments that led to blindness. The Relic was probably opened and everyone who looked inside it became blind; First with power, then with their sight. She had to do something. That Coffin couldn't be opened for any reason.

Dyenarus looked at Vindar and Condarin and said, "Follow me. I need to get to the Relic, but I think they might stop me. Help me get there."

They nodded as she walked forward. Neeza was about to open it before Dyenarus interrupted him.

"Hold it, my great Master Neeza. We can't open it yet. The ritual must first be performed."

Joakon asked, "Ritual? What ritual?"

Dyenarus explained, "The ritual of the amulet. The Coffin is surrounded by a powerful shield, one I can sense because of my knowledge in the area of Illusions, but is blind to you all. Why do you think it is so heavy to lift? Let me put the amulet on top of it, and then we can begin the ritual. We can open it once the seal is broken."

She sure hoped that worked. It was a long shot, but it was the only way she could think of being able to get it on the coffin without fighting. It was a better option than just trying to run it there.

Neeza began to evaluate her request, examining the amulet and then her eyes. She had to keep that conviction in them if she was going to pull off this farce. She also hoped that Neeza didn't recognize it. He was the one who gave it to her after all, and if he remembered what it did, the running option would look pretty darn good.

Surprisingly, Neeza was allowing her through. Just as she was about to walk past him, a hand grabbed her arm. She saw it was Neeza's, and it was quite a firm one as well. He tossed her back with a strength she didn't expect from 800 year-old arms.

Neeza said, "Don't play me stupid! I know there is no seal on it. It wants us to open it."

Lindaris and Mimerck yelled, "Liar! Betrayer!"

Neeza began slowly walking her back toward the end of the room. She was going the wrong way. She had to find an opening and fast otherwise they would subdue her and stop any chance of leaving.

Dyenarus, knowing the ploy was over, no longer tried to hide it, "Neeza, I need to put this on it. We can still take the Relic, but let me just put this amulet on it. It will do no harm."

Lindaris yelled, "Liar!"

Neeza replied, "By how you state it, I highly doubt that. Joakon, retrieve this amulet and smash it against a stone."

Joakon walked over to Dyenarus, but never quite made it. Vindar tackled him and punched him in the face, dazing him. Gerran began running toward Vindar seeing his mate in trouble.

"Dyenarus! Go, now!"

Gerran rammed into Vindar, knocking him off Joakon. The Divination mage recovered faster and began hitting their navigator mage with his fist and whenever he could, his staff. Gerran began attacking relentlessly, something he didn't expect from him. Dyenarus tried to run, but Neeza was blocking her at every turn.

"Where do you think you're going? Time to put an end to this now!"

Neeza brought his hands back to use a spell, but it was negated when he felt something hit his shoulder. Condarin was in back throwing rocks at him. It was not the most intimidating thing she could do, but it peeled his attention off Dyenarus as she continued forward.

Neeza instantly began firing spells in her direction, causing her to run for cover. She finally hid behind a decent-sized rock and covered her face. Rock and dust flew everywhere from the spells.

Condarin yelled as tears ran down her cheek, "Please, Neeza! Stop this! This isn't you!"

Dyenarus was about halfway when she noticed Lindaris coming hard from the side. He was the most athletic between the two, but she was the smarter of them. She reached down and grabbed some sand on the ground and as he neared, she blew the powder into his face. He negated his tackle and fell to the ground trying to wipe the dust from his eyes. The Coffin was only ten feet away when she was finally brought down from behind by Mimerck, who was holding on tightly to her legs.

She looked back to see how the others were fairing. Vindar was now getting double teamed by Gerran and Joakon, who recovered from Vindar's opening assault. Haldirin joined in as well. As she looked back at Neeza, he was chanting to cast a spell at Condarin. No, not just chanting . . . he was pleading. He was pleading to their gods . . . oh no! He was trying to cast one of the forbidden spells! If he got that off, they were all dead. She had to get to the Relic and get to it now.

She was able to free one of her legs as she hobbled to reach it. She was no more than two feet from the Coffin, but Mimerck's resistance was causing her to lose ground fast. Taking the amulet, she drove one of the edges into his hand, puncturing it deeply. He let go of her leg finally as blood began to flow. Dyenarus dove, slamming the amulet on the Relic.

The jewel lit brightly like the sun for a few seconds as everything suddenly went quiet. Dyenarus looked back to see all the mages possessed before grabbing their heads.

Neeza asked, "What . . . happened?"

Gerran answered, "I don't know but my head feels like it had rocks thrown at it."

Thank the gods! It worked! Dyenarus relaxed her body as everyone began to stand up. Haldirin helped her up as they all surrounded her.

Dyenarus explained, "You were all consumed by the Relic's power. You were going to open it, so I stopped you by placing the amulet on it."

Neeza and the others could see the amulet giving off a soft yellowish glow. It was strange that he couldn't remember anything after their eyes first gazed on the Relic. *Was it purely evil? Whatever the case, they were going to need to be very careful with it.*

Mimerck stood up finally and yelled, "What in the bloody version of hell happened to my hand?"

Dyenarus commented, "You hit a sharp stone. You should really be more careful."

She walked over to Vindar and Condarin, who patted her shoulder. Condarin had some scrapes from the rocks that hit her while Vindar had some bruises on his face that she was certain were going to leave their mark. Both had smiles on their faces despite that.

"We thank you for saving us, Dyenarus. Now, let's get the Relic to the ship and get out of here."

She had to stop. Did her ears deceive her? Was Neeza still intending on taking the relic even after what just transpired?

Dyenarus pleaded, "What are you doing? How is this still an option after what just happened? This Relic is evil! You must see this! Let it go, Neeza. Whatever you need it for is not worth the pain it causes!"

Condarin and Vindar both voiced their concerns as well. Neeza put his head down. *You were all right.* He could see now that this was truly a dangerous item that they were next to. It was probably even a mistake coming in the first place. They lost one man on the expedition and nearly more just a few moments ago. But his thoughts referred back to Mierena. He was here because this might be the last thing in the known world that could save her . . . and their family in his lifetime. On Dyyros years ago, he was so close, but never got the chance. Here, he was actually touching the item of her salvation. As much as this was a threat, he couldn't abandon it.

Neeza answered solemnly, "I sense you might be right. I haven't come all this way to fail. I have to try and see if what I think this can do works. When we are done, I promise you, we will willingly hand it over to the elves so that it can be destroyed. I know you might not understand, but I must try."

As Neeza tried to pass, Dyenarus blocked his progress. The look she gave, he had never seen from her before. It was one of anger and concern.

"Neeza, please! Leave it. I know Biverin said to get the Relic, but he didn't know what I know now. Don't let your guilt for his death make you do something we all might regret."

Condarin and Vindar supported her as her legs looked weak. Neeza didn't say a word. He patted her on the shoulder as he continued toward the Relic. The others followed hesitantly, nearly driving Dyenarus to tears.

Dyenarus didn't like their leader's suggestion. It was a mistake to bring the object back home. What else could she do, though? He was aware of the risk of what he was doing. Her words, as true as they were, failed to sway his opinion. This was the first time that she allowed her curiosity as to why the Relic was this important to him dominate her mind.

Neeza ordered, "Secure the amulet to the Coffin. I'll need one man to each handle. Let's go home."

The mages reached the southern island after spending most of the afternoon crossing atoll after atoll. Mimerck anchored in a very ideal location. The atolls led right to the island, where he was ten miles away. Good thing too. Valendri's Relic was bulky in all the right spots making it difficult to maneuver. Surprisingly, the Coffin was light in weight. Quite amazing for something made entirely of what appeared to be a heavy metal.

Haldirin, Lindaris, Joakon and Vindar were charged with holding the Relic. Condarin was excused because she was the first to regain her magic back after the spell. Gerran and Mimerck were leading them toward the ship. Neeza stayed back with Dyenarus as he wanted to speak with her alone while they traveled.

Neeza said, "Dyenarus. I know that this may not be the proper time, but Haldirin had told me how brave you were when we all separated. Plus, if not for you, we would probably still be in the relic room doing . . . well, who knows what we would have been doing. Your disapproval of us taking the Relic was out of place, but it's one I understand why you feel as such. When we return home, I am giving you the full endorsement."

She was honored. It was what she had hoped for on this trip. With the honor bestowed to her, she was one step closer to being able to reveal her half-mage origins. Although she was honored, she was surprised others didn't receive it.

"This is a blessing, and I am grateful to receive it, but I was certain others like Condarin would get it. She did save your life after all."

Neeza said, "This is true. Her judgment in that situation was immaculate. However, this entire journey you have shown the leadership skill and the magical know-how to prove to me that you are deserving of this award. Plus, your mates really like you and trust you. Those are two qualities that will earn you respect and as you will find, will be key as you go on with your life."

She replied, "Then I would be honored to accept this upon our return. But let's not get ahead of ourselves. We still have to return before it becomes relevant."

That was why he chose her. She wouldn't feel safe until they were back on the shore of Myyril. She shouldn't feel safe, either. They went unopposed as they exited Mount Hrithgorn, but they weren't on their boat yet. And the Relic did slow them down. Mimerck assured him that the damage to the boat was not serious enough that it would stop them from departing. Repairs had to be made, but most could be done enroute.

He took another glance at Mount Hrithgorn, probably the last time he would ever look upon it. He remembered the awe they felt when they first saw it. The mystery that it held, and the excitement and fear they experienced upon arriving seemed like a distant memory. As much as he was happy to go home, he was sad to go as well. So much had happened here, so many good and bad memories. It was something he was certain neither he nor the students would ever forget.

It was then that he saw something climbing down the side of the mountain. To be able to see it from that far, that clearly meant that they were big. There was only one thing that big that he was aware of. *This couldn't have ended easy, could it?*

Neeza asked, "How far are we from the ship?"

Mimerck said, "I'd say about seven miles. Why?"

The roars in the distance were all they needed to hear to understand what he meant.

Neeza answered anyway, "Because we're going to have company very soon. Everyone move! Someone be sure that the amulet stays secure."

They began to run as fast as they could. It was not going to be easy to run seven miles carrying the Relic. They were going to need to change positions every couple miles to keep people fresh. They had to reach the ship. There was no way they would be able to fight the Garchai, not with only three of them being able to cast magic.

They reached a more heavily wooded section about three miles in. The uneven ground was making it difficult to keep a steady pace, slowing them down even more. The roars were getting closer. By the gods, he forgot how fast these things were out in the open.

About four miles from where they started running, they came to a small clearing. Before they could re-enter the woods, one Garchai jumped in their way. They were soon joined by about five others. They were surrounded. The mages huddled in the center, surrounding the Relic. Neeza, Mimerck, and Condarin each readied a spell, but they didn't think it was going to do them any good. Two of the Garchai charged forward.

Suddenly, every other sound was muffled by many things whizzing against the wind. Three of the Garchai dropped dead in mere seconds. A fourth one suffered many wounds before escaping. The fifth, unsure as to what was happening, retreated.

The mages were not sure what was going on either. Neeza moved away from the pack to examine one of the Garchai. When he reached him, he pulled out the arrow and stared in disbelief. Unbelievable! He didn't need to study it to know where these came from. The design and make of the arrow made it easy enough.

Neeza said, "Elves."

He barely finished saying it before another set of whizzing was heard, followed by a collective cry of pain from the mages.

Lindaris grabbed whatever hit him in the back of the neck and yelled, "What in everything was that?"

Dyenarus pulled it out of her neck too. Whatever it was, it was short, black, and very elaborately made. Also, whatever the liquid was at the end of it, it was making her and the rest incredibly woozy. What was going on? Joakon and Condarin were the first to go down, followed by Haldirin, Mimerck, and Gerran. Lindaris and she fought as hard as they could, but they too succumbed to the numbing strength of that dart.

Neeza had seen them before. *This couldn't be happening!* They were so damn close! He couldn't be denied a second time. Damn the elves! Damn them to the deepest hell he could think of! He blacked out shortly moments later.

15

Neeza woke up suddenly as a sharp breeze hit his face. He had expected to be lying on the ground somewhere or not waking up at all. Yet, here he was in a very comfortable bed with silken sheets. He was no longer donning his robes, but an equally comfortable silk tunic and pants. The room was large and exquisite, with beautiful tiling and paintings on the wall. The windows were large open slots in the wall, offering a very beautiful sight of the ocean. He knew instantly by the design that they were in an elvish building, but where in the devil was he? And where were the rest of the mages?

The sun was rising, so they were out at least for twenty or so hours. Maybe it was longer. The place they were at was very high just by going off the distance he was from the sea.

The door opened and a nicely dressed elf walked in. He was wearing fine leather boots and a well-made tunic and pants. Like most elves, he was wearing his quiver of arrows on his back, but a bow was nowhere in sight. That didn't mean he was defenseless. I just meant that death wouldn't be coming from a bow. Most usually carried a strong knife or short sword and were very proficient in both.

The courier said, "The esteemed Vindimar will see you in a few minutes. Make any preparations you'd like beforehand. Knock thrice when you are ready to go."

The elf didn't wait for a response, only closing the door and locking it. Neeza walked over to a chair and table. Resting on it was a plate of fruits and bread as well as a goblet filled with some reddish drink. It was most likely a wine of some kind as they did like the finer things in life. Beer or ale was below their palate. On the chair, he saw his robe. It was cleaned and pressed to almost new. The tears and wears that he had donned on them were repaired. His staff, which received quite a bit of damage from his fight with Orznaii, had been patched up and made stronger. One wouldn't be able to tell he was even in a fight had he not remembered it.

As much as he wanted to find out what was going on, his growling stomach was a much stronger force. He sat down and began eating the fruit and bread, feeling almost instantly relieved. It was said that elvish food had an incredible effect on most of the other races so long as it wasn't a salad. To get fruit or bread was considered an honor to receive. That meant they must know who he was.

After he ravaged the food, he looked at the robe that rested peacefully on the chair backing. As comfortable as these clothes were (and as a mage who was supposed to desire nothing but his robe, this was even a hard choice), he decided that if he was going to be meeting an Elvish dignitary, he was going to do it in the clothes of his people. He dressed in his robe and grabbed his staff as he walked toward the door, knocking three times.

"Ah, Honorable Neeza! It is a great honor to see you. Welcome to Hiierland! My name is Vindimar, the one in charge of this facility."

Neeza progressed forward closer to his elvish host. The space was fashioned in the same way a throne room was normally dressed. A long red carpet that led from the doors to the throne was over marble tile. Behind the throne were more open slots for windows that reached from the floor almost to the top of the fifty foot ceiling. A tapestry could be dropped for when it rained, no doubt.

He had heard many stories about Hiierland. It was one of only three of the active island fortifications that remained when the elves were still residing in Mount Hrithgorn, deserting most of them after the Ettui Island Wars. The palace fortress was situated on the tip of a long piece of rock that elevated on one side. It was the perfect defense because there was only one way up and any army charging had to run entirely uphill just to reach it. It had a dock large enough to hold two ships at most. He had heard stories that even this place was abandoned and lost to time like Mount Hrithgorn.

Neeza, trying to be polite but stern, answered, "It is my honor to be here. Where is here, exactly? And where are the rest of my mage friends? You know who I am! Release us at once!"

Vindimar laughed and said, "You certainly do get to the point. This place is located in between The Simorgan Chain and Fort Za, much closer to the Dragonian continent west of here."

He stood up showing his true size. He was nearly seven and a half feet with pale skin and fine hair. There was another elf that was slightly shorter than the one that stood next to him, but he remained silent for the time being. He wore a robe and seemed to be some sort of chancellor.

"Since you are in a hurry to get to the point, let me first begin by apologizing how you were treated back on the Simorgan South. But we couldn't take any chances. We didn't know how influenced you were by the Relic. Your people are currently being held in rooms such as you were. Comfortable, I assure you. Well except that one that called himself your captain. His tongue has gained him temporary stay in the cells. I give you my word that once we have concluded our business here, you all will be free to go as you please."

Somehow he didn't seem surprised by Mimerck's actions. He could imagine him waking up and being infuriated about what had happened. Neeza supposed he could demand Vindimar to free him, but he figured that a little lockdown time would do him good. There were other more important things on his mind then trying to spell his captain thirty minutes of relief.

Neeza asked, "And what about the Relic?"

Vindimar replied, "The Relic will stay here until we have some idea how to handle it. When we first observed you heading toward the island chain, we meant well to stop you before you arrived. But we too had felt the Relic reaching out, calling to be discovered. If we had gone, the Valendritaii would have found us the moment we stepped foot there. They would have recognized our taste."

He wasn't surprised that they did see them, but that is where things got confusing to him.

"What does that mean? How can they recognize your taste?" asked Neeza.

Vindimar sat down again, the normal elf hint that he was going to tell a story of sorts, "To answer that I should tell you a little of the history of Valendri's Coffin and of Mount Hrithgorn after the Ettui Island Wars were won.

"Valendri's Coffin was created by an outcast elf named Wilnmis, who decided it would be amusing to dabble in necromancy. Legend says Valendri used the elf to create a doorway for him to easily enter the mortal world. What he opened was something that not even he could control. He disappeared shortly after. He must stayed with it until he died, driven mad by the power he unleashed. With no one to consume, the Relic waited for the right moment to spill new blood.

"In all the years we held onto Mount Hrithgorn, we had never felt a strange presence there. We were there for nearly 200 years before the Ettui began their assaults.

"After our victory, a newly appointed commander-in-chief was named. He examined the battle and sought to find ways to correct our mistakes. One of which was the enemy sneaking into underground passages. He ordered more rooms be made from below the throne room and to make an escape route only usable from the inside. That is when he found it.

"It seemed simple; a coffin and nothing more. But then everything changed. The people began to lose their minds. The Twin Dragons who guarded the gold supply became fearful of the relic's power and locked themselves in. Physically the people began to mutate. As you know, when an elf destroys the land instead of nurturing it, they turn into Ettui. The Relic . . . did something different. It changed them into monsters. They became known as the Valendritaii, or Valendri's minions. I'm sure you met a few of them on your journey there.

"In fact, the only reason you are all alive is because they had never acquired the taste of mages. Their years of being exposed to the Relic ate away their sight, so they relied on the races they had eaten to be able to track their prey. Because of this, whenever they tracked you, to them you were nothing more than a log on the ground. If even one had licked some mage blood, then everything on the Chain would have been able to sense you."

Although hard to believe, he began to think about all the previous encounters with the Garchai. Before they entered Hrithgorn, it was true they couldn't find them. Yet when they left, the Garchai knew exactly which island the mages were on. He thought their cargo was responsible for that. But his thoughts returned to their fallen brethren, Biverin. Zondiir or one of the other Garchai could have licked the pool of blood that he was told was at the mage farmer's feet. If that happened, then it was possible to find them fast.

Vindimar concluded, "The remnants of the fort didn't disappear as legends say, you see. They never left."

That meant the Garchai were actually the elves that stayed and were corrupted by the Relic's power. Incredible! Would that have happened to them had they stayed exposed to it for long? It was difficult to accept that those used to be elves.

Vindimar asked, "What I want to know primarily is why you want the Relic?"

Neeza heard the question, but it was something he didn't want to answer. He knew the elves were going to say no if he gave his real request. Even if he gave the lie he told the students, they would see right through it.

"So, the commander of the Mount, was his name Zondiir?"

Vindimar said, "I don't appreciate you changing the subject, though I am curious how you know his name? Zondiir's name is just as forbidden as speaking the Eratuu language."

Neeza explained, "I know him because I spoke with him. He still lives in the Mount. Another elf still lived there too. His name was Higalmos, but he died during the Ettui attack there. Why were they there?"

Hearing this surprised the elf captain. It must have been assumed that he died by the power of the Relic. As it turned out, the Coffin made him the strongest of them all.

"He did discover the Relic, so he had a unique bond with its desires. It is shocking, but not so much. I don't know why the Ettui were there, just as much as I don't know why *you* were there."

This elf was a clever one that was for sure. No matter how he asked the question, he turned it back onto him. Just as before, it was a question he didn't want to answer, especially not to him.

Vindimar guessed, "Did you want it for the power it gave? If so, you are wasting your time. You would never be able to complete the task required to activate it."

Neeza put on a blank face, instead demanding, "The Relic is ours by recovery. After we are done with it, we would be more than happy to return it to you, and you may do whatever you wish to it."

"I'm afraid that's not how it works," stated Vindimar.

Neeza said, "I'm leaving here with the Relic. What are you going to do? Torture me?"

"I hardly see that as necessary."

Vindimar and Neeza looked to the right. Out of the shadows stepped a seemingly young elf. He was different than the one sitting high on his throne. He had a presence to him. Neeza had actually met him, but only once. It was also a long time ago.

The mage leader respectfully bowed, "Arionn, leader of the Wood Elves. What brings you here?"

Arionn answered, "It is good to see you well again. I feared for you once I felt you going to Mount Hrithgorn. That is the reason I am here. Why won't you answer Vindimar's question?"

"It is an answer he would not understand and frankly, doesn't have any business knowing," explained Neeza.

The mage leader was just as Arionn remembered. He was head-strong, but was also easier than a book to read. Vindimar could have sensed it if he wasn't so uptight about finding his answers. One would say he had spent too many years with the humans in his younger days that he forgot how to observe like the true Wood Elf he was. No matter. This was a situation that must be resolved carefully and quickly.

Arionn said, "Neeza, Vindimar is correct in saying that your desire for the Relic is fruitless. You have no idea how it works, do you? The legends of the Coffin are true, but it is the sacrifice that must be given which is why I bid you to forget it. The Relic has no happy endings."

Neeza asked, "And how do you know that?"

"Valendri is the god of Mortality. Souls are what he strives for. What else could he want? I know you better than you might think. You are not one that would purposely take innocent lives for the sake of saving one," said Arionn.

Neeza didn't want to believe it. Was he saying he would have to kill people to make it work? Normally that was the only time sacrifice was ever used in this day and age. It was what Biverin did to save them.

Vindimar said again, "That still does not tell me why he sought out the Relic."

Arionn looked over at Neeza. He wanted to end this swiftly. He hated to have to divulge into the mage leader's personal feelings and emotions, but it would be the only way this confrontation ended with Neeza leaving and without desiring the relic. He would give him one last chance.

Arionn asked, "Will you volunteer to explain or must I tell him?"

Neeza remained silent. Although he had only met the Wood Elf leader once, the tales about how he was able to know things about people were legendary. Did he truly know why? He was pretty certain he was trying to call his bluff. He had never seen Arionn do it and many aspects of elvish tales had to be taken with a grain of salt.

Arionn finally answered, his eyes never leaving Neeza, "He wants it because he blames himself for the death of his wife. He feels that claiming the Relic will be able to bring her back. Neeza, know that there was nothing you could have done to save her. You must accept this."

Neeza dropped his head. The elf could see he was hitting every point correctly, but he was still teetering. He disliked having to bash the mage leader with this reality, but he had to hear it aloud.

Arionn continued, "You always say to yourself that you were never able to give your wife anything because you couldn't find a cure for her disease. That is not true. You had actually given her the one thing that she desired most in this world . . . a child. You have a beautiful daughter back home, one who is more important than you can imagine. Instead of trying to save the dead, you might want to consider protecting what you still have and love."

Neeza couldn't hold the tears. The leader in him was embarrassed, but the father in him was sorrowful by the realization. How could he have been so blind?

Arionn placed his hand on his shoulder as he looked up, not even bothering to hide the tears on his face, "Honorable Neeza, let the Relic go."

Arionn didn't have to be in his position to know that after what he said, there was no way that the mage leader would be leaving Hiierland with the Coffin. And what he said was all true as well, including the part about his daughter, Divi. He couldn't see too far into the future, but he did foresee that he and Divi would one day cross paths, and that she would soon play an important role in the upcoming events.

Neeza hated to admit it, but the Wood Elf was correct. He was painfully, one-hundred percent correct. The time to go home was now. He had to face the facts with the students . . . and with his own daughter.

The mage leader didn't even bother to say any more as he turned around. There was nothing more to be said. He knew there were questions they weren't answering about the Relic; ones he was very curious to at least know the truth about. He would probably never learn them from the elves. One thing he was certain about: any desire to bring the Relic back to Myyril had lost its luster.

Arionn didn't show it, but inside he was smiling. He made a wise choice. The Coffin was a tool of evil, and if they would have kept it, who knows the chaos it would have created. The Relic and its fate would be something to discuss, but later when the mages had left. These were trying times, and they needed to use the upmost caution about who they took into their confidence. He liked Neeza, but he wasn't ready, nor were the mages.

Neeza left the room as soon as Vindimar ordered that his friends be released and fed before their departure.

Neeza and the other mages left Hiierland after sharing one last complimentary meal in the Great Hall. It was at least a five day journey back and the feast would assure at least they wouldn't go hungry during that time. Mimerck's ship was even improved as the elves included a special liquid so that his spells would make the ship travel faster for a month at the very most two.

The mage captain was a little upset that they made an Elf Eye travel with them on the return home. They were told it was a requirement for any vessel leaving an elvish site that one travels with them, but it also was to ensure a safe trip home. Neeza thought it was perhaps because Vindimar didn't fully trust them. The two races may never fully get along, but he did respect them. He was so blinded by trying to save his wife that he forgot and pushed aside the only piece of her that truly mattered.

The students were all conversing while Neeza stood by Mimerck. The Elf Eye, named Firamos, stood over near the mage captain, making him feel uncomfortable. Yet, he could understand why. Mimerck cared most about gold and riches due to his profession. When that was what mattered most, one usually had to keep a watchful eye. Still, he learned to respect their captain's ability and even if he was loyal to the coin only, at the very least they found a good sailor they can call upon.

Mimerck yelled, "Would you stop staring at me! It makes me feel naked!"

Firamos answered, "That's the point."

Neeza intervened, "Firamos, may I just have a private word with Mimerck? After that you can continue making him as unpleasant as you wish. I have no doubt he earned it."

Firamos, who was appointed by Arionn, nodded to him and walked to the other side of the ship until Neeza was finished. Mimerck seemed relieved just to be away from the elf, even if it was only going to be for a few moments.

"I guess I should thank you, even if this is only temporary. But come on! What did I do to deserve him?"

Both mages laughed as Neeza replied, "Nothing I know of, but I'm sure there has been some event you wondered if you would regret it later. Consider this as your payback."

Mimerck commented, "Well, when you put it that way, this is making up for a lot of miscues of mine."

Neeza decided to get to the point, "I'm sorry you didn't find your riches. I know that was one of the reasons that drove you to volunteer for this journey. I am grateful that you agreed to captain us here."

Mimerck smiled and said, "Let's just say that I learned that gold . . . is a fickle thing. That and there is always someone out there who wants it more than you ever could. Besides, you're still paying me on our return, so not a wasted trip at all. I have regretted many things in my life. This is not one of them. If you ever need a captain again, Your Highness, you know where to find me."

Neeza smiled and turned around, but not before hearing Mimerck yell, "Get back over here, elf! I miss your eyes piercing my soul every minute of the day already!"

That was the Mimerck he knew and . . . well, appreciated. Neeza went to join the students as they sat in a circle near the bow of the boat.

Neeza asked, "So, what have you been talking about?"

Haldirin stood up and said, "Well, they wanted to tell you something. I need to check some things with Mimerck."

As he left, Dyenarus stood up. She had already been chosen to be the group voice for their party, giving him much proof of his decision to give her the highest endorsement. She not only stood up, but confidently and with conviction. He was so proud of her.

She said, "We all wanted to thank you for taking us on this adventure. I know you doubted us in the beginning. I'm sure most of us doubted ourselves when we stepped on this boat the first time. But this allowed us to grow like no other exercise in a classroom or words in a tome ever could. You did as you said, you got us home, and I guarantee that none of us are returning from this journey the same person."

Neeza tried to say, "But Biverin . . . and we aren't coming back with the Relic."

"Biverin died for something he believed in. He didn't believe in the mission. He believed in us, in you. We would have all died for each other as you were willing to die for us. We couldn't ask for much more from our leader."

Lindaris stood up and said, "I know I haven't been the easiest to deal with here. I can be snobby, unwilling to listen to others . . ." Dyenarus elbowed him as he paused, "Yeah, I'm getting to that. And I have issues thinking I'm better than others, but this trip has showed me that as I high as I think myself, I still have a lot of room to grow. Thank you, Honorable Neeza."

Condarin and Vindar stood up next as she said, "I will admit, I did doubt my abilities when I came here. Vindar helped me much along the way, but I didn't start putting faith in my abilities and pushing myself to the limits until I came here. My teachers are going to be surprised that the once reserved girl they knew died out there on Mount Hrithgorn and was replaced by a better mage. Thank you, Honorable Neeza."

Neeza added, "I should be the one thanking you. If not for your willingness to try something you may have felt you couldn't do, I wouldn't be here today."

As each and every student gave their heart-felt reason for thanking him, his memories were coming back to him and why he had started the mission in the first place. He had lied to them since day one and for the first time, that guilt was eating at him. He had to come clean. No more lies. They weren't the only ones that changed on Mount Hrithgorn.

As the last student finished, Neeza said, "Thank you, all of you. I do appreciate your gratitude. I must say more about why . . . "

Dyenarus stopped him and said, "Why we went is unimportant now. What we came back with is all that matters."

She was right. He still felt bad that they wouldn't know the real reason about why he wanted the Relic, but he should stop looking at the past. The past is what got him in this predicament in the first place. It was going to be easy for Haldirin to let go. Inno was going to be another story. He was certain his friend and messenger would be there to help him. He patted Dyenarus on the shoulder and went to join Haldirin.

Lindaris walked up to Dyenarus and said, "Look, about that kiss and everything. I know how you are just pining to go out with me, but I think I have someone back home who will be impressed how much I've changed. I just wanted to let you down easy and not string you out. Still friends?"

Dyenarus almost laughed as he hit the sarcasm to a whole new level. She was happy for him. It seemed small, but he had changed the most, just behind Condarin. Haldirin was also right, if things had been different, perhaps her and Lindaris might have worked. But she knew, as he just realized, that their futures went down different paths. She shook his extended hand.

"Friends. And to a lifetime of annoying each other."

Both laughed as Neeza reached Haldirin, who was looking toward the east and home.

"Well, Haldirin, looks like we survived another adventure together."

"Indeed. To be honest, I think I'm going to need a break after this one."

Neeza commented, "Trust me. If I can, this will be the last great journey I take for a very long time."

The moons were beginning to show apart from the setting sun to the west. They were still a few days away, but he couldn't wait to get home. Primarily, he wanted to see Divi. He had begun to realize how much he had wronged her over the years. No one deserved that, especially from their own father. Then again, that prophecy he received from a soothsayer didn't help matters either. Regardless, things were going to change when they got back.

Haldirin asked, "What are you going to tell the council about what happened?"

He did have some explaining to do, that was for sure. He was quite certain the teachers would come to him on fire once they learned they went to Mount Hrithgorn. They may have already known because Sydis had found out some way. It was something he wouldn't worry about until they got to that bridge.

Neeza answered, "I'm going to tell them the truth. No use hiding behind a lie anymore. We shall see."

They continued to watch as the boat steadily made its way back east.

****

"Are the mages on their way?"

Arionn confirmed, "Yes, Firamos tells me that none of them desire to return and try and claim the Relic. It seems we reached them in time."

Vindimar was joined by the chancellor, an elf named Gornimos, Arionn, Killiam and Hortimus, their twin captains, and Bargalmos, their head of the guard. The throne room was beginning to show signs of the darkness of night as they lit as many torches as necessary. Now that the mages had departed, they could talk freely. Neeza had attempted to listen in to their conversations after their meeting, so he couldn't say much until they were gone.

Arionn added, "That was quite an entertaining story about the origin of Valendri's Relic for it being a false one. We are still trying to figure out who built and put the Coffin there, in addition to what its ultimate purpose is. We don't even know if it belongs to Valendri. He remains quite silent on the matter. All we know is that it's a tool of evil."

Vindimar commented, "Not all of us are as skilled as you are by telling the truth to influence others. It was necessary. At least I was truthful about the Valendritaii. Now, what to do about the Coffin?"

Gornimos said, "It cannot stay here. It might do the same to us as it did the residents of Mount Hrithgorn."

Bargalmos replied, "I say we take it back to Hrithgorn. It took extraordinary circumstances for it to be retrieved. I doubt anyone will be coming close to it again."

Arionn added, "We put it back there, more will go after it. It might even urge the Ettui to once again try and acquire it."

The Ettui. That was one of the most chilling revelations about what transpired on the Simorgan Chain. For generations they had been held strictly to the Barbatan continent after the Ettui Island Wars, only making any real offensive when they decided to take an army by boat to Fort Za. They had been trying for a long time to re-establish colonies elsewhere, making the remaining island fortresses a must for the elves. As far as they knew, they had yet to accomplish this.

Vindimar said, "That is the other troubling news. Not that the Ettui were involved. Arionn foresaw that they might try and acquire the Relic once its power began to expand. What is concerning is we don't know where they came from. Hortimus, you are certain that Fort Za saw nothing?"

"Quite. They noticed the mages sail past from a great distance, but nothing more."

Killiam suggested, "They must have a colony somewhere up north, but where? There are far less land masses that way than there are to the south. Our last northern fort, Fort Ghiiverlan, has reported no changes to the old Ettui stronghold, Dhallik val-Ghull."

Arionn said, "This is truly disturbing news. I will ponder on this when I return home. We must find out where they came from. If they have been able to hide from our sight, then there might be a darker power involved."

Vindimar didn't like the sound of that. The Ettui were formidable enough when their enemy knew they were coming. If they were in the dark about the Ettui's plans, that put them at a huge disadvantage.

"Arionn is right. Let him focus on the Ettui situation for the time being. Now, for the Relic. We all agree that its timing has been strange. It has done this before, but not so powerful that it could be felt on the mainland. These are odd times indeed. Arionn has warned that an ominous darkness was growing stronger. If acquiring this Relic is part of that, we must find a safe place where no one would think of looking. Is there any place on the mainland that might be safe?"

Gornimos, as he was most familiar with the mainland being a chancellor to the elvish people, said, "I would avoid the mage lands for obvious reasons. I don't think the Human realms would be any better. Rudann and Garlock, two nations struggling for acceptance and power, might try and use it if they could acquire it. Cordcan lands are too populated. There would be no place for it to go. If I may suggest, what about Dyyros? It has many unpopulated areas and their ruler, Lord Ulcinar, has re-established some order since he overthrew the ruling kingdom there."

Arionn was the first and only to answer because there was no reason to question his logic, "I would avoid there too. I have felt a different kind of darkness coming from there. Ever since this governmental transition from king to dictator occurred, a strange shadow has been coming from that direction."

Gornimos asked, "Then where? The Dragonians would never agree, and quite frankly, I would fear what the Relic would do to our dragon friends."

Vindimar saw only one way to rid it from here and safe enough to where no one could realistically retrieve it.

"Someone will take one of our weakest ships, go out to the deepest waters they can find and sink it with the Coffin aboard. Let Nighalmais do the deed. He is more seasoned on the seas than most of our kind. Be sure he secures the amulet to it. It will block the Relic's power and be out of the way. With any luck, the pressure will destroy it once and for all since the hottest fires don't seem to work."

The elves nodded and left except for Arionn and Vindimar. There must have been something still on Arionn's mind if he stayed. He knew the leader of his people well. If he waited around, it meant that he withheld information . . . information he wanted to keep private.

Vindimar asked, "What is it that still troubles you?"

Arionn explained, "The way of the world is bothering me. A dark storm is coming and I don't think we are ready for it."

"I wouldn't worry too much. We'll most likely find these Ettui were part of a pack that found a way to migrate north, and in an attempt to gain some kind of advantage, tried to acquire the Relic," said Vindimar.

Vindimar stood up and walked out, leaving Arionn alone. Now it was like he was at home in the Forbidden Forest. It's how he did his best work. He began to recall his interviews with each of the students prior to this one, heeding particular attention to the one he had with Dyenarus. She told him *many* interesting things about their journey, just as he learned many interesting things about her. As he paced, he began to speak aloud, realizing more things.

"The magic involved here; that is another distressing revelation. For the humans to be consumed by strong magic is quite common. Mages and elves have a unique bond with magic, making them difficult to corrupt. We can sense when something is wrong and move away from it. From the way Dyenarus explained it to me, the change happened almost instantly, attracting them instead. What power does this Coffin have that it can turn one so sensitive to the life particles just as fast as it would a human? It is truly frightening."

Arionn began to wish that Vindimar's conclusion was the case, but everything in his gut was telling him otherwise. The fall of the Aranian kingdom, the rise of its cruel dictator, the section of the woods to the north that was suddenly hit by plague, the calling of the Relic from Mount Hrithgorn, and the increased actions or movements of the Ettui, were all happening for a reason. If these were natural, he wouldn't show any mind. But there were some unnatural things happening here being directed by some puppeteer and they all were the puppets putting on the show.

Arionn said before he walked out of the empty throne room, "I pray you are right. If you are wrong, I pray that we are ready."

16

The mages arrived at the Myyrilian docks on the fourth day since they left Hiierland. It was quite an uneventful trip considering the storm they ran into on the way to Mount Hrithgorn. Regardless, they returned to the mage capital near midday when the sun was at its hottest.

As Neeza stood at the front of the ship, he couldn't see anyone waiting on the dock, which surprised him. He knew Firamos contacted the most powerful mage when they were nearby because Myyril didn't have an Elf Eye present in the city. That mage was none other than Sydis. He was expecting him to at least be there. Yet, there was no one but the minimal staff of dock hands to help with anchoring the ship. At least he didn't have to deal with any of the political mayhem this may have caused the moment he got off the boat.

He took a deep breath and exhaled. It was good to be home! Yes, a part of him would always love the adventures and the excitement they brought. But as Dyenarus and Condarin had said, their old selves died up there in Mount Hrithgorn. That adventurer's spirit in him was slowly beginning to dwindle and lose its sparkle. Arionn was right. He had everything he wanted here in Myyril. He had his comfortable lifestyle, he had his job, and most importantly . . . he had Divi. He resolved to no longer be distracted by false hopes. His wife was always going to be gone, but she was still alive in his daughter.

It took nearly twenty minutes, but finally Sydis and a small group of the council came marching down the path. None of them were heads of the Schools of Magic as he noticed. Only the elected members accompanied him as they made their way to their leader. These men and women he had some influence over. The school heads would be more difficult for him to persuade. He also couldn't miss the couple members of the Kittara alongside of him. Where the right hand went, the left hand followed.

Haldirin asked, "Do you want me by your side?"

Neeza said, "No, I'll be all right. Find Biverin's family and offer them our deepest condolences. I will be sure that financially they will be compensated for their loss, and they will be welcome anytime they want in my home. I'll see you when you return."

"I will tell stories of his bravery so that they remember the man that we knew, and not the one they might remember," said Haldirin.

Haldirin left moments before Sydis and the others arrived, "Welcome back home, Honorable Neeza. When you failed to return in the time you allotted, we feared the worst. Did you find what you were looking for in Mount Hrithgorn?"

Neeza looked back to see the smiling students as they disembarked from the ship, gathering whatever supplies they had left. Did he get what he originally came to find? No, the Relic was long gone if his theory was correct. What he did find in its place, however, was worth more than ten Relics.

Neeza replied, "Yes and no, Honorable Sydis. I have no regrets for going. I'm certain the teachers at their respective schools will have no complaints either."

Sydis asked, "Who is getting your endorsement? It must be recorded properly so the ceremony can take place with haste."

"Dyenarus of the School of Illusions. She proved her worth more times than I can count."

Sydis began examining Neeza and the students as best as he could. He didn't seem to be looking at anything in particular, which had him very curious. His vision once again focused on Neeza.

"You all have scars of some kind. And you are one short if I seem to recall your original count. What in the name of our merciful gods did you face there?"

So that was it. He was trying to see the condition they were in. He also wanted to know what happened. Could he tell him now? No, most of this trip would be something that would be written in his logs to be read when his soul returned to the life force. Not now or sooner.

Neeza simply answered, "Nothing we couldn't handle. We did lose one, sadly. The farmer. His family is being notified as we speak and his name will be remembered at the next seasonal ceremony with honors. Come walk with me. You must share what I missed in my absence."

Neeza and Sydis walked ahead while the rest followed behind. It was customary for the more powerful to walk in the front while the rest would not be far. He had been gone for nearly two weeks, so he expected something to have happened.

Sydis reported, "Our Kittara forces defeated a rebel group near the edge of the Rim, but we couldn't destroy them as a pack of Midenbeasts attacked."

The Rim was a made up circular line that marked the territories it was safe for mages to settle. The capital was the epicenter and the edge of the Rim was about 100 miles outward. Past the Rim one would run into the danger of meeting Midenbeast or worse. One would need a great guide and fighter to survive on those plains. It was quite sad. They owned so much land, but because of the wildlife, couldn't settle on most of it.

Sydis continued, "The fall festival committee has been pestering me since you left about approving their plans. I wish you would meet them as quickly as possible so they can bother me no more. And your daughter was angry that you left on yet another adventure without telling her in person."

That was normal. He felt sorry for Tasi. She must have given him hell. Well, that was something he would hopefully change soon.

Sydis concluded, "And I think that is about it."

"What about the visit from the strange man?"

Sydis tried to silence the councilman, but it was too late. Neeza had heard it and was curious what that meant.

"What strange man?"

Sydis reluctantly explained, "Two nights ago, a man came to the front gates of our city, demanding he meet with you. We told him you were gone away on a mission, but he refused to leave. I would have had him executed for his actions had he not already surrendered his weapons to the gate guard before he even asked."

Strange. *What would a man want with him?* It was rare to have human visitors, mainly because they knew how much mages hated them. Whoever this person was had to be very stupid, or perhaps he came from a land who was not familiar with their customs. Humans in Arten would have been smart enough to hire a mage driver to take them to the city gates.

Neeza asked, "What did he want?"

Sydis said, "Nothing but rubbish. Only thing I could make out was that he repeated a man's name. Ulcinar it was I believe. The name most likely has no meaning to you."

Neeza froze as he suddenly saw Orznaii's face gleaming him in the eye saying that exact same name to him in the depths of Mount Hrithgorn. Could it possibly be the same person? Ulcinar was quite a unique name. It had to be. Coincidences were something he was beginning to believe in less and less.

"Where is he? In one of our guest houses or held under watch in our inns?"

"Neither," answered Sydis. "I put him in the Casteel. I had no idea his intentions! At least there he wouldn't escape."

Neeza was disappointed and angry by what was done, shown by the redness of his face, "You placed an unarmed man who followed protocol for a peaceful entrance in prison? He doesn't want to escape; he wants to talk to me! Hopefully after your actions, he still will. Take me to him immediately! I want to hear what he has to say. Have a couple guards stand watch outside in case I need them."

The councilmen present nodded and began to lead him toward the Casteel. Sydis stepped back as there was nothing he could do to stop him. He knew their leader was making a huge mistake. The problems of Man were no problems for a Mage. Let them deal with their issues alone. They had a hard fought peace they were able to keep. The truce, as unstable as it was, held true all these years. Pray to their gods that this would not undo what years of hard work had loosely cemented.

Haldirin waited outside the Casteel as Neeza had instructed him telepathically. He had just arrived from the Biverin Ranch where he got to meet the wife and child of the late-Biverin. He recalled him saying he had one daughter, but he failed to mention that his wife was still pregnant with their second . . . his unborn son. This made it even harder to report the already difficult news.

They took the news with sadness, almost as if they were expecting this when he said he was going. Yet, as Haldirin spoke of how he stood up to Ettui forces and was able to subdue the much stronger Garchai, his widow felt more honored, more at peace. They cried when he told him Biverin's last words to them and the promise. She thanked him, and he made as much haste as he could to join Neeza.

From what the guard had told him, he had been in there for a couple hours talking to the prisoner. He couldn't tell him more than that. He may be the right hand man for Neeza, but that gave him no authority in the Casteel. The famous prison had its own set of rules and its own hierarchy. The only position that had the same power outside the prison was Neeza's.

After about another hour, Neeza finally emerged from the door. Instead of going straight to Haldirin, he went to the guard first.

"I want you to release the prisoner in cell 87H-5A immediately. Assure him safe passage to the borders cities into Arten."

The guard acknowledged and went inside. Neeza walked quickly past Haldirin, forcing him to run and catch up.

Haldirin asked, "Neeza! Neeza! What's the matter?"

Neeza ordered, "Get the council assembled for an emergency meeting. And ask Mimerck if he'd be willing to stay in port. We might need him. Give him this manifest and have him try and load as much as possible. I will compensate him his costs."

Neeza handed him a paper as Haldirin looked at it. There wasn't much on the list. Food, knives, and survival supplies made up most of it. The one item he noticed was the request for a small boat. It was apparent that he didn't want to be left without that option this time around. Mount Hrithgorn taught him the value of having a portable vessel at least.

"What's the matter?"

Neeza replied, "Remember on the third day of our trip home I was mentioning that I thought Mount Hrithgorn was just a small piece of a much larger puzzle? I just may be correct. Please hurry."

He certainly did. He called him, Mimerck, and even their Elf Eye to discuss how he believed something major would happen soon while the students slept. They had Dyenarus to thank for that as she reported everything she heard Orznaii say to the mysterious white-haired man. Haldirin admitted that there were many strange coincidences that happened at Hrithgorn, but he just couldn't believe what Neeza was telling them on the boat. It just seemed too large and unrealistic.

Neeza quickly made for the palace as Haldirin stopped. Whatever it was that man had told him, the mage leader was very determined. So much for no more adventures. It had been a while since they had called one of these late meetings, but if Neeza felt it important enough to do it, then it must have been quite urgent. Haldirin rushed to inform all the members of the news.

It was nearing the long hours of the night. Haldirin had been sitting around the outside of the council chambers as were a couple couriers, named Calidis and Hortis. They were brothers and young, but it was all they had available at such late notice. They had been in the council chamber lobby at least two hours, but that was probably inaccurate. It took him that long to locate Mimerck, who was nearly drunk when he found him. Yet, when he told him Neeza needed him, he quickly got ready, paid his tab, and headed toward his ship with the manifest Neeza made.

Haldirin first arrived to an unforgivable scene: the couriers asleep. He knew it was late, but they had to be sure they were awake when the meeting was adjourned. Even if they weren't needed, they still had to be ready. Haldirin was tired and hungry as well. He had been running around all day. The only food he'd eaten was an orange and a wheat cake from Biverin's family, which was quite delicious!

Time ticked away as the moon moved from the left side of the window to the center. Finally, after it seemed like they were never going to leave, the council began to exit the chamber. A couple filed out before Neeza emerged. Haldirin found him first and met him.

"What is going on?"

Neeza said, "Inform Mimerck to prepare his ship immediately. I and a group of the council will be leaving tonight."

Tonight? He was thinking whatever it was wouldn't go until morning. It must have been more dire than he even could have imagined.

Haldirin asked, "Where are you off to?"

"All I can say is that we are heading toward Dyyros."

Dyyros? Of all the places, why there, the birthplace of Man? The last time Neeza was there he was trying to invade it, so the humans claimed. The only reason he wasn't executed for the act was because he promised he would never step foot on those lands again unless invited. It was a long standing truce that he kept all these years. Did that man invite him over? Possibly, but it couldn't have been sanctioned by the governing body of that continent. This was too hushed to be something official.

Haldirin said, "Very well. I will inform him to be prepared with haste. I shall get my supplies as well."

"You will stay here."

Haldirin looked at his boss shocked, "Like the hells I am! This business sounds like it might be very serious . . .

Neeza interrupted, "Which is why I need you to stay in Myyril. There are forces at work here which have me scared. I want you to try and keep things at home going. We should be back in about a week."

Haldirin didn't like it at all. Not one bit. Neeza had never refused his company on a mission before. What was so important that he was demanding him not to go? Whatever it was, he must have had his reasoning.

Haldirin, doing his duty, asked the next obvious question, "Should I inform Tasi to keep his watchful eye on Divi?"

Neeza paused and finally said, "No, wake her up and tell her to get dressed. She's coming with me. For years you have been telling me I should spend more time with her. I know this trip won't resolve the years of hardship I caused her, but at least I can get a start here and now."

All of Haldirin's concerns went to the wayside. At last, after all these years, he was going to spend time with his daughter with the intention of trying to bring them closer instead of drive them further apart. He was right that it was going to take more than just one trip to fix their relationship, but he knew his boss. When he wanted something, he would do whatever it took to complete it. Besides, with this newfound appreciation for her, he doubted he would take her on a mission that was going to be dangerous. Just because something was important didn't mean it would be deadly.

Haldirin said, "I will do as you say. She will be there."

Neeza replied, "Thank you. I will tell you what is going on when I get back, but we must make haste. If for some reason I don't return, I want you and Frari to have a hold onto the stewardship for a couple months."

Haldirin said, "Don't talk like that! If you can survive Mount Hrithgorn, this should be easy."

He hoped that would be the case. That was why he was leaving. The sooner they did, the better . . . and the easier it would be to move around. He might not be able to say that in a week if what the man said was true. If everything went to plan, they would be off the continent with plenty of time to spare. But time was of the essence.

Neeza just replied, "I hope you are right."

He began to walk out as Haldirin followed. Calidis watched as the councilmen were all leaving the hallway. His brother had already begun to follow them out as none of them were asking for any messages to be sent. Sure, it happened, but it was quite rare. Who would be up at this hour to receive them anyway? He supposed it was safe for him to do the same as his brother.

"Calidis! I have a message for you to deliver!"

He turned around to see Sydis standing there holding a large envelope. Just his luck! Of all the people who would have a letter tonight, it would be Sydis. He really didn't like him because he seemed to elevate himself above everyone else. He was certainly powerful enough to have that right, but Neeza rarely ever did that, and he was even stronger than Sydis.

Calidis met the second-most powerful mage in Myyril as he handed him a plain white envelope.

"Be sure this gets sent out immediately. It is of the upmost importance that this gets to its destination before we arrive. If I find out it wasn't, I will be most displeased on my return."

Sydis began to walk out after the courier acknowledged he understood. One thing he knew about him was that he was serious with his threats. That was something he didn't want to worry about. He started lightly jogging toward the Emergency Delivery Center, or EDC, located on the lower levels of the council building.

As he did, curiosity got the best of him and he looked at the front of the envelope. Most of the words were written in invisible ink so that only the EDC master would know where it was going. As he did, a reddish rune appeared on it. That was normal for something important. What wasn't normal was that it appeared he had begun to write the destination before the initial rune spell was cast, as a result he was able to read one word on it: Dyyros.

His mind began to race as he walked. What could be on Dyyros that was so important? Sydis did this in such haste that he probably didn't even realize the mistake. He did know that they had a couple of contacts there that despite the truce, they were able to blend in to the human population. It had been years since an envelope was sent to them, and it was normally the green rune, which allowed the address to be seen. The red one was supposed to hide everything. Was this to one of them?

There would be time to ponder it later. If they were leaving immediately, then time would be short for him to get to the EDC and deliver it. His jog became a full out run as he quickly maneuvered through the empty hallway to make up time.

At the boat, most of the mage council was there, with only a couple excused because of age or of ailments not allowing them to make the trip. The night was still young, being as this was the longest night of the year. The ship was nearly ready to go when Mimerck walked up to Neeza.

"Well, ship's as ready as ever. I put the rowboat in it as requested, so it might be a little tighter than it was going to Hrithgorn. And that elvish stuff is still there, so if I go at full throttle, we should be able to make it there in four hours. Five or six is more realistic. Point being, we should still arrive while its night there. Pirate attacks won't be a concern. We should be able to outrun all the ships we might come across."

Neeza said, "Good. We'll have to slow down once we grow near Dyyros. You probably know that they tend to not like our kind, so secrecy will be of the upmost importance. Where did you say we would port?"

Mimerck said, "Porsita. It is the last free port on the western sea of Dyyros. Tartus would have been better, but too many people and too much paperwork. We'd never be able to sneak in. Furthermore, it's under Ulcinar's control. I've been to Porsita before. You'll get there safely."

Porsita. He had been there a couple times. That was the exact same port he entered on during the assault over 300 years ago. Thankfully human lifespans are much shorter than a mage's. No one there is apt to remember the incident.

Mimerck asked, "You really think this is wise? I know I shouldn't doubt you, but it is part of my nature."

Neeza explained, "If I didn't think it was important to do this, I wouldn't be risking my life to do it."

The mage captain heard that before. That is precisely what he told the students back on the way to Mount Hrithgorn. He seemed less worried now. He wasn't carrying just students. He was carrying some of the most important and seasoned mages of Myyril on this trip. If they ran into any opposition, he was certain they would be able to handle it much better. Still, he did miss those wily kids.

Sydis finally made an appearance from the boat as he bowed to both Mimerck and Neeza, "We are ready to go as soon as you are. The ship is ready."

Neeza replied, "Excellent. Once my daughter arrives, then we will leave."

He truly hoped that Haldirin was having success in getting her. He had a feeling she wasn't going to be happy being woken in the middle of the night for something that he couldn't explain to her quite yet. He would make it up to her. This was only the beginning for them in their new life together.

No sooner then he thought, it he saw Divi storming ahead of Haldirin, carrying nothing but a small satchel and her staff. She was wearing a half robe for the hood because the night was quite cold. Otherwise she wore her rebellious wears. Just seeing her bare uncovered legs made Neeza shiver and he was dressed for the occasion. If not for the staff, he would have had trouble knowing she was a mage at all. She definitely never dressed the part.

Mimerck greeted, "Ah, so you must be the Honorable Divi! Welcome to my . . ."

She walked past the captain not even lifting her head and intentionally bumping into her father. All three watched as she instantly went on the deck of the boat and sat at the edge, watching the sea.

Mimerck commented, "She's quite the fireball isn't she?"

Neeza said, "You have no idea."

The mage captain laughed and said, "Well, all I'll say is good luck with her. It looks like you're going to need it."

Mimerck moved to the ship leaving Neeza with Haldirin. They were silent for the first few moments. It was a strange scene. Neeza believed he wouldn't be coming home from his new mission. Mount Hrithgorn was dangerous, but the current situation was much graver.

Haldirin finally said, "Have a safe journey. Be sure you come back."

Neeza said, "I will. I know this isn't goodbye, but I wanted to thank you for all the years of service you have given me. I don't always show it, but I wanted to just let you know."

"It is a dubious honor to serve under you, Honorable Neeza."

Neeza said before turning to get on the boat, "Please, just call me Neeza."

Haldirin smiled as Neeza got on board. He nodded toward Mimerck to signal for him to move.

Mimerck yelled, "All right! We are about to make the Porsita run in record time. Hold onto your hoods! It's going to be a ride!"

Mimerck got the ship going as they began to head northeast to toward the Gulf of Dyyros, where the port town of Porsita rested. Although he was scared, he was getting that adventurous excitement back a little. He wanted to apologize to Dyenarus and the others that he wouldn't be there at the ceremony, but he signed what he needed to, paid who needed their coin, so at least he took care of those that risked their lives for him.

As he looked toward the east, his mind began to race with many questions. Would they get there in time? Would they run into any opposition? Would he be able to finally make things up with his daughter so she would at least give him the chance to make it work? He didn't know the answers. All he knew was what was in front of him.

Meanwhile, Divi sat looking forward at the sea, filled with anger for the late night wake-up, but excitement for getting out of Myyril for a while. Why did her father want her to join him all of a sudden? If it was another attempt to embarrass her or try and encourage her to learn magic, he would be sadly disappointed. Whatever the reasons, she would find out one way or the other. As her mom would tell her even while on her deathbed: Only time would tell.

About the Author

TOM ROGAL

Born and raised in northern Illinois. Graduated with Honors from Northern Illinois University in Communications in the Media Studies and English. History has always been a large interest as one can always learn from the mistakes and successes of the past. Primary areas of interest is Alexander the Great, The Greek and Roman Empires, Medieval times, and WWII.

A big sports fan and is very active athletically. Loves running, doing at least six races a year. Also an avid movie lover and can be found often in a theater.

*In a Time's history, there is always a conflict . . . one that
changes the world one lives in. It is how that conflict ends
which determines the future . . . or lack there of.
One perception that all deny is that no matter how minor, everyone
plays a role in said events. Every action, good or bad, is
important. How will the future play?
Time will tell.*

---- Time Sage

The Saga Continues in . . .

Brinks in Time: The Unification

Book 1 of the Ulcinaric Conflict

Coming soon.

For more information on the *Brinks In Time* series, check
out the website www.brinksintime.com.

Be sure to check out and Like the Facebook page at
https://www.facebook.com/BrinksInTime for updates.

CPSIA information can be obtained at www.ICGtesting.com
Printed in the USA
LVOW10s1701310516

490597LV00023BB/479/P